FREE LOVE

FREE LOVE

A NOVEL

TESSA HADLEY

HARPER

An Imprint of HarperCollins*Publishers*

FREE LOVE. Copyright © 2022 by Tessa Hadley. All rights reserved. Printed in
the United States of America. No part of this book may be used or reproduced
in any manner whatsoever without written permission except in the case of brief
quotations embodied in critical articles and reviews. For information, address
HarperCollins Publishers, 195 Broadway, New York, NY 10007.

HarperCollins books may be purchased for educational, business,
or sales promotional use. For information, please email the Special Markets
Department at SPsales@harpercollins.com.

First published in the United Kingdom in 2022 by Jonathan Cape,
an imprint of Vintage.

FIRST U.S. EDITION

Library of Congress Cataloging-in-Publication Data has been applied for.

ISBN 978-0-06-313777-6

21 22 23 24 25 26   LSC   10 9 8 7 6 5 4 3 2 1

FOR ERIC AND FOR DAN FRANKLIN

ONE

This Friday evening in late summer was so lovely that Phyllis Fischer sat at her dressing table with the window wide open onto the garden. Life flowed into the room from beyond the window in its drowsy suburban evening stream: the steady relieving splash of a hose in a herbaceous border, confiding clack of shears, distant thwack of balls from the tennis club, broken sharp cries of children playing, fragrance of cut grass and roasting meat, jiggling of ice in the first weekend gin and tonics. When slanting low sunlight was suddenly blinding in one wing of the dressing-table mirror, Phyllis adjusted it and the light ran instead around the cut-glass toiletry set and her bottles of L'Air du Temps and witch hazel and cleansing milk. She sat forward in her petticoat, leaning on her elbows to see more clearly in the mirror, feeling the flirting of the breeze on her bare shoulders, smelling the soap on her skin. She was forty but still had an expectant, animated prettiness: her sandy, tanned face was brushed with faint freckles across the upturned nose, her rather dry fair hair – not yellow, but a shadowed gold like washed-out straw – was backcombed into volume for tonight, and stiff with hairspray. She put on pale lipstick carefully, pressing her lips together, frowning at the mirror because she thought that her mouth was too big – too soft and indefinite, as if she might blurt out something coarse or raw. In fact she was easy, an easy person, easily made happy, glad to make others happy. She was pleased with her life. The year was 1967.

Her dress for this evening waited like a friend, hooked on its hanger over the wardrobe door: empire-line with a skirt that ended above the knee, green chiffon with bold vertical red and orange stripes, green grosgrain ribbon sewn under the bust, fastened in a bow in front. She had asked Mandy Verey to press it for her, before she went home – no need to keep Mandy on to help serve dinner, because it wasn't a formal dinner party. The young man who was coming, Nicholas Knight, might turn out anyway to be a bore; Phyllis had a dim memory that he'd been a bore as a small boy. She'd met him long ago, when she was first married to Roger and her daughter Colette was a colicky baby. At nine or ten years old, Nicholas had been owlish, with a big heavy head and black-framed thick glasses, brimming with factual knowledge, insisting that they test him on flags and capitals of the world; patiently Roger had obliged. Nicholas was the son of Roger's friends Peter and Jean Knight – who were really his parents' friends, older than he was. Phyllis's anticipation of Nicholas's visit this evening was only buoyant because she liked entertaining – and because he was a man after all, even if he turned out to be gauche and unattractive. She liked men, she couldn't help herself. Though there was no question of her flirting with Nicholas, who was nearer to the age of her own daughter.

The children playing outside were screaming now with excitement at the climax of some pursuit, weaving on their secret paths around the gardens in the hot light, ducking behind clipped high privet hedges or pushing through thickets of rank shrubbery: rhododendron and hydrangea, poisonous spotted laurel, stiff bamboo. Some of these gardens ran to half an acre or more, and the children had made dens in the scraps of woodland at their far ends, where they arrived at the river, out of parental reach; one garden of an abandoned house was an overgrown wilderness, and they had worked themselves up into a horror of coming upon dead things in there. They knew all the broken places in fences for squeezing through, streaking their clothes with lichen stains or tearing them on nails. An adult opened an upstairs window in one of the nearby houses in the Fischers' cul-de-sac, to shout at them: with a splash and cry a child missed a stepping stone in a fish pond, lifted in dismay a dripping sandal, a soaked sock – but there was no time to stop, the others were pitiless. — You idiot! one of them sharply exclaimed. Phyllis thought with exhilaration that her son Hugh would be running with them, perhaps out at the front of the tribe, leading the way. She ought to lean out of the window and call to Hugh to come inside, it was time for his supper – but she was still in her petticoat, and anyway couldn't make herself be offended by the children's exuberance. She felt with them the promise of the evening, the gathering shadows, the pang of ending.

Roger Fischer arrived home from the Foreign Office where he was a senior civil servant, a respected and subtle Arabist, taking off his coat downstairs in a dazzle of coloured lights from the stained glass in the porch door, calling out to his family as he hung it on the coat stand, appraising himself only for tidiness, not vanity, in the small square of mirror with its bevelled edges. He was tidy: medium height and stocky, waist turning to softness, striking jowly face, dog-heavy eyes, dark shadow of beard growth, black hair slicked back. The hallway was savoury with cooking smells and through the open dining-room door he saw the table laid ready with flowers, a colourful check cloth and napkins, wine glasses. Upstairs at the dressing table Phyllis paused with her mascara wand held to her eye and met her own glance for one moment in the mirror, unfathomable – although her expression was arranging itself brightly in welcome already, she was singing out her greeting. Roger would go in first to see poor Colette, who was struggling as usual with her homework. Phyllis had time to put on her nylons, slip the dress over her head, dab L'Air du Temps on the pressure points at her wrists and behind her ears.

If Colette was struggling it wasn't because she wasn't clever. She was very clever, but everything was a struggle with her. English Literature homework ought to have been easy, but too much was at stake: she was supposed to be writing an essay on imagery of growth and decay in *Twelfth Night*, which she could have done standing on her head, except that through it she was trying to communicate, in a veiled language, her passionate affinity with her new English teacher – who was in her forties, slim, equivocal, elegant, dry, divorced. Colette attended a private girls' day school, dragging her reluctant feet each day, in their regulation brown lace-up outdoor shoes, all the way up the steep hill from where her father dropped her off, through ominous wrought-iron abandon-all-hope gates, down into the Underground Cloakroom with its mineral smell of hockey boots and cold sweat, where she must take off her bottle-green mac and change into indoor sandals.

Girls at Otterley High were hearty and sporting and blithe, gifted with unconsciousness of themselves; Colette was a lonely tortured intellectual. She thought of setting up, like Viola, a willow cabin at her new teacher's gate, but knew she couldn't play the part: Viola had to be exquisite, poignant, pocket-sized. Colette was substantial and square-jawed, bosomy, with curling dark hair at a moment when only dead-straight hair was beautiful. And she wore glasses – stubbornly, she had insisted on standard-issue National Health glasses with transparent pink frames. — I'll buy you some more attractive ones, her mother had pleaded. — Your father won't mind paying.

— I don't want more attractive ones, Colette had bleakly said.

Although she read everything, she refused to read the novelist her mother said she was named after. She could guess what her mother's idea had been, calling her Colette in the first place: she'd been imagining some fey imp of a child, skinny and lithe and French-looking, blinking appealingly through the fringe hanging in her eyes. Some child who was not her. Bitterly Colette applied herself to her essay, her bedroom window shut tight against the seductions of the evening outside. She always did her weekend homework on Friday, as if she were clearing the way for something, although when she'd cleared it she didn't know what the something was. Through the glass and the sealed-in stale heat of her room she was aware of the children calling outside as they hurtled headlong, and was swamped with regret for a time when she'd been one of them – which seemed centuries ago, although she was only fifteen.

Colette hadn't ever been a skinny imp. She'd been hot-faced and barrel-shaped and bossy, pumping her fists like pistons when she ran – she knew, because her brother had imitated her. But in those days she was powerful; she could remember standing with her legs apart, in wellingtons, on top of the rockery, hands on hips, tummy thrust out under her dress, shouting out orders to her gang of friends – who were being Egyptian slaves building the pyramids. Her fantasies had often involved an element of historical instruction; but the others had wanted to play with her nonetheless, because she made up the best games, the most terrifying ones. They'd launched a leaky raft in the river and nearly drowned – she'd lost her then glasses, they'd lost two oars borrowed from somebody's parents' boathouse. They had kneeled in the dusk with a torch in the ruined greenhouse in the abandoned garden and made chalk marks on the stone floor to call up spirits. They had found dead cats and rats in that garden, and once in a stream they'd sordidly killed an eel by stoning it, because they were too afraid to touch it – afterwards they'd been ashamed of this, and never spoke of it.

Her pen spluttered, she mopped at the mess and then her fingers were inky; she was suddenly sweaty and wondered if the room smelled of her unpleasantly, because she had her period. When she heard her father come in downstairs, she leaped up to open a window, then sat down at her desk again, in a posture of absorbed study. At least her father always came to say hello to her first, because Colette was still his little muffin – though tactfully these days neither of them mentioned it. He knocked before he peered around the door.

— Hard at it? he enquired sympathetically.

— Rotten idiotic essay. *Twelfth Night*.

— Lovely play.

— I know but . . .

— Horrid putting a lovely play through the mincer. What's your theme?

She crossed her eyes comically, which her mother said she shouldn't. — Imagery of growth and decay.

Roger laughed. Her father's intelligence was so much stronger than her mother's, Colette thought; yet it was the slippery labyrinth of her mother's mind – illogical, working through self-suggestion and hunches according to her hidden purposes – which was closed to Colette, and therefore more dangerous for her. Phyllis appeared in the doorway behind her husband, lipsticked brilliantly, wafting scent, draping herself against his shoulder and not-quite-kissing his cheek, because of the lipstick. How was Colette supposed to perform as a young girl while her mother persisted in wearing girlish dresses like this one, with its short skirt and high bustline, trailing ribbons tied in a bow?

— Colette's going to eat with us tonight, Phyllis said in her pleased, encouraging voice. — I'm going to do Hughie beans on toast in a moment, get him out of the way and off to bed.

Roger smiled steadily between his wife and daughter. — Let's hope the occasion lives up to such good company.

— Just don't get any ideas, Colette warned her mother darkly.

— You're always telling me that I don't have ideas.

— But you have stupid ones. Like about me chumming up with this Nicholas Knight, whoever he is. I can tell you right now that he'll hate me.

— He won't hate you. It's much more likely you'll hate him, he's probably dreadfully dull.

— We ought to be nice to him, even if he's dull, Roger said.

8 | TESSA HADLEY

— His mother's a very dear old friend. Because of her, I feel an affinity for this young man. Let's give him our best shot.

Phyllis asked Colette what she was going to wear, she said she refused to wear anything.

Her father said that should sharpen Nicholas's concentration.

Phyllis tied an apron over her dress in the bright modern kitchen which was all yellows and blues, with flowered curtains she'd sewn herself, at the window over the sink. Everything was ready, the pork terrine decorated with bay leaves and glazed in its aspic in the fridge, the charlotte russe inside its palisade of sponge biscuits on the counter, beef fragrant and spitting in the oven. She was an adventurous cook and read Elizabeth David, cut out Len Deighton's columns from the newspaper; over the years she'd educated Roger to like his meat cooked with herbs and garlic. They bought strings of garlic and onions on their holidays in France. It might of course turn out that their guest preferred plain food; hadn't Jean Knight, now she came to think of it, been a funny old stick, the boiled potato type? Well, if Nicholas was fussy then it was time he tried something new.

Stepping out of the kitchen door, she passed down the side of the house and out into the garden. The children's voices had quieted, and the pregnant warm light seemed dense and suspenseful as amber; nothing stirred until a blackbird gave off its clucking alarm cry, burrowing into the dusky, dusty foot of the hedge. Then even before she called for him, Hugh came racing suddenly full pelt from among the trees, alone because the others must have gone in for tea: he was stripped to the waist and wearing his Red

Indian trousers with the white plastic fringe down each seam, aiming his rifle at her, dropping to one knee behind the hammock to squint along his sights until he fired at her, making that pee-yong noise which was supposed to be bullets ricocheting off the rocks. Phyllis died, although feebly, because she didn't want to risk her dress – sometimes she managed almost to frighten him, dropping so authentically in a heap. She closed her eyes and crossed her arms across her chest, staggering and groaning. Hugh came running then, cannoning into her so hard that she spun round under his force, laughing and protesting and hanging on to him so as not to lose her balance. The top of his head came up to her chin, he pressed his probably dirty and snotty face into her breast, she put her face down into his hair and smelled the sun-warmed salty heat of him, undertones of shrubbery and foliage, metallic tang of his gun.

— Confess, Mother, you didn't see that coming.

She was always *Mother*, with this affectionate irony, not Mummy.

— Hughie, get off me, you're ruining my dress!

— The watchword is vigilance! he said.

This happiness can't last, Phyllis thought.

Hugh was nine, he had to go away to school, to grow up and forget her. Phyllis made an effort to hide how much she loved her little son, treating him breezily with a special lightness, bantering and joking, because she believed her too-much-love could damage and pervert his nature. She half hoped that he would lose some of his beauty when he grew to be a man: his good looks were un-canny, like an angel's in a painting, with white-blond hair and wide-open blue eyes, skin that turned in summer to golden brown. He had almost killed her when he was born, in the nursing home after such a long and difficult labour, because he was breech, and the doctors couldn't turn him. And Hugh wasn't ashamed of playing a teasing game of close affection with his mother, indifferent to what his friends might say, supremely confident in his own actions. He sometimes kissed her openly in front of them.

At the kitchen table he shovelled in baked beans on toast with ketchup, swinging his feet out restlessly from the stool where he sat, his gaze roaming around the room but without much interest, telling her about his adventures which she could hardly follow – some woman in Elm Rise was an old witch, it wasn't fair that Smithy had the ARP helmet for two days in a row, they were supposed to capture something from the enemy but Barnes-Pryce got his foot wet, lost his sandal, his folks would blow their tops. When he'd finished a bowl of tinned mandarin oranges, Hugh retreated upstairs – he dreaded visitors, their horrible questioning and fondling. Gregarious outdoors, he was fierce in defence of his privacy inside their home. Only his mother was permitted to cross the threshold of his bedroom; a paper sellotaped to the door warned trespassers, *especially Miss Colette Fischer*, that entry was *Stricly Forbiden and punishable by very Severe Mesures, including Torchure and Death.* Hugh's relationship with his father was amiably superficial, they left each other alone – Roger only took him out on Sundays for cricket practice. Everything that mattered between them was postponed, by tacit agreement, until the time came for Hugh to be sent away to Roger's old school. Once he was at Abingdon he'd understand his father.

Colette had corrected the spelling on her brother's notice with a red pen, and made a point of going into his room whenever

Hugh was out, monitoring the progress of his various collections – which amounted to mania, she privately thought. The room was a chaos, heaped up with penknives, stamp albums, cigar boxes, notebooks. The butterflies he asphyxiated himself in jam jars with laurel leaves, before spearing them with glass-headed pins onto polystyrene ceiling tiles, where gradually they turned brown and fell apart. She was touched, despite herself, by the idea of her little brother so absorbed and solitary in the evenings, sitting on the bed cross-legged in his pyjamas, sorting solemnly through these mad heaps of his possessions, listing and cataloguing. When he was a bonny, beloved, laughing baby, delighted for hours on end with his blue-lustre plastic rattle, tanned from sleeping in the sun in his pram, she hadn't thought he had this seriousness in him.

Nicky Knight was over an hour late for dinner with some old friends of his parents, who were probably appallingly dreary. He had no memory of these people from the past, and couldn't think why he'd agreed to this visit. Was he supposed to get something out of them? But the husband was at the Foreign Office, full of fascists and colonial types – surely even his own fond mother couldn't believe that her son's future lay in that direction? Nicky imagined complacently that there was a file on him in MI5, and that this file must be thick by now with reasons a Foreign Office career was unlikely. The suburban train out to Otterley – trundling between the tamed, meek house backs and allotments, crowded with commuters sweating in their suits, barricaded behind their newspapers – had so filled him with flatness and despair that as soon as he'd got off it he'd fallen into the nearest pub, where he was on his second pint.

Nicky was almost unrecognisable from the unappealing child he'd been when Phyllis Fischer met him years ago. He'd never quite convincingly looked childish: his long nose, full lower lip and dense eyelashes had seemed exaggerated in a little boy, and his ears too had been comically adult-sized, a significant item among his humiliations at school, where he was known as Fat Bat – he had been plump then, with a mop of curls. His parents had moved to live abroad when he was eleven, because his father got into oil: they had lived first in Kuwait and then Teheran, and Nicky had boarded at school and gone out to them in the holidays. He hated his father. Because Peter Knight had wanted him to go to his old college in Cambridge, Nicky had insisted on doing history at Leeds. And now he was long and thin, and his ungainliness answered perfectly to the style of the times. His black curls had grown out straight and his hair hung down well past his collar, so that it was his habitual gesture – almost a tic – to shake it back, raking through it with nicotine-stained fingers, pushing it out of his short-sighted eyes; his glasses were delicately gold-rimmed. The flesh was thick under his eyes and his nose was distinctively crooked, nostrils flared like a thoroughbred; his face seemed marked already with efforts of thought. In concession to the occasion of dinner with the Fischers he had put on a not-quite-clean white shirt and a navy blazer with brass buttons his mother had bought for him, which he wore in a spirit of military parody. No tie: partly because ties symbolised a conformity he despised, and partly because he'd never mastered tying one. At school he'd anxiously preserved the pre-tied noose at the end of each day, slipped it over his head again each morning. If ever he pulled out the knot by accident, he went with it shamefacedly to Matron.

In the pub he huddled in concentration over a paperback of *Tristes Tropiques*, which he was manhandling as he always manhandled books, bending it back so he could hold it and lift his glass and smoke at the same time, turning down corners, dripping ash and beer onto its pages. He claimed it was capitalistic to put a value on books as physical objects – but his mother said he'd wrecked his picture books when he was small, long before he was against capitalism. When he returned her loans she was rueful over swollen pages and broken spines, trying with her competent freckled hands to press them back into shape. — You're not supposed to actually devour them, Nicky, you know, she protested mildly. — It's only a metaphor.

The brown electric light in the pub gathered intensity as the evening grew dusky outside. Everything once pure and whole in primeval life, he thought as he read, was broken and contaminated in the modern era. He was filled with Lévi-Straussian desolation; there remained only the astringency and high style of pessimism. Lifting his head from the page he shook it as if a fly buzzed at him: engraved backwards on the opaque glass of the window he read the words *Commercial and Smoke Rooms* and was afflicted suddenly with unease, because he was late for dinner. Perhaps he was too late, and couldn't face the Fischers after all? But he was hungry, imagining chops, peas, boiled potatoes, mint sauce. Getting up to go, he shoved *Tristes Tropiques* inside out into his blazer pocket.

———

They had been about to start on the terrine without him. It was Colette who came to open the front door, looking – in her own opinion – like a pink blancmange in her dress, peering out blindly into the drive because the lights were bright inside. Nicky's relief at having found the place subsided when he saw her. He had feared that the Fischers would have just such a daughter, lumpy and un-gracious; no hope there of any sex interest, to help while away the tedium of the evening. He would have fled then if he could.

— Oh hello, Colette suspiciously said, not budging from the entrance to the brick front porch, in which they kept umbrellas and wellingtons and mackintoshes, along with the leashes and chewed rubber balls belonging to a couple of dogs long deceased, which no one could bring themselves to throw away. From beyond her, it seemed to Nicky, there shone out the whole deadly entice-ment of a bourgeois life, ordered and upholstered and bathed in warm light, smelling of dinner.

— I've got no sense of direction, he apologised.

They stood confronted, antagonistic. — It's a straight walk up from the station.

Colette might have added, but didn't quite dare – because Nicky had every advantage over her, his age and his freedom and his good looks, and he might have just laughed – that she could smell beer and smoke on him from the pub. He'd probably been in the Queens Head, where she intended to begin drinking herself at some point in the near future.

— You'd be surprised. I mean, how easily I can get lost. On a straight walk, even.

In the dining room Phyllis stood up from where she'd hovered with a knife over the terrine on its plate, striped with glistening pink-and-white bacon; waiting for their guest, they'd lost their appetites. They had been buoyant over the first stiff gin, hardly noticing that he was late; then when Roger proposed a second one, Phyllis had progressed through dizziness to hollow irritability, and began to have a headache. They'd both kept up, however, their veneer of wry humour – unlike Colette prowling angrily in her pink dress, which had a ribbon under the bust just like her mother's, except that Colette's bust was more cumbersome. She'd picked at a bowl of stuffed olives until they were all gone. They were relieved now that Nicholas had turned up at last, but it was too late; a light ash of disappointment had settled over everything. Phyllis couldn't help feeling annoyed with Jean Knight, Roger's old connection. It was Jean who had brought this evening about, writing to Roger out of the blue to ask whether they would be kind to her son, who had moved to London recently and might be short of friends. It was obvious to Phyllis, as soon as she saw Nicky, that they weren't the kind of friends he'd ever choose.

He told them that he'd got lost, and even though none of them believed him – they could smell what Colette had smelled – it was extraordinary what lengths they went to, commiserating and fussing, trying to work out where he'd gone wrong, which streets he had mistaken. Had he unfortunately gone along Beech Avenue, rather than up Dorlcote Lane? With his bemused loose grin, wiping his glasses on his shirt tail, he hardly seemed to make any effort to pass off his lie. They offered him gin and tonic, and when he said he'd rather have beer they were covered in consternation because they didn't have any. Roger had opened a bottle of Moselle to go with the pork, would he like to try that? To be honest, Nicky said, not quite putting them at ease, he would drink anything. Probably not meths, he added, but registered that their laughter was uneasy. They might as well eat right away, Phyllis suggested, with a hint of severity. He must be very hungry.

Nicky seemed outsize in their low-ceilinged dining room, and when they sat down at the table his knees bumped up somehow against its underside, dragging at the tablecloth and the blanket put down to protect the surface; Roger only just saved the water jug. How could this young man, Phyllis wondered crossly, inept and intoxicated in a dirty shirt, make her surroundings seem so absurd and miniature? Yet she loved this house with a protective tenderness. It was all Arts and Crafts, stained glass and gleaming copper fittings, parquet flooring, padded window seats. A dresser in the dining room was set out with rows of the painted plates they'd bought in France; the brick fireplace was filled for the summer with her arrangement of dried flowers and tissue paper. It had been their first real English home, after they returned from years in Cairo.

She squeezed her hand for a moment on Nicky's shoulder as she leaned across from behind him, setting his gin and tonic down beside his place: to placate him and suggest a truce. He was a man, after all. Phyllis was used to communicating with men through these light sexual touches, as much as through her chatter: soothing and bolstering and enticing them, then holding them off. She'd been faithful to Roger always; before him she'd only had one other lover, a terrible mistake. Nicky was supposed to look up at her appreciatively now, or lean back into her grasp of his shoulder; but because her fingers were cold from fishing in the ice bucket – the tongs were lost somewhere – her touch penetrated through the thin material of his shirt, and he recoiled from her unmistakably, with nervous violence, almost knocking the gin out of her hand. And his recoil startled Phyllis, though she carried off her discomfiture in perfect style; no one could have known that she was in the least hurt, sitting down and smiling and picking up her knife again, to serve the terrine. Yet she scalded with humiliation. Nicky had shied away from her touch, and she thought that he could hardly bear to look at her: he was frowning, stabbing with his fork at the tablecloth.

— So, Nicholas, Roger asked with strained joviality. — How are you enjoying London? Making a go of things?

Nicky smiled dimly, blinking – it seemed to take several seconds for the question to arrive with him. — 'Making a go of things', he repeated, as if these words were a strange language. — Yes, I suppose I am doing that.

— And what's next? What's your plan?

— The trouble is, he explained thoughtfully, — that I just don't think about the future in that kind of way. You know, as a series of steps, advancement, arriving at an end goal. Because the end goal really, after all, is death, isn't it? So I wanted to travel: open myself up to other ways of looking at the world. And now that I've stopped travelling, I don't want to just 'get a job', close everything down again.

— Oh tosh, said Colette, but not loudly; she thought that her father must be finding Nicholas Knight preposterous. Yet Roger seemed determined not to give up on him.

— Your mother said you're writing.

Nicky flinched. — Did she? Oh well, you know mothers. She's probably saved up some glorious essay I wrote in primary school, building her hopes on that. It's true though that I did write a novel, last year when I was living in Teheran with them. But then I burned it.

He obviously hated the terrine, pushing it around his plate with his fork.

— Literally burned the whole thing? Colette doubted it. — I'll bet you're keeping it on a shelf, ready to bring out sometime when you're famous.

He looked at her narrowly. — I literally burned it. The gardener was burning weeds in an old oil drum. I fed months of work into his fire, a few pages at a time.

She was impressed in spite of herself. — That must have been hideous.

— It was liberating. I felt more free afterwards. It was supposed to be about the people in the places I'd visited in Iran and Afghanistan, but the truth was that I didn't know what those people were thinking. So there was only me on every page, thinking about them: that was fairly sickening. Then when I came back to England to find some material I could get inside, I discovered I didn't want to write novels after all. It's a dead form.

— No it isn't, Colette protested, but Nicky ignored her.

— So I don't quite know what to do with myself, he went on to Roger. — Because the novel's dead, and the political system's pretty filthy – if you don't mind me saying so.

— No offence taken, Roger said. — We probably don't disagree quite as much as you imagine. Only I'm more resigned to my part in the filthy system.

Nicky said he didn't hold it against him, and Roger asked if Nicky was a Marxist. But Marxism was such a drag, Nicky complained. Getting up at dawn, going out to make a fool of yourself, handing out leaflets to dockers who don't want them, who only want to keep out the West Indians. — They look at your soft hands as if they're already making plans to line you up against a wall somewhere, if the revolution you're idiotically advocating were ever actually to come to pass.

Colette watched to see if her father disapproved of Nicky's flippancy, but he was smiling. The socialists were even drearier, Nicky added glumly: vegetarianism, CND, folk music. — I can see your dilemma, Roger said. — Frustrating, if you can't even campaign for the overthrow of anything.

— I'm just looking around, Nicky said, — to see what happens next. I'm writing a few articles. Perhaps there's another way of doing things. Or I'll go back to Iran and live like a peasant. I suppose you go all over the place for your work, Mr Fischer. Carrying abroad the light of civilisation, or whatever it is that Her Majesty's Government imagines it's doing.

— Mostly a desk job these days, alas, Roger said. — But I have liked to travel. I was sent to improve my Arabic when I was about your age, a set-up the FO has in Lebanon, not far from Beirut, in an old silk factory. That was a marvellous time.

He hardly pretended to be interested. — Oh, really?

Roger said they were lodged with local people, and studied in the evenings by the light of Aladdin lamps; at weekends they hiked in the mountains. — But you're quite right of course – what you said about your novel. The more we began to get hold of the language, the more we realised we didn't know what our hosts were thinking. A salutary lesson for diplomacy.

— You're a linguist.

— Classics at Oxford. Not a bad preparation.

— Roger loves the Middle East, Phyllis said. — We met in Cairo, I'd taken a job out there, I thought I wanted to see the world. It's all my fault that we came home to live in England. I loved Egypt but it didn't agree with me, it made me ill.

— So inconvenient, Nicky said. He was buttering his toast with childish concentration, spreading right to the edges. — What I can't stand are the smiling bright faces of the expats in all those places. No offence to you, Mrs Fischer. I've been one of them, I know: although, in my own defence, I've never smiled much. But it's the British and American expats in particular: steeped in crime for so long, and yet those bright guileless faces like infants, wiped clean of bloody deeds, so innocently ugly. While the faces of the oppressed are weighed down with sin, and ancient. As old as the hills.

— I can see you might make a writer, Roger said.

Phyllis was hardly listening to Nicky, except to note his disapproval. She was still reacting to his recoil from her, when she squeezed his shoulder. She'd begun joking recently about becoming an old woman: she'd pictured herself sliding across serenely into middle age, fulfilled and busy with her house and her hobbies. But all this cheerful resignation, she recognised now, had been a sham, mere self-deception. It hadn't seriously occurred to her, in her deeper awareness, that anything had changed or must ever change; she'd taken for granted that at her core her sexual self would continue for ever, a nugget of radioactive material charged with its power, irreducible. Now she was afraid that she'd sickened Nicky when she touched him, just as she'd been sickened by the leering older men who'd groped at her when she was his age.

It was her turn to be old and repulsive. Wasn't that what he meant by what he was saying? Women like her, and of her class, were repulsive to the young. Probably no one would desire her ever again, apart from Roger.

They were all more or less drunk by this time: apart from Colette, who judged them from the lonely eminence of her sobriety. Every last detail of Nicky's presence seemed significant for Phyllis, because she might be shut out from now on from youth and beauty: purple smudges under his eyes, taut creases that came beside his lips when he smiled to himself in irony, nicotine-stained fingertips which trembled when he lit up a cigarette after finishing his toast. She had been careless of these things, she thought, when they were easily attainable. His movements were so loosely spontaneous, outraging all the conventions the Fischers lived by: she seemed to see their constraint and formality through his eyes. Nicky stubbed out his cigarette, right in the middle of his slice of her terrine. Phyllis hadn't known that the young had this power, to reduce the present of the middle-aged to rubble.

It was only when she touched him that Nicky noticed Phyllis Fischer properly. He had seen her, until that moment, through the fog of all the things he'd taken for granted about her: for instance, that she was somewhere about the age and sexlessness of his own mother. He had taken in a familiar enveloping solicitousness, a pointless fussing: these weren't unwelcome but weren't interesting. However, when Phyllis claimed him with her cold hand, he was jolted: something at least was alive, beneath the stultifying surface of this conversation. He had been looking for sexual interest in the wrong place. It wasn't the daughter whose attractions might pass the tedious time this evening, but the mother: younger than he'd thought and eager, with that pretty, sandy muzzle of a face. The blurred big mouth – pink lipstick seeping into the cracks in her lips – gave her away somehow as playful and irresponsible, for all her performance as the ideal housewife. No doubt she was as bored as he was, bored to death. It was unfortunate, though, that she cooked this kind of French food. He couldn't bring himself to touch the meat she'd served as a first course, because there were white lumps of fat in it, he hated fat. The beef at least was eatable: her potatoes were too rich, she'd sliced them and cooked them with cream and butter. He tried hiding the gratin dauphinois under his knife, an old boarding-school trick.

Her husband, of course, was Nicky's enemy, with his frozen conversation, his well-worn ironies. Roger was the Establishment: his starred first from Oxbridge, his good war, decorated at Monte Cassino – Nicky's mother had enumerated all these, proud to be the friend of such a man. What was more natural, faced with this unanswerable force of his rival, than to seduce the wife? That is, not actually seduce her: after all, these were his parents' friends. But seduce her at least in his thoughts. He wondered, if he pulled at that ribbon on Phyllis's dress, what would come undone? When she stood up to fetch a bowl of salad from the sideboard, he saw that the ribbon was purely decorative, the dress undid in fact at the back with a zip. Refusing salad, and between elements of his conversation with her husband, fending off the pestiferous daughter, he imagined holding Phyllis's body against his, reaching down across her shoulders to undo the dress. She would be silky and complicated in his arms in only her slip and brassiere, smearing him with pink lipstick, mysteriously experienced.

Nicky had had an acceptable number of sexual adventures, but worried that none of them had been transforming. Uncomfortably, he shifted from where his knees were jammed up under the table. The schoolgirl in her unfortunate pink – Cornelia? Caroline? – was obdurate, and her gaze made him uneasy, so that he could only glance furtively every so often at her mother; his attention was glued of necessity to Roger Fischer. He noticed that Roger used his fork to cut his food, resting his right hand in a fist on the checked cloth beside his place.

— Is that an old war wound, sir?

Who knew where that *sir* came from: out of his childhood comics, maybe? Or a shaming remainder from the school he'd hated. Nicky knew even as he used it that it sounded too much like mockery, though mockery wasn't exactly what he'd meant. Roger looked down at his hand as if he'd forgotten it: something in its shape was wrong, fingers curling weakly against the palm, tendons withered and sunken, skin taut and purplish: thinking about it, he made an effort to stretch it out. — Nothing so glorious, he said. — I've learned to mostly use the other one.

— Oh Roger, it is a war wound! Phyllis exclaimed, relieved by an opportunity to display her wifely devotion. — Only not the actual war: afterwards, in Egypt, over Palestine. The Stern Gang bombed a train, a shard of metal pierced his hand, he nearly lost it. This was before I knew him, but I heard all about it – though not from Roger, you can be sure of that. His friends told me.

— Cairo to Haifa train, February '48, carrying a lot of military. Wrong place at the wrong time. No heroics.

— It's not true, Phyllis eagerly said. — He was heroic, helping with the wounded, although he was in such pain himself. There were hundreds of soldiers dead.

— Not hundreds, Phyl.

— You ought to be grateful to him. I mean, we all ought to be grateful. I know I am.

— Now you're really embarrassing me. But is there pudding? I'm holding out hopes for pudding: you have laid spoons. Perhaps a glass of Madeira with it? Shall I get the Madeira out?

— I suppose you despise my generation, Nicky said bitterly.

— Our generation, Colette corrected him, but Nicky said it didn't count in the same way for a girl, girls were lucky. Roger said he didn't despise their generation, not in the least. He thought they had an opportunity to look around them with clear heads.

— I suppose you think, Nicky went on, — that we'll never be heroes, because we'll never be tested in the way you were. But we don't want to be. At least I don't. I'm happy to come clean: I'd fail every test you want to put to me. And I don't care. I'm a coward and I glory in it. A world built by cowards would be a better place. We could all sleep in peace and read our books.

— Somebody would still have to make the beds and cook the dinner, Phyllis said merrily, trying to lighten the tone.

— You don't make the beds, Colette said. — Mandy Verey does.

She was surprised to see her mother blush darkly then, as if she were ashamed of something – which she never was. Phyllis was thinking that now Nicky Knight would despise her thoroughly. She was not only old and repulsive but she had servants too.

———

At that point the telephone rang in the hall and Phyllis went to answer it. It was the mother of one of Hugh's friends, complaining that her son had come home minus a sandal. Phyllis pretended to know nothing about it. — Such naughty boys, she commiserated, but too flippantly. Patsy Barnes-Pryce seemed to reproach her.

— I don't know if they think we're made of money.

The Barnes-Pryces *were* made of money though, Phyllis thought. Patsy's husband was a stockbroker, they were stinking rich. — It would be much appreciated if you or Roger could go out and take a look, Patsy was saying.

— But we don't have a fish pond!

— No, but the Chidgelys do, and they're away in Switzerland. Don't you have a key? I thought you were feeding their cat.

— I suppose I could look for it in the morning, Phyllis said doubtfully.

— I'm worried about foxes, Patsy firmly said. — I think you should go now. Take a torch. He says it's by the nymph.

— What nymph?

— No idea. But surely you'll know a nymph when you see one?

Phyllis felt quite dizzy, and thought that she must collect herself: the Barnes-Pryces were churchy types and wouldn't approve if they thought that she'd been drinking. Twisting the telephone cord around her hand, standing on the Turkey rug, flexing her stockinged feet up and down – she must have kicked off her shoes under the dining table, she did that sometimes when she was tipsy – she could hear her own voice, charming and hesitating, trying to refuse Patsy without offending her, explaining that they had a dinner guest. But really! she exclaimed to herself. It was dark outside! And why on earth should she go looking for Milo's soggy sandal?

With its boxed-in oak staircase and panelled oak doors, she thought then that this hall she loved was like a stage set, for a play by somebody out of fashion. And it was as if not only Patsy's voice but her own continued at some distance, far off along the telephone wires, and was quite unreal. The only reality was the present moment gathered around her in this deep well of quiet and velvety dimness, its light tinged pink by the shades on the lamps she had made out of glass demijohns, gleaming on the brass pots with her arrangements of ostrich feathers, dried seed heads. Talk went on without her in the dining room whose door was just ajar, some argument rising and falling. Phyllis felt the present moment on her nerve ends, prickling with sensation; unseeing, she rifled the pages of their address book, soft with use, stuffed with cards and lists, a few names of friends and relations who had died crossed out respectfully. In all that stillness one pulse was racing: hers. Her life was passing, passing. Catching sight of her own face unclearly in the square of mirror in the hallstand, she thought that she looked bewildered, victim of something, assaulted.

— The thing is, Patsy went on inexorably, — that I've found a little man, a specialist maker, frightfully expensive. Because altogether we've had a nightmare with Milo's feet.

Upstairs, Hugh's bedroom door creaked open: he had a sixth sense for when any business on the telephone concerned himself, and he crept to sit cross-legged, with folded arms, in his striped pyjamas on the half landing, where the staircase turned to descend into the hall. Sighing, eventually Phyllis agreed to go and look, and to call Patsy back. — You're terribly kind, said Patsy insincerely.

— I'll bet that was the egregious Madame Barnes-Pryce, Hugh sagely said when Phyllis had replaced the receiver. — About the sandal scandal.

— That woman's the limit!

— I'll tell you something else. The sandal's in.

— What d'you mean, in? In the pond? But she says he took it off and left it by a nymph.

— He did. But someone else, following after, kicked it in.

— Not you, Hugh?

— Mother, how could you think? Scout's honour. But I saw.

Phyllis couldn't help herself laughing. She thought that her son was like her, he understood her. — Go back to bed at once, she said. — What time do you call this?

Colette cleared the plates grudgingly, while her mother was on the phone. The two men were left awkwardly alone together; surely when they'd had pudding, Nicky thought, he could make his escape. Roger asked after Cressing, the Knights' house in Suffolk; they'd let the place for years while they lived abroad, and now they'd decided at last to settle at home in England. Nicky said he didn't go often to Cressing himself, the house gave him asthma, he was allergic to his own childhood – but his mother was very happy there. His father didn't like the country, spent more time in the flat in Woburn Square. Roger said that he'd grown fond of Cressing when he'd been there during the war, as a young man. He'd visited on leave because Peter Knight had been a friend of Roger's father, the two men had worked together for a while – though his father hadn't had anything like Peter's success. Roger had held on to the idea of a place like Cressing, he said, during tough times. — That somewhere there was a cosy old house in the country, you know. Nothing vast, but with a library, a few swans on a moat, and an observatory. Ridiculous, of course. Because the place wasn't mine, nor anything like it. I don't come from that kind of property, nor from that class: your class, Nicholas, I suppose. I don't even really approve of a landowning class, theoretically.

— Oh, *my* class. I disown my class.

— Easier said than done. I was a scholarship boy. My father was an accountant.

— It's striking, incidentally, Nicky mused, embarrassed by the older man's confession, — that every day my mother discovers more things broken or stolen by the tenants who had the house while she was away. It's making her slightly unhinged. It's as if she goes around wanting her heart to be torn: hunting in the backs of cupboards for pieces of smashed vases that she'd forgotten she even possessed until she lost them.

— I don't think of Jean as in the least concerned for material possessions.

— It's an overreaction probably. After her years of wandering. Oh, and they send their love. At least, my mother does. I don't really talk to my father. I've no idea whether he has love to spare from himself and his ghastly mistress to send to anyone, although I doubt it.

Roger smoothed the tablecloth, perturbed: perhaps it wasn't good form, Nicky thought, for him to have mentioned the mistress.

Then just as Colette brought in the charlotte russe, Phyllis arrived from the hall with a stricken face, her wellington boots in her hand, and said that she had to go out. — What do you mean, out? Roger asked in concern, half standing up from the table. — Where?

— Honestly, that bloody woman. Excuse my French.

The sandal problem was irresistibly ridiculous: all of them were glad to be breaking up the party around the table. Windows had been open all evening onto the garden, but when Phyllis opened the doors onto the paved terrace, the room was all at once alive with night air, laden with scent from the Albertine rose that grew in pink profusion over a pergola. On the terrace she began pulling on her wellingtons, explaining over her shoulder to her lit-up audience, from a half crouch, that she couldn't actually go through the Chidgelys' house into their garden because she'd temporarily mislaid their key, only she hadn't wanted Patsy Barnes-Pryce to know that. It would only have added to Patsy's sense of her incompetence – the key must be somewhere. She'd been feeding the Chidgelys' cat – or rather Colette had, she was the one they were paying to do it – by getting into their garden the same way the children had got out of it in their game earlier on, through a gap in the hedge at the far end. Luckily the Chidgelys kept a spare back door key under a flowerpot. — So I have to go this way, if I'm going to fish Milo's bloody sandal out of their pond – if it's even really in there in the first place. Do we have a torch?

— You should have just stood up to her, Colette said.

— We'll all come with you, Nicky suggested, wanting to escape Roger's interrogation. Colette said that she could feed the cat at the same time. Phyllis was cross that she hadn't already fed it.

— Poor Sim: what if he starved? Now, *you* could look for the sandal, on your way.

But she only suggested it half-heartedly: she was ready in her wellingtons and wanted to get out, away from whatever she'd found around the dinner table. Colette said that if anyone thought she was fishing in ponds for the Barnes-Pryces at this time of night they had another think coming. — We ought to bring a slotted spoon or something. We don't want to actually use our hands, Phyllis said, seizing an unsuitable silver serving spoon. Roger went off to look for a torch in the garage, and while he was gone Colette found a red plastic one in the dresser drawer: then they couldn't wait for him to begin. Because of the absurdity of their quest, they were infected with childish irresponsibility, plunging away from the sociable bright lights into darkness, re-turned inside their private selves under its cover, aware of one another with a renewed intensity.

Halfway down the garden, lawn and flower beds gave way to a few sparsely planted young birch trees, blotched trunks spectral in the torchlight. The torch was weak and flickered; Colette shook it hard and it went out altogether. Nicky tripped over a tree root and the other two, yelping, grabbed at him: they all hung on to one another. Then the blackness yielded to their eyes strained open, and they began to make out shapes again: upright inky pen-strokes of the trees, numbly squatting tool shed to their left, dark mass of the tall hedge dividing them from the Chidgelys' garden to their right. Above them, stars. Roger called amiably from the house: outlined against the light inside, he appeared when they looked back like someone left onshore when a ship has sailed. The night was ripe with the earth's exhalations: mushroom-pungent leaf mould, hint of reeking fox, foliage sour from fermenting all day in the sun. The broad brown significant river, close at hand, flowed too fast and was too full to lap or babble; coiling mud-rich against its banks, it seemed, if you knew it was there, to damp off sound like a felt blanket; cries of late-settling birds rent it sharply. Phyllis's arm was hooked into Nicky Knight's and she was aware, through the thin wool of his blazer, of the sharpness of his elbows and his preoccupied loose lope. Colette led them confidently, despite the darkness, to the gap in the hedge. A fox barked. — It's a tight squeeze, she warned, and then after a tussle she was on the other side. Nicky went next and helped pull Phyllis after him, although the hedge, which was taller than they were, felt at first impenetrably dense: she was prodded and scratched, its twigs caught stiffly in her dress and her hair, she almost dropped the spoon.

Once they were safely through, Colette said she would leave them to it, and set off towards the lightless back of the Chidgelys' house; when she shook the torch again it began this time to work. The cat poured sinuously from nowhere to impede her progress even against his own interests, winding around her ankles; she found the key under the flowerpot, let herself inside, forked out cat's meat from the horrid tin in the fridge, turning her face away, grimacing, from the stink. Then when she'd washed her hands she wandered; the Chidgelys' house was interesting in their absence as it wasn't when they were in residence. They were a dull family and the house was unlovely, without any signs of art – the nymph beside the pond wasn't characteristic, she'd been inherited from previous owners and they were merely resigned to her. Kitchen cupboards were full of greasy Tupperware, used instant-coffee jars were labelled for self-raising flour and pudding rice, a grandma had crocheted covers for their saggy feather cushions. At school Colette avoided any appearance of acquaintance with Anthea Chidgely, who was two years younger and sang hymns eagerly in morning assembly, enjoyed hockey and maths: she had pale hair and eyes and her downy skin smelled of the ointment she put on her spots.

Yet in Anthea's bedroom, poking through her things, Colette was moved: the material evidence of a life was eloquently suggestive, as long as you didn't have the life thrust in your face. She thought about how it would feel to be in here if the Chidgelys, all five of them, had been wiped out in a car accident in Switzerland: Anthea's collection of costume dolls under those circumstances would seem poignant, eloquent. Who knew how these Red Indian squaws and Macedonian peasants and Eskimos had figured in her imagination? Colette made herself comfortable on Anthea's raspberry-pink eiderdown, looking probably, she considered, like blancmange on jelly. Sim came to sit purring on her stomach, helping with the pain, kneading it with his paws – she only protested when he licked her face, his breath was too disgusting. Each evening while she was cat-sitting, she allowed herself two from the tall pile of Anthea's *Bunty* comics.

– Without the torch, can we see the pond, or will we just fall into it? Nicky said.

—— We have to look out for a nymph.

—— Oh, Mrs Fischer, but . . . Do you still believe in nymphs, hasn't anyone . . . ?

— I've led a very sheltered life, Nicholas.

— I hate to awaken you from your dream.

He found matches in his pocket, managed to strike one, they peered around them in the little den of light it made. Phyllis said she supposed this nymph was some kind of awful fake statue. — We can't quite see their pond from our upstairs. But the Chidgelys have terrible taste.

— *The Chidgelys have terrible taste.*

Nicky imitated her, teasing her. But somehow this wasn't rude, it was flirting, it was his kind of flirting, she basked in it. He shook out the match and swore when it burned his fingers. — *Christ.* What's taste, anyway? What about your taste? Perhaps the Chidgelys think that's awful?

And Nicky all the time was thinking, I'm flirting with her, but I'd better not go too far, they're Mummy's friends. On the other hand, they had both of them been drinking and weren't quite responsible for their actions. Nicky almost fell over the nymph before he saw her, by the light of another match: a pale form, child-sized, with her hands upraised, her back to them, backside chastely draped, enchanting in the dark as she might not have been in daylight. There came a secretive trickling, presumably some kind of system for aeration, from the small pond beyond her. Phyllis and Nicky kneeled together warily on its crazy-paving edge, and made out, by the light of a third match, lily pads against a surface of dark water which was somehow repellent, so that Phyllis couldn't imagine plunging her hand through it, though she held her spoon ready hopefully. — It all seems more complicated now that we're actually here. What was I thinking of, agreeing to look at this time of night? That woman's too used to getting her own way. I must have been mad. Who knows what's in here? Worse than fish . . .

In a fit of bravado, rolling up his sleeve, Nicky plunged his hand in, then quickly pulled it out again. — Slimy, he grimaced. — Are there fish, do we know?

— Here, try the spoon. Though it's entirely the wrong kind of spoon.

Nicky felt around with it unconvincingly, not quite reaching the pond's bottom. Each could make out the other's darker form against the darkness.

— Oh come on, give it here.

She was suddenly bold and desperate, raking with the spoon, cursing Patsy Barnes-Pryce, heedless, giving up on the spoon, splashing, groping with her hand.

— There! Success! Ha!

Triumphantly she lifted up Milo's sandal out of the water, which streamed everywhere: it had been kicked almost to the middle of the pond. Nicky hadn't ever believed they would find it: in fact he'd pretty much forgotten what they were looking for, out here insanely fishing in someone's garden pond in the middle of the night. Under the placid surface of suburbia, something was unhinged. The influence of *Tristes Tropiques*, kept at bay in the Fischers' bourgeois domain, had come flooding back in the dark while they searched: as Phyllis stirred up the rotten bottom of the pond, he'd seemed to breathe in the vegetable, tropical, hothouse flowering of Brazil. The little nymph was a symbol of some ruined civilisation, keeping watch over their violation of the place; Nicky felt himself a pinprick in the scale of history. When Phyllis jubilantly laughed, sitting back on her heels, holding the dripping sandal away from her, he swayed across the space between them: the thought had come from somewhere that he ought to kiss her, if he wasn't bourgeois, didn't care for their niceties. Wasn't this dangerous life, and shouldn't he seize it?

He aimed for her cheek in the dimness, but she turned her mouth hungrily to his. Her kiss was arousing, alarmingly garlicky – he imagined himself fallen into a hot cave of grown-up pleasures which was somehow also Brazilian. The sodden sandal was suddenly nothing. Phyllis dropped it indifferently with the spoon on the paving behind her; her hand came up exploring inside his blazer, gripping his shoulder, pond water soaking his shirt. Their kiss went on, opening and closing, aching, slippery. At last they fell back from each other, breathing hard, close enough to make out the form of each other's faces, her palm on his neck, wet fingers pushed into his hair. — I thought you hated me, she said.

Actually he had no idea what he felt about her.

But Phyllis was thinking already that Nicky was her lover, or would become it. No one had kissed her like that, so wetly and hungrily, in all the years of her marriage; that space had been un-filled in her passionate nature. There had been one other man she'd briefly loved – long ago in Cairo, before Roger. But that affair had turned into something ugly and she'd buried the memory of it, marrying Roger instead and reacting against passion, seeming to see through it and believing she could live without it. This version of her life story was spooling through her mind even as she kissed Nicky: now she thought that she'd been waiting all this time, to find him. She was intoxicated with Nicky's thinness, his jaw lean and smooth as a girl's, his mouth sour from cigarette smoke, everything in him that was unfinished and casual and impolite. The thud of desire, plummeting through her body like a weight, rearranged everything inside her, changed her beyond recognition; *he's my lover,* she thought with finality. Phyllis was quick and adaptable, responsive: she took things with an outward grace and lightness. But she was also superstitious and stubborn. Once she had told herself a certain story it became fixed, and no reasoning or evidence to the contrary could shake it.

Before there was even time for them to kiss again, Roger called to them from the far side of the hedge. — Any luck?

Phyllis pulled away from Nicky, touching his cheek with a tenderness that was almost motherly. — We have to go back, she murmured in his ear. — Don't be afraid, I'll come to you, I'll find a way. But you must leave a telephone number, he'll expect you to do that. Then I can call you.

Roger must have brought out a better torch with a strong light. The hedge was too tall, fortunately, for him to see over or shine the torch on them – its beam combed the night above them futilely. Nicky was still bemused, dizzy and swollen with desire, ashamed; Phyllis stood up, pulling down her dress, collecting the soaked sandal and the spoon. She shouted out ringingly into the darkness, exultant like a child in a game who's got the prize: *We found it!* Her performance as a contented wife was consummately good. It frightened Nicky: what depths of experience had he stumbled into? He had taken the Fischers at their face value, as respectable and innocent. Now it appeared that he might have been the innocent himself. By matchlight, though the matches shook in his fingers, they found the gap in the hedge and pushed through again, Phyllis first; as he emerged on the far side where Roger waited, they all saw by the light of his torch that Nicky's white shirt wasn't only soaked with pond water, it was smeared and filthy with mud and green slime from the bottom of the pond, which matched exactly the mud on Phyllis's hands and her dress. — Look at the state of you both! Roger exclaimed. — How did that happen?

Nicky was appalled, contemplating his shirt in the beam of light, which made him feel like a target. He expected Roger Fischer at any moment to see through this criminal evidence to what had happened beside the pond with his wife. Also, the wet material clung to the skin of his chest unpleasantly.

— Look at me, Phyllis cried. — This dress is dry-clean only! And poor Nicky, you are in a mess! I'll have to find you a clean shirt: you can borrow one of Roger's. Because it was all in a good cause, darling: Nicky fished it out. Look! We found Milo Barnes-Pryce's wretched sandal. In pitch-darkness too, which is why we've made such a hash of it. I can phone Patsy and tell her what trials we've put our dinner guest through for her sake.

— But where's Colette? I presumed she at least had a torch.

— She did, but took it up to the Chidgelys' with her naturally, to feed the cat.

— I'm embarrassed by what our family's inflicted on you, Nicholas.

— Don't worry about me, Nicky assured him. — Happy to help.

— The whole thing was too silly, Roger said. — We're not usually so silly. Can we make it up to you? Won't you stay over? We have a spare room. I'm thinking you must have missed that last train already. Phyl can rinse out your shirt, have it dry by morning, give you a good breakfast.

— Oh, the shirt's not a problem, Nicky said desperately. — I can go like this, it doesn't matter. What time is it? I have to get back. Surely I haven't missed the train?

— Of course you haven't missed it. Phyllis was suavely reassuring. — Roger can run you to the station. And as soon as we're inside you can get that wet shirt off and have a wash and tidy-up, while he backs the car out of the garage. Your blazer's not too bad. I'd just hang it up to dry if I were you, when you get home. Then give it a good brushing.

She brought a clean shirt to the bathroom door while Nicky was washing, running the hot tap hard so that the pipes squealed, clouding the mirrors with steam, sobering up, burying his face in the towel to obliterate his wincing awareness of what had happened. Discreetly, she knocked. — The sleeves will be too short on you, but that won't show under your blazer, she called out loud. Nicky opened the door dismayed, naked to the waist. — I'm so sorry, Mrs Fischer, he whispered urgently. — I must have drunk too much.

Phyllis touched with her fingertips his chest where the skin was pale and hairless, clammy with steam, taut over his ribs so that she thought of some delicate boat, a coracle. Bending her head she quickly kissed his shoulder, and he felt the light mass of her hair compress against his neck. In the bathroom's harsh light, when she raised her face to his he saw that she wasn't young. Not old either, her flesh wasn't drooping or loosening, but a strain was gathering in it: tension at the edge of her lips, under her eyes the skin faintly blue. Her vivid colour was crisp, autumnal. — Leave your number, don't forget, she said.

When he didn't give Roger his number Phyllis wasn't worried. She only thought that he must have forgotten, in his confusion at having to be alone with her husband in the car, after what had happened. She felt for his trepidation, knew herself fearless and ruthless enough for both of them. Phyllis could find him easily, anyhow; she only had to ask his parents, she could think up some excuse. In the hall after they'd left for the station, telephoning Patsy Barnes-Pryce about the sandal, stretching up on her toes, turning in slow circles on the rug, invisible to Patsy, she had heard the joy bubbling in her own voice, irrepressible. There wasn't a thought in her head, she wasn't thinking. It was too soon, she would begin thinking tomorrow. Patsy was interrogating her suspiciously, as if something was her fault. — But how did it get into the water in the first place? she protested. — I only hope it's not ruined.

In fact Nicky never meant to leave his number, he had no serious idea that evening that he'd started anything with Phyllis Fischer. The only moment he came close to mumbling some politeness about staying in touch was when Roger dropped him off at the station and got out of the car to shake hands under the station lights, seeming reluctant to part with him. He extracted *Tristes Tropiques* from where it was mangled in Nicky's blazer pocket. — Treat your books a bit more kindly, old man, he'd said, folding its covers back into place, trying to press it into shape with his good hand. — Are you enjoying it? I liked this a lot. Incurably romantic, though.

— It's the saddest thing I've ever read, Nicky exclaimed. He said that civilisation was an appalling error; Roger assured him it didn't do to take these things too much to heart.

— It's the French, you know. They go in for that high style.

No one else was about, the suburbs were sunk late at night in their deathly torpor. Roger put his arm on the young man's shoulder and let it weigh there for a few moments heavily, consoling him.

Colette came in half an hour after her parents had gone to bed, through the French windows which they'd left unlocked for her. One lamp in the dining room was left on: she had an opportunity for a moment, before the film of familiarity settled on everything, to see her own home in the same alienated light as she'd seen the Chidgelys'. Phyllis had cleared the table and stacked dishes in the kitchen, ready for Mandy in the morning. The room seemed smaller than Colette remembered from two hours ago, more crowded with furniture, stuffier with smells from dinner, stupider. Needlepoint chair backs – English wild flowers against bottle-green – had come with the house, pointlessly stitched by some unknown woman with nothing better to do, probably long dead. For an instant Colette seemed to see that something had happened in this room just now: it showed like a bright thread flicked across the floor, pulled out of sight at once. But there was no outward sign of any disorder – except that her mother had kicked off her high-heeled shoes under the table and forgotten them, tipped ungainly on their sides, scuffed, with the heels crossed like swords.

TWO

Almost, Phyllis turned back.

She had never been to this part of London before. Usually when she caught the train up to town for the day it was for shopping at Dickins & Jones, or to meet one of her sisters for lunch at Simpson's in the Strand. In Ladbroke Grove – where Jean Knight had told Phyllis her son was renting a *pretty ghastly* room – there was rubbish lying out on the street, windows were broken in cavernous brooding houses which must have been grand once. Now they were subdivided into flats and bedsits, their pillared and porticoed grandeur was decayed and rotten, their front gardens were heaped with discarded mattresses and old sinks, overgrown with ash saplings and buddleia. Filthy old bedspreads were pinned across inside the windows for curtains; the end wall of one terrace was painted with two disembodied red mouths, smoke coiling out of them between laughing white teeth. Phyllis supposed with a frisson of fear that these mouths were smoking pot.

And she'd never seen so many coloured faces before, anywhere in England. Of course she had lived in Cairo for all those years, she was used to moving among brown-skinned people in the streets – but that was not the same. There, you knew you were an outsider, shut out from their way of life – and yet at the same time felt yourself sealed off from them, safe inside your whiteness, which made you immune and invisible. Anyway, those were Arabs, which was different. She didn't feel invisible now, she felt conspicuous in her beige mac, beige shoes, pretty mauve flowered blouse and silk scarf, chosen to be careless and joyful; it was spitting with rain and the afternoon light was bruised and lurid, making the streets tunnel-like. When she'd chosen her clothes so carefully it hadn't occurred to her to imagine wearing them in a deprived area like this, where their expensive smartness seemed flagrant and ill-advised. She'd only been thinking of showing herself to Nicky, making him love her.

Jean Knight had laughed when Phyllis telephoned about the shirt.

— Poor old Roger, she said. — I hope he gets his shirt back in one piece – laundered would probably be too much to hope for. Nicky's a disaster with other people's belongings, I'm so sorry. But did the shirt fit? Nicky's such a scarecrow, he gets that from me. Roger's quite a different physique. How did your evening go? Was Nicky well behaved?

Phyllis had liked Jean, talking to her on the phone: she was warm and direct, no subterfuges. In all the days since Nicky had kissed her at the dinner party, Phyllis had been in such a strange condition of absorption, as if she moved and acted just as normal, yet in a trance; when she talked to his mother, shaming recognitions loomed for a moment in this mist of vagueness, almost burning through it, so that she would be forced to know what she was doing. But she prevented the recognition, thrust it back to where it was harmless, outside the cocoon of the absolute preoccupation that wrapped her up. It wasn't Nicky's words she played over and over to herself, it was rather the wordless minutes of their one long kiss, until she wore out the freshness of her own recollection of it. Then she was frantic – silently, invisibly, rigidly frantic – in her need to renew the freshness, kiss him again. It was only now, searching for his room in Ladbroke Grove, that Phyllis properly understood the unsoundness and risk in this pursuit of him. She was afraid of danger as she'd never been in Cairo, and couldn't stop and consult her A–Z map, because she didn't want to betray herself as a foolish outsider. It was best to stride on purposefully, heels tapping and echoing with authority, down these dark streets where she was lost.

She almost turned back.

But then when she tried to imagine turning and retracing her steps to the Underground station, going back on the train to tell Roger she'd been up to town clothes shopping but hadn't found anything she liked, putting macaroni cheese in the oven for supper, it was as if she saw herself turning round and walking with her so purposeful stride, in her pretty mauve blouse, slam into a blank wall across her path, beyond which there was nothing. A few weeks ago, before Nicky kissed her, she'd have laughed at such exaggeration. Now she couldn't laugh at it because she felt it: the violence of that blow, the nothingness of her self, crumpled at the foot of this wall across her life.

And anyway, just as she tried to imagine turning back, she saw that she'd arrived, more by luck than judgement, at Everglade Buildings – where Nicky Knight in any case would probably not be at home. He was not waiting for her, he had no idea that she was coming.

The Everglade was a crumbling vast art nouveau palace, built at the turn of the century to contain sixty luxury serviced apartments. There were a few old ladies left, too penniless to move anywhere else and certainly no longer serviced, who wore gloves when they went out and were in mourning for a time when the place was select and elegant, with a restaurant and hairdressers on the ground floor. Now it had fallen from grace, broken up into who knew how many run-down bedsits and sublets, taken over by ex-boxers, theatricals, members of occult sects, tarot-card readers, revolutionaries. Every-one who was anyone in the counterculture had stayed in the Ever-glade at some point. The roof leaked in a thousand places and no one seemed to be responsible for mending it; once or twice an excess of stone ornamentation from the façade had crashed into the street below. Nicky Knight's room was on the top floor, inside the roof space, so that its walls slanted spectacularly; it was freezing in win-ter, broiling in summer, and lit by half of an outsized flamboyant round mansard window, partitioned so that its other half was in the bathroom he shared with five other tenants.

Nicky had tried to forget about kissing his parents' old friend; every so often the scene would flash on his inner eye, making him clammy with embarrassment and vaguely excited. His sexual life otherwise was humiliatingly unsatisfactory. An idyll of playful sex-ual ease seemed to lie only just out of reach — what prevented him from arriving at it? You heard about everyone sleeping with every-body. And there were so many attractive and fascinating women, he saw them all around on the streets and in bars; the films he watched were knee-deep in possibilities. Whenever he did manage to get hold of a girl, she was a disaster, too silly or too plain, too awkward or too keen, so that he was eager to get rid of her next morning.

Idly, and ashamed, he had made use of Phyllis now and again in his fantasies. Then suddenly, one Wednesday afternoon, rapping with a brisk little fist at his door, she was actually there – the least plausible person to materialise amid his sordid solitude. His first instinct was to apologise for the stuffy smell and the unmade bed, for himself. He should open the window, he suggested. — I'm so sorry.

— I brought back your shirt, she said, smiling.

She had it in a little wicker basket, slung over her arm. Phyllis didn't look dishevelled even from climbing the five flights of stairs; she looked fresh and eager, more petite than he remembered, bright with her veneer of female charm. In these surroundings, in her fashionable clothes, he thought she was like a charity worker visiting the less fortunate – he half expected her to take nourishing food for him out of her basket as well as the laundered and ironed shirt, which was folded in tissue paper. — You didn't use the lift? he hoped, playing for time. — Because it gets stuck. It probably hasn't been inspected since before the war. Unwary strangers have been stuck between floors for hours on end.

— Thank goodness I wasn't tempted then. I didn't know which floor you were on.

— It's this one, at the very top. I mean, obviously, as you're here.

— I'm lucky you're at home. Aren't you going to invite me in?

— It isn't very nice inside.

— I don't care what it's like. I'm not such an old square as you think.

Nicky wasn't dressed, he was still in his dressing gown; he was writing something on R.D. Laing for a new periodical started by one of his friends from university, and he'd promised to deliver it by tomorrow morning. His consciousness swung round only slowly from intense absorption in ideas to face in this new direction, processing Phyllis Fischer's appearance. How had she found out where he lived? Was she really simply returning his shirt? God knew what he'd done with the shirt he'd borrowed; certainly he hadn't taken it yet to the launderette. This woman was old enough to be his mother, and respectably married to a good man. What did she mean, by her pursuit of him? He didn't want to become entangled in her world of table napkins and candelabra and French food. Yet the idea of making love to her was also flattering. She was good-looking, she smelled nice. With a mature woman, presumably you could to some extent leave her in charge.

Phyllis slipped off her mac as if she were staying, dropped it over the back of his chair; Nicky remembered that at her dinner table, even before he kissed her, he'd liked her breasts, which showed as small and shapely now under her flowered blouse. She said this was just how she'd imagined his room would be – typewriter on the desk, coffee cups, books everywhere; she stood looking around with an exalted expression at the mess he lived in. Women were entranced, Nicky thought, by the external fittings of the intellectual life. They loved the *idea* of thought, the outward look of it; Phyllis had probably never read a book, apart from novels. As a matter of fact, he said, glancing half enviously at the page rolled into his typewriter, he was in the middle of writing something. Phyllis made a teasing face of mock regret. — Oh, and I've interrupted you.

— It's very kind of you to bring back my shirt.

He asked how she'd found out where he was, and winced when she said she'd contacted his mother. Phyllis ploughed on. — But that's not why I've come.

— I know I've got your husband's shirt here somewhere.

— Wasn't that such an extraordinary evening, though? It was magical for me, like a midsummer night's dream. I haven't stopped thinking about it.

Nicky mentioned that it hadn't actually been midsummer. — Let me make you coffee, he said, — while I look for this shirt. Only instant coffee, I'm afraid. I keep the milk out in the gutter that runs along the front of these top windows – in winter it's as good as a fridge. All mod cons in this apartment. In hot weather it tends to go off. Do you take milk?

— Nicky, I don't want coffee, I don't want Roger's shirt.

Phyllis had wondered whether, in Nicky's real presence, she'd be disappointed in him, at the end of all her frenzy of longing. But he was as powerful and desirable in his angular awkwardness as she had imagined: unshaven, slightly stooped, black hair flopping forward into his face. His skinny legs were hairy under his boy's wool dressing gown tied with a cord, his bony long feet comical in old-man carpet slippers, his gold-rimmed glasses bent hopelessly out of shape: yet this indifference to his appearance only showed his beauty to more advantage, because he was so perfectly young, and so complete in his absorption in his mind-work, which lay beyond her imagining. It wasn't exactly desire that kept her here, however, blocking her from saving herself and exiting the humiliating scene. It was a fanatical persistence, rather. She had to try to get what she'd come for, couldn't face going down into those alien streets again without it, retracing her torturous journey. If he won't have me then I'll die, she thought. Although she also knew that she wouldn't really die, she'd go home and put macaroni cheese in the oven. And that would be worse.

Almost exasperatedly Nicky asked, — What *do* you want?

He had put his kettle to boil on the gas ring and now, to fetch in the milk, opened the round French-chateau window, disproportionate to the attic room in its size and showiness, like a pantomime set. Someone bellowed, splashing, from the bath next door, at the blast of air. The light outside was mineral and greenish, the afternoon smelled sooty, and he felt on his skin the first portentous drops of a rainstorm; he pulled the window shut again and in the changed acoustic they were suddenly closed in together, intimate. When Nicky looked at Phyllis he saw that she was anxious; uncomfortably he remembered his mother in that moment. If his mother were ever pitiable it touched a nerve of anguish in him.

— I can't stop thinking about that evening, she said in a low stumbling voice, different to her ringing, sociable one. — You kissed me. I didn't know what you meant.

— I didn't know what I meant either.

— I thought that perhaps . . .

They were standing so close together that he felt her body's heat; holding the bottle half full of sour milk, he frowned down at her as if she were a puzzle presented to him. Kindly, to reassure her, he did something to the Peter Pan collar of her blouse with the fingers of his free hand, straightening and smoothing it although it was perfectly straight. She was so much older than he was, with a lifetime of experience behind her: and yet she was also weaker and smaller than him, childish. Phyllis let her head fall against his shoulder, his nose was in her perfumed hair, stiffened with hairspray; his fingers found their way up from her collar onto her warm skin, she threw her arms around his neck and stretched like a cat against him, making a little mewing thankful noise. Ducking down his head he began to kiss her for the second time. The taste of her mouth was familiar, though less garlicky. Then he stopped to laugh at himself: he was still hanging on to the milk bottle, the kettle was coming to the boil.

After they'd made love twice that afternoon, to the sound of rain insistent on the roof, in his cramped single bed where the sheets smelled of his feet and the pillow smelled of his hair, Nicky thought this was the best sex he'd ever had. Prudently, he didn't say exactly this to Phyllis, believing he must preserve something of his mystique. It was absurd that this married, bourgeois, middle-aged woman, friend of his parents, was unclothed and delivered up to him in his bed. Phyllis's body had surprised him: he'd expected it to be more marked by age. She looked so different from her public self at close quarters, very close quarters, without her clothes – although unexpectedly it was her face which was most changed, revealed when she was naked as if what she'd taken off was a bland mask of beauty. He saw how her make-up drew an image over the real face underneath, close to the original but taming something in it that was more ruddy, blunt, open. Her lips were darker and more fleshy under her pink lipstick. She was both more shy and more slyly audacious than her outward persona, not ashamed at letting him look at her when he pulled the blankets down, asked her to roll over to show herself, front and back; pale marks left on her tanned skin where she'd worn her bikini, sunbathing in the South of France, seemed luminous in the dingy afternoon. Although she'd had two children, she was as slight as a girl. He'd never made love before to a woman who'd had children, and had been squeamish in case he felt any difference; the idea of childbirth sickened him. But then, after all, he hadn't cared about squeamishness or anything.

He had to call her Phyl, she said, everyone did. Phyllis was impossible, a name for an old lady; she was called after a great-aunt who'd died, and had always hated it. Her sisters were plain Jane and Anne, they were the lucky ones. Phyllis found herself chattering away to Nicky inconsequentially and happily, although she'd expected that taking a lover would be moodily sophisticated, like a French film. When she was a child, she told him, she used to pretend she was a boy, that Phyl was short for Philip; she'd always wished she'd been born a boy, boys had all the best adventures. Nicky said her name made him think of an eighteenth-century shepherdess in a poem; she exclaimed that she'd love him to read poetry to her. And had he noticed she wasn't wearing her wedding ring? She'd taken it off on the train and put it in her purse, wrapped in a scrap of paper. — I don't know why you wear one anyway, Nicky teased. — Isn't it a sign of bondage? Showing you're his possession.

— Oh no, Roger isn't like that.

— It isn't a question of Roger. I'm sure he's a very good type.

— I shouldn't talk about him with you. But he is.

— It's the whole system that's rotten. Marriage is an aspect of capitalistic exchange. Your husband owns you, he buys you with his income – quite a reasonable one no doubt as he's at the Foreign Office – and in return you bear his children and keep his house. Quite possibly you've been contented with your bargain. But whatever any individual couple imagine they've chosen – *falling in love* and all that — there's an element of delusion in it. The system's bigger than any individual.

Phyllis was frowning and smiling, prodding at his bare shoulder with her fingertip, not really perturbed. This was just how she imagined young men might think. — Don't you believe falling in love is real, then?

Nicky said sternly that romantic love was a Western invention, sugar coating on a contractual arrangement. — But what if I loved you? Phyllis said.

— You wouldn't really. You'd just think you did.

All this was a game between them, while they lay touching together in his bed. — I have to go, Phyllis eventually said. — Hugh's having tea with one of his friends. I told them I was coming up to town to shop. Usually I catch the five thirty home.

— You see? Nicky said complacently. — A prisoner of the system. Who's Hugh?

She couldn't talk with him about Hugh, she said. Not now, not like this; and Nicky was relieved, because people's children were boring, at least as subjects for conversation. He pretended to hold her down in the bed when she tried to get up, admiring her nakedness, kissing the dark mole on her ribs, the fine bones of her wrist. She was like a slave, he insisted, marked with the tokens of her master's wealth: the watch on its dainty gold bracelet, stylish knots of gold clipped to her ears, under her hair.

— What nonsense you talk, said Phyllis happily.

But she had to get up, venture in his dressing gown into the sordid bathroom next door to use the WC, wash between her legs, make herself decent. He watched from the bed while she moved around in his room, putting on her clothes with grace as if this ordinary act were a special skill or an art, looking in a little mirror in her powder compact while she applied fresh lipstick, smoothing cream into her hands from a tube in her bag. How hard these dressed-up women had to work, he reflected, to achieve their effect of careless elegance. A girl his own age would have pulled on a T-shirt and jeans. She asked whether he'd ever got that mud off his blazer, after their adventure in the Chidgelys' garden. He couldn't remember, and when she hunted for it she found the blazer thrown in a corner, still streaked with pond dirt. Arranging it on a hanger, she did her best, batting out the creases with her palms, trying to brush off the dried mud.

— Can you come back tomorrow? Nicky asked eagerly.

— Oh no, not tomorrow. I'm involved in the afternoon with the Church Education Group.

— You're not a Christian! Won't you have to make a penitential confession or something? Fasting, stretched out all night on a stone floor.

— Don't be silly. I'm C of E, we don't go in for those extremes.

This idea of her faith was as exotic to him as if she'd said she was a pagan, or believed in sticking pins into wax dolls. — Still, your conscience must be nagging at you, he insisted with serious interest.

— But look at me, she said seriously, sitting down on the bed beside him in the chaos of his blankets, putting her cool hand to his cheek. — I'm so wicked, the only thing I care about in the whole world is making love to you again. I'm not really a good Christian anyway, not the whole Creed, rising again on the third day and everything. Only you have to believe in something, don't you?

— Absolutely not. I don't believe in anything, outside this room, outside myself.

— Don't you believe in me?

He turned his nose into her palm, which smelled of hand cream, lily of the valley. — You're pretty implausible, he said, — erupting into my afternoon, throwing your clothes off, jumping into my bed. I'd be mad to believe in you. You're clearly a fantasy projection of my desires.

Phyllis drank in the sight of his face unguarded in profile, deep lids closed over his eyes, down of dark hair on his upper lip, muscle that tightened in his cheek when he smiled. Those thin smiles, meant only for himself, were her treasures to dwell upon, when she was apart from him. — I'd better come back soon, try and convince you I exist. I'll come next week, Wednesday again. I should be able to get away, Wednesday's usually my day out. I'll write to you.

— But I can't wait till next week.

Gratified, she said he had to wait.

— And don't write, he said. — Letters get lost here. People take them, they hope there's money inside. Just turn up. I'll be here on Wednesday.

When Phyllis opened the door at home with her latchkey, shook out her umbrella on the doorstep, left it to dry in the porch, she felt no qualms. Her bones ached from sex, she was raw from it, but that awareness, coarse and exulting, was safely hidden beneath her pretty clothes and underwear. This evening she would take a bath, wash herself clean. What had been unthinkable yesterday, now felt inevitable and necessary: she saw that she was capable of being two contradictory things at once, wife and lover. The two selves existed as separate sealed chambers, both were necessary to her, only she had the key to both – how could that harm anyone? No one she knew at home was likely to venture into Ladbroke Grove, let alone into Everglade Buildings. Although there was Jean Knight, of course, who must have visited her son, because she'd said his room was *pretty ghastly.* Phyllis must watch out for her.

Stepping into her own hallway, unbuttoning her mac and ducking her head to see herself in the hallstand's square of mirror, for a moment by contrast her own home seemed the ghastly one, embalmed in its order and its turpentine smell of polish, unopened letters from this morning arrayed beside the telephone: its air so still that for the length of her glance at herself she couldn't breathe. Nicky's room, inhabited with such different carelessness, was freedom; you could live in it shedding responsibility, as easily as dropping your clothes on the floor. A petal fell from bronze chrysanthemums in a vase in the hall, stair rods gleamed dully; even the high ceiling with its vaulted white plasterwork, from which they'd hung a wrought-iron candelabra fitted with electric bulbs, felt cramped after her ascent of the Everglade stairs. At the top of those she had seemed to breathe a purer air. Externally at any rate, she reassured herself in the mirror, she was unchanged from when she went out, her expression bright and capable – only her nose was reddened, hair misted with rain. Realising she'd left her silk scarf in his room, she was glad, imagining it spilled out on his chair like her mark left behind.

Colette leaned over the balustrade on the landing, still in her uniform, voice scratchy with dissatisfaction. — Where have you been? What did you buy?

— Nothing, couldn't find what I wanted. How was school?

— School was desolating. I don't think Mrs Bernhardt likes me. Did you have lunch with Aunt Anne? I wish I'd been there.

— Just by myself. A wasted journey, really.

— Why didn't you buy something for me?

— You know I wouldn't dare. You don't like anything I choose for you.

— But you never choose anything any more.

— I wish you'd take off your school things, dear, so they don't get too creased.

Phyllis slipped her mac on its hanger to dry and stepped out of her heels, inspected their mud splashes, carried them upstairs to change into her flats: even the stair carpet compressing under the soles of her feet in nylon stockings was sensual. She thought she could smell the freshness of rain on the shrubbery outside, green beyond the frosted, patterned window glass on the staircase. Colette reappeared on the landing half undressed, remembering to tell her something. — Hugh's here. They brought him back, the other boy was sick apparently. Mrs Whatsit telephoned first: luckily I was here.

— Oh, that was lucky.

— They hoped that Hugh won't get it too.

— Let's hope so. He never gets anything. Has he had his tea?

— I heard him thieving in the cupboards just now, so probably not.

— Poor Hughie, he must be starving. You both must be. As

soon as I've changed my shoes, I'll put the supper on. Daddy will be home any minute.

Knocking at Hugh's door Phyllis heard furtive rustling. — You can't come in!

— But I am coming in.

Cross-legged on the bed in his school shorts and socks, scabbed knees presented, he presided over his feast spread on a torn-open paper bag: sultanas, pickled cocktail onions leaking vinegar, squares of cooking chocolate, crumbled stock cube. His tie was pulled loose, white-gold hair stuck up around his head like a ruff. Phyllis remembered how Colette's nursemaid in Cairo had said perfection attracted the evil eye. — As you've seen my secret, Hugh calmly said, — I'll have to kill you. Anyway, where were you? Neil puked, they had to deliver me home early.

— I'm sorry, darling, I've been up to town. And really I don't care if you kill me, but I wish you wouldn't go foraging in my ingredients.

— Now that I've foraged, however, I might as well eat. Buy anything nice?

— No, a wasted journey.

Throwing a sultana in the air to catch it in his mouth, missing, he commiserated. — Feet aching, little Mother? Head?

Hugh feels what I feel, Phyllis thought with a rush of love. She sat down on his bed and the small white onions rolled off the paper bag, into the folds of his counterpane. — I don't know how you can eat those by themselves, she said, — they're meant for cocktails. Goodness knows how long we've had them.

— I don't know how you can drink cocktails, Mother, they're too foul.

Recapturing one of the onions, he tried to feed it to her so that she squealed, laughing at him, twisting her mouth away from his seeking fingers. — Go on, he said, — try one! They're really not too bad.

— Hughie, I don't want to, get off me.

In the midst of their wrestling he dropped his nose to her neck suspiciously, holding her in place in his tight grip: although he was small he was strong, his torso muscled from rugby at school. — You smell funny! You're different.

— No I don't! It's your blasted onions.

But she leaped to her feet; Hugh grabbed at her left hand.

— And where's your wedding ring?

She was shocked, and said she must have taken it off just now when she washed her hands in the downstairs cloakroom. — Let me look, stay here, Hugh sternly said. He ran as if this were an emergency, thudding down the stairs three at a time as he was forbidden to do. Hurrying into her bedroom Phyllis fumbled in her purse, unwrapping the stupid ring from its scrap of paper – insisting, when Hugh returned upstairs with a severe face, that it had been on her dressing table all along.

— But why did you take it off? You never take it off!

She pretended to be annoyed, asked him to leave her alone while she got on with supper, said she did have a headache after all.

The false headache developed into a real one over their meal, so that Phyllis was hardly able to lift three forkfuls of macaroni cheese from her plate; she went to lie down in the bedroom with her eyes closed and the curtains drawn. Roger was so considerate when she was ill. She heard him piling their dishes in the kitchen for the morning, then running a bath for Hugh; Colette broke a plate and raised her voice, defending herself indignantly although no one accused her. Hugh recited his times tables monotonously as he undressed in the bathroom; Roger's sister Marnie, who lived alone with their widowed mother, telephoned to make arrangements – they were to go to her for Sunday lunch. Phyllis's awareness floated above all this as if she were dead and they carried on without her. She wasn't asleep but lay on her side under the coverlet with her knees jackknifed, watching the alarm clock ticking on the bed-side table: how cruelly slowly it jerked around towards next week, the white plastic minute hand with its phosphorescent-green tip! Outside the sluggish twilight in her room, she guessed that the weather changed: the evening sky stretched tall and was washed clean, wetness glinted in trees and grass. Pale light slid over the wallpaper.

Roger would smoke his pipe and read over papers in his study, once Hugh was in bed. There was so much for him to do, with war having broken out in the Middle East, between Israel and the Arab countries. When she thought about war, what she saw was Roger's round tobacco tin with its concertinaed paper lining, piled up inside with fragrant tobacco strands. — It was a good thing, though, wasn't it, this war, she had said. — I mean, that they won. Don't the Jews deserve their own country, after what happened to them?

— Of course, incontrovertibly.

He bent over his pipe cleaner, scraping out mess from the bowl of his pipe into an ashtray; his liquorice-black hair was the same colour as the sticky tar, only threaded with grey. He answered Phyllis's questions with meticulous fullness always, and yet while he was speaking never quite looked at her, as if he deflected whatever was harsh and pessimistic in his analysis, making it more tentative to spare her. — The trouble is, this country of theirs belonged just yesterday to someone else. One can see the thing both ways.

— At least it was quickly over.

— It's a great blow to the Arabs. They don't come out of it well.

— To Nasser and his sort. But didn't he need taking down a peg or two?

— No doubt. But who comes in his place?

When he looked up, his brown eyes set in the thick folds of his face were hazel-flecked, faintly bloodshot, apologetic, full of intelligence. The idea of war made Phyllis impatient and jumpy. If she'd been only a few years older she'd have been one of those plucky Waafs monitoring troop movements or listening to radar on headphones: but on D-Day in 1944 she was seventeen, staying with an aunt on the Sussex downs. She had walked for miles just to get away from a stuffy whist drive, listening to the skylarks with her hands pushed in her pockets, deep in private reverie and quite unconscious of what was happening: in the evening when she came home they were all so full of the news, the whist drive had been abandoned. And of course she had cared about the news too, intensely: but always felt afterwards as if she'd absented herself from a significant initiation. She was hollow inside where her wartime spirit ought to have been.

Hugh called out from his bed – *Daddy!* – and his voice was

musical and full of warning, like a bird settling for the night. He was buoyant and alert in the mornings, but the evenings were an anxious time for him. Phyllis knew how to touch his forehead, help him make the leap down into sleep. In sympathy now with the child's effort, she fell asleep herself and only woke again hours later – she could see by their little glow the figures on the clock – to darkness as muffling in the room as cloth. She was still in her clothes, in the same position on her side under the coverlet; as if, while awareness fled, her body left behind was empty as a husk. Her headache was gone, the clarity of her mind was glassy, the quiet so tangible that she could hear Roger downstairs, turning a page, clearing his throat, getting up from his desk.

He couldn't possibly know what she'd done. But it seemed to Phyllis that he came upstairs heavily, forbearing and resigned, like an old man; she leaped up and pressed the light switch, the room sprang into its mundane daily character. He mustn't find her abandoned to herself – she must be busy, pulling off her earrings at the dressing table, fussing with her hair.

— How's your poor head?

— So much better, thanks. But I want a bath, I'm filthy from town.

— Shall I run it in for you? By the way, where's the boy's shirt, Phyl?

— Yes please, that's so kind. Which boy? Oh, that shirt. I posted it, telephoned his mother for the address. But I don't suppose that you'll see yours again.

— Funnily enough, he was such a bright spark, I don't mind the thought of him wearing it out, pulling off all the buttons. So you telephoned Jean. How was she?

— Settling in, I think. I mean, I hardly know her. I remember thinking, visiting their place when Colette was a baby, that an old house like that has character but takes it out of you.

— I gather Peter doesn't like the house. Jean's from the kind of gentry family whose name goes back to Adam, Peter's a different sort altogether. Though apparently very good at what he does.

— Oil, isn't it?

— Oil. But he's older than her, must be thinking of retirement soon.

Taking off her make-up, face clownish with cold cream, Phyllis smiled at Roger's reflection in the mirror, and it was a relief when he turned on the taps in the bathroom. The water pipes groaned, filled the house with the purposeful rushing of water, steam, clean perfume of Badedas. — I think we won't ask Nicholas Knight again, she said. — Don't you think he's a bit of a bore? So idealistic, young. He's too far out for us.

— I liked him.

— I can't imagine mixing him up with our friends.

— You're usually right about those things. Although perhaps it's our friends who are the bores. Hughie took a long time to settle, by the way. I hope he hasn't caught anything.

But he had. And only an hour or so after they fell asleep – chastely, back to back, touching hands behind their backs lightly under the bedclothes, wordlessly taking leave before they parted for the night – Phyllis was awake again and out of the bed. She held Hugh's head, stroking his sweaty hair while he vomited into a bowl – sultanas, chocolate, macaroni cheese, the lot. Then she emptied the bowl, fetched a bucket of hot water with Dettol to clean up the mess on the floor and scrub it off his bedside mat, tugged the soiled sheets off his bed for rinsing and boiling in the morning, found clean ones in the linen cupboard, made up the bed again – tucking a towel over the turndown in case of more accidents. Hugh sat blanched and shivering in a chair, hunched over the rinsed sick bowl on his knees. — It was those onions of yours, he ruefully said. — I hate the stink of them.

— I shouldn't think so. I should think it's whatever Neil got.

It wasn't anything serious. The bug only lasted a couple of days.

Colette disliked her aunt Marnie, her father's sister, partly because people said they looked alike: she dreaded that when she grew old she too would be unmarried and mean and stout, with a pneumatic shelf of bosom and mannish gruff voice. Marnie wore her hair rolled into a kind of sausage round her head; her face was like a Dutch doll's, with its eyes painted very wide open – small stub of nose, circles of high colour from the broken blood vessels in her cheeks. Aunt and niece had the same uneasy way of standing, fists clenched hanging at their sides, lower lip thrust out. Marnie had studied French at university and could answer the questions on *Brain of Britain* on the wireless; she wrote a weekly column for a Guildford newspaper, campaigned for the Liberals, smoked forty Capstan Full Strength a day.

When she cooked Sunday lunch, dropping cigarette ash unapologetically in the gravy, she had the unfeminine air, amid steaming bubbling pans, of a captain on the bridge executing a tricky manoeuvre. The food she served up was filling and functional, conventional; at the table she perspired, fanning herself with her linen napkin, and was triumphant while Roger carved.

Surreptitiously Hugh transferred things he didn't like onto his mother's plate. After they'd finished eating, their linen napkins would go back into little matching pouches, each embroidered with the user's name in chain stitch. Roger's mother had sewed new pouches for Colette and Hugh when they were born, but Phyllis still had to use the one marked X for visitors – she told this as a funny story. And it was true that after all these years she was still an outsider in that house. Roger was appreciatively aware, against its sombre background, blinds at half mast to keep out the ravaging light, of his wife's bright face and fresh fashionable clothes, her quick spirit and slight figure.

Marnie, ferociously atheistic, tried to pick quarrels with Phyllis over her churchgoing. Phyllis agreed, there wasn't much evidence in the world for a benevolent Providence. But she couldn't help it, she loved the atmosphere in a church service, the flowers and the singing, found it uplifting even if it didn't make sense.

— How you can sit there listening to all that mumbo jumbo!

— Don't call it mumbo jumbo though, Roger mildly suggested.

— Why ever not?

— Because it's a cliché, used by old bores.

Marnie reddened and Phyllis was sorry for her: she admired her brother's cleverness so much. Long ago, before the war, the Fischer household – in this same big, ugly, detached Guildford house behind its ramparts of yew hedge – must have been feverish with cultural improvement: amateur theatre, word games, a baby grand piano. Roger had escaped – first to school and then to war; Marnie had come unprotestingly home from university to help nurse their father, who'd had an accountancy business, when he had his stroke.

And although Marnie mostly preferred men and boys and was bored in the company of women, she made an exception, fortunately, for her own very dull mother, to whom she was devoted. — You have to give her credit, Phyllis said fairly. — Your aunt must have the patience of a saint. I couldn't put up with looking after your grandma all day every day.

Guiltily she felt a repugnance herself for the harmless old widow with her big soft body and mild sheep's face, mop of white curls, muddled mind. She admired how Marnie resolutely was not martyred, returning to the library romances whose plots and characters Mrs Fischer forgot as soon as she closed them up. Marnie accepted as law the worn groove of her mother's routine, her ailments and medicines, TV programmes, knitting, supply of Mintoes. Hugh was adored by his grandmother and his aunt, and tried to dodge their embraces; when they lunged and squeezed, he flexed his shoulders quizzically afterwards in recovery, or rubbed his jaw. Mrs Fischer was preoccupied with finding the right moment to press half-crowns, hot from her clutching, upon both grandchildren. Marnie deplored Phyllis's child-rearing system but knew better than to mention it; when she and Roger were small they'd been smacked and shut in the understairs cupboard for much less than her niece got away with. Suspicious of something difficult – *bolshie*, she called it – in Colette, she was vigilant against whatever threatened family tradition, just as she kept watch for shoddy vocabulary on the BBC.

Meanwhile, head down over her plate, hair falling into her gravy, as her aunt pointed out, Colette ate up her roast dinner, despising herself for enjoying it; they had discussed Hugh's sickness bug exhaustively beforehand, which cast a pall over the food. In

her dreams she was ethereal, didn't need glasses and had a dainty appetite. Her father pushed watery cauliflower to the side of his plate; Marnie protested. — Roger, I cooked the cauli especially for you! It's your favourite!

— Oh really? I rather thought I didn't like it.

— You always *used* to like it, old Mrs Fischer weakly said.

— He doesn't mind it in cheese sauce, Phyllis offered hopefully, as if these were peace talks and she'd suggested a compromise. Scowling, gripping her bone-handled knife convulsively, Colette made an effort to visualise Mrs Bernhardt, who was the opposite of everything banal and philistine here – *philistine* was one of her English teacher's own expressions. She must surely at this moment be dipping madeleines in a *tisane* while browsing among the Silver Poets; or was perhaps at a matinee at the cinema, watching a licentious French film in black and white. Her teacher was fine-boned, thin-lipped, her grey-brown hair draped in a chignon, eyelids heavy with weary irony; she looked like a hardened, professional Virginia Woolf, brushing off the chalk dust from nicotine-stained fingers. She had given Colette A plus for her *Twelfth Night* essay – but coldly, Colette felt. *Ingenious and accomplished*, she'd written. The more Colette dwelt on *ingenious* and *accomplished*, the more she was convinced they contained a reproof, even distaste. It was unfortunate to be clever; it was better to be natural, not to try too hard. If Colette raised her hand in class, she thought that Mrs B., dropping those heavy lids, pretended to see anyone but her. Eventually – when everyone else had been stupid – as though exhausted, accepting the inevitable: *Well, Colette?*

Old Mrs Fischer ploughed through conversation as she ate her lunch, dogged and oblivious; she remarked over steamed pudding and custard that it was a good thing young Hugh was off to school soon, if he was getting into mischief. Phyllis had entertained them with Milo Barnes-Pryce's sandal. Hugh looked up alertly, interested in their talk for the first time; Roger and Phyllis sat with straighter backs. This quarrel was not resolved between them yet.

— I don't think he's quite ready for boarding. Phyllis smiled brightly round the dining table, putting down her spoon with her pudding unfinished. — And we're very satisfied with the local school.

— Roger was perfectly happy at Abingdon. We packed his little trunk, I sent him a tuck box every half, with home-made fruit cake.

— But times have changed.

— You don't want him getting into bad habits, Marnie warned. — Boys can get very clingy, if you don't act soon enough.

— Hugh doesn't have bad habits. It's ordinary childish fun, it's good for him.

— Yet Roger said he won't go to sleep without you.

— Did you tell her that, Roger?

He demurred, annoyed with his sister. — It isn't the right time or place for this.

— But is that what you think?

— I don't mind going to Abingdon, Hugh stoutly offered to his father. — If you think I'm ready.

Mrs Fischer beamed at him. — That's my good boy!

Colette heard Hugh whisper into his napkin, *I'm not your boy.*

She was thinking that no one took so much interest in her education: it didn't matter apparently if girls were clingy. She was relieved, though, in truth, that the question of boarding hadn't ever seriously cropped up for her. Vividly she could imagine the horror of sharing a dormitory — and worse, a bathroom, all that humiliating intimacy of smells — with the very girls at school she could hardly bear to sit with to eat lunch. She'd have been delivered over finally inside their system, with no privacy to retreat to where she could belong to herself. Also she knew that what awaited Hugh wasn't actually about education, or knowing and understanding things. You didn't need boarding for that; you could get it all more or less out of books, along with throwaway remarks, guides to discrimination, from one or two good teachers. From Mrs B. especially; even if she hated Colette, she threw out enough clues to help her find her way, like a life-saving trail of breadcrumbs in a dark wood. No one cared what Hugh would actually *learn*, at Abingdon. What they intended was that the school should change him, through its alchemy, into its own mysterious substance, which was supposed to be golden and superior. Well, it had changed their father once, and he was superior. But Colette was not envious of Hugh. She didn't want to be changed, or initiated into anyone's tribe.

— Hugh doesn't know what he's talking about, Phyllis crossly said. — He's got so many good friends here. The Barnes-Pryces aren't sending Milo anywhere yet.

— You're wrong there, Mother. Apparently there are plans afoot, for after Christmas.

Lighting up her post-pudding cigarette before coffee, vigorously shaking out the match — Mrs Fischer collected in a drawer jokes cut off the backs of her matchboxes — Marnie shot a Dutch-doll glance triumphally at Phyllis. Roger put an end to the subject, saying he hadn't made his mind up yet. — Phyl and I need to talk it all over. I'm not sure how it's become a matter for general discussion.

Phyllis felt Hugh's betrayal sharply. Something had changed be-tween them since that silly fuss over the wedding ring. He had been cooler, was beginning to detach from her; it was what she had dreaded, although she'd also accepted it as necessary and even a good thing. Some vision of compensation flashed in her thoughts, as bril-liantly illogical as those floating objects made of light that swam in front of her eyes before a migraine; though she hadn't meant to think about Nicky Knight while she was in Guildford, *couldn't* think about him. He couldn't exist, not here, in this company today – not with his long hair, scruffy flared trousers, unbuttoned unironed shirt, drawling mockery, thin smiles, offensive opinions, deliciously offen-sive everything. It wasn't exactly, though, that she thought of him. It was more like sensation, a finger drawn down her body, melting and undoing her, assuaging the impending loss of her little son, which hurt so absurdly much. To block out the hurt she imagined herself bargaining, accepting Abingdon in exchange for that room in Ladbroke Grove, as if the two places existed in some significant and consoling relation, although she knew they didn't.

THREE

When she went next to the Everglade, their second Wednesday, she was blind almost from love of Nicky; afterwards she could hardly remember making her way through those streets which had seemed so forbidding the first time. This time the sun was shining; an old horse had snorted through pink-and-black nostrils bristling with white hair, waiting patiently, stamping its feet, dropping its affronting straw-green dung in the road between the shafts of a rag-and-bone cart, which was piled up with a broken gas stove, kitchen chairs, filthy bedding, a gilt mirror, the bowl from a washstand cracked right across, edged with a pattern of rosebuds. Workmen had wolf-whistled at her, from where they were demolishing a row of houses; behind her she'd heard, a few minutes later, the luxuriant slow release of a wall falling. The entrance hall in the Everglade was still beautiful underneath its veil of filth and age: black-and-white marble floor tiles, a plaster frieze of dancing maenads, the curved stone staircase circling dizzyingly – with its balustrade of swirling wrought iron, and slender handrail in dark mahogany – all the way to the great skylight at the top. Phyllis was so obliviously happy that she ran into a coloured girl coming the other way, knocking down the pile of medical textbooks she was carrying; she picked them up while the girl reproachfully waited. Phyllis apologised with no shyness, overflowed with companionable warmth, wanting to belong here. — How wonderful! Are you training to be a nurse?

— I am a nurse, the other austerely said.

Phyllis barely registered any hostility, only the forceful Caribbean accent; the palms of the girl's hands when she took back the books were pearly shell-pale, like her neatly trimmed nails. She didn't thank Phyllis but it didn't matter. A strong nip of fear as she continued upstairs, then along the corridor to his door, in case Nicky had forgotten she was coming: but he hadn't forgotten, of course he hadn't. He'd even anxiously prepared for her visit, not tidying exactly but picking up clothes and books from the middle of the room and heaping them around its edges; she was touched that he'd put ready a bottle of Mateus Rosé wine with a corkscrew and two glasses. When he tried to pull out the cork his hands shook, so that Phyllis took over from him: she was capable of anything. It was warm under the roof in that late September spell of burnished ripe fine weather; he had the pantomime window propped open.

— My dear Mrs Fischer, Nicky said, marvelling over her, when she was naked again and in his bed. — What are you doing here? I hardly know you.

His lascivious uninhibited gaze was as arousing, almost, as if he touched her. She had never been seen like this before, or allowed herself to be seen, without any ironic deflection: not with Roger, nor that other man. Getting his pleasure, Nicky was so heedless and unconstrained – so that she, too, was unconstrained, and didn't care how he saw her. Married love was too kind, she thought, it hovered on the threshold of this knowledge and never went inside, never took the necessary liberties. Because her shared life with her husband was grown-up and considerate, they had made love considerately, like innocents. Also, she'd been ill with miscarriages after giving birth to Colette – which was why in the end they had come home to England. This had shadowed their lovemaking with the gravity of failure, made them apologetic. Nicky had no history of failure, and no grown-up authority in the world, so when he made love to her it was with his whole frank concentration – and with such urgency, as if nothing else was important. That was what Phyllis thought then too. Nothing else was important.

She remembered those first few weeks afterwards as coinciding with a long-drawn-out Indian summer, when the light and heat were thick as oil; later on there were bright, taut, chilly Wednesdays, when even without wind the trees felt the bite of the change of seasons, letting go a first few leaves to lie around listlessly, improbable on the city pavements. Phyllis postponed for a long time any acknowledgement of the difficulty in their love affair. She didn't mention the difference in their ages, or bring up the subject of her husband. In her thoughts she held away, too, any idea that they were doing wrong. Morality she pictured as an inexorable mill grinding out its judgements, irrefutable but ugly, like the machinery in a factory, alien to the subtlety of her inner life. She knew that her betrayal of her husband and children was wrong, but in the same impersonal dulled way that she knew from school about the Treaty of Vienna, or the abolition of the Corn Laws.

It's true that when Phyllis had to tell lies at home, it wrenched something in the fabric of her idea of herself: and yet it was also so easy, and she carried it off blithely, offhandedly. When Roger remarked on how regularly she was travelling into town, she explained that it cheered her up to have a change of scene. He mustn't worry, she said, she wasn't spending all his money; she didn't go for the shopping, really. Sometimes she visited the British Museum – or the Tate Gallery, to see the Constables. Roger said he didn't mind her spending his money anyway. Within reason, of course, he joked. The lies flowing so smoothly, smilingly out of her seemed to cost Phyllis nothing. Once or twice she really spent the morning with her sisters, and had lunch with them, to provide authentic cover for her trips. She loved Jane and Anne, and was used to feeling herself rather a baby beside their earnestness and solidity: they were both big-boned and tall. Anne taught painting at Chelsea College of Art; Jane with her waspish ironies was married to a vicar, very high church. It should have been horrible to Phyllis, even frightening, using her beloved, distinguished sisters in her deception. But it wasn't.

And after they'd parted at Piccadilly tube station, exchanging affectionate messages for one another's families, she hurried on, not to Waterloo to catch the next train home, but to Ladbroke Grove and Nicky's room, dismissing behind her everything that got in the way of their being together. On those afternoons, cheated of so many hours of him, she was careless of the time, took off the little gold wristwatch and dropped it in her handbag where she couldn't see it. The days were getting shorter, the room darkened around them as they lay wrapped in each other's arms, his young body angular in the shadows. She told Nicky about the tomboy she'd once been, climbing trees and running away from home; he told her about his childhood in Suffolk, how he used to keep newts and grass snakes. For a while, he said, before his parents went abroad, he'd attended the village school, where they still wrote on slates, and the poorest children had ringworm and went barefoot. When he'd fallen asleep one afternoon with his head on the desk, the teacher told the others not to wake him. He'd suffered with his asthma, and his father had disapproved of his having any medication for it, believing it was a nervous disorder and could be overcome by mental discipline. — My mother hid my drops in the drawer of an old card table, until our doctor thought it his duty to speak to my father, man to man, and Mum got into trouble. My father's a beast, I loathe him. She was teaching me history and Latin in the evenings, and reading me poetry: but I had to be torn out of my happy life eventually. At boarding school they torture boys like me.

Phyllis never spoke to him about Hugh going away to school; superstitiously she hardly mentioned even her son's name to Nicky, although quite often she told him stories about Colette. She stored in her imagination every detail of Nicky's past, which seemed magical to her, like something out of a storybook. He had no memory of her visiting Cressing with Roger when he was a child, and she skimmed over her account of that day, not wanting to remind him that she belonged in any sense to his parents' generation. Pressed against Nicky in bed, she felt as though the skin between them, dividing them, was stretched so fine that they were almost one form, and she ached when they parted as if a portion of her own body was torn away. It was very late, on those afternoons, by the time she arrived home. Often Roger was there before her, and the children were irritably hungry. — You could have made yourselves toast! Phyllis said gaily, refusing to feel stricken or be cheated of her happiness. Wasn't she always there when they got back, on all the other days of the week? — Your father could have put the dinner on.

— Don't be silly, he's working in his study, Hugh said. — Anyway, men can't cook. I'm never going to learn.

— All the world's best chefs are men.

Hugh said they must be sissies then.

— We kept thinking you were about to come, Colette protested sulkily, — and then you didn't.

She hung around in the kitchen while Phyllis put the potatoes on and began frying the little meat rissoles she'd prepared and left in the fridge the night before. Phyllis wasn't aware of it, but on the days when she'd been with Nicky, although her cheerful performance of herself was impenetrable, she gave off nonetheless a warning air: her cheeks were hot and there was something acerbic and brittle in her remarks and her glancing quick looks, as if she held off from her family at some sceptical distance. Colette was drawn to her mother in this mood, she longed for female confidences. Despairingly she spread out, for Phyllis to see, her inky short fingers with their bitten nails. — Don't you think that to be truly beautiful, a woman has to have good hands?

Phyllis was flipping the rissoles with a spatula. — I could put something on your nails, to stop you biting.

— But my hands are so stubby! There's no hope. I wanted long expressive ones like yours, with tapering fingers: not these horrors.

— You've got nice practical hands, dear, like your father's. Would you mind using them to lay the table in the dining room?

Phyllis was conscious on those Wednesdays of her own absence, like a ghost in all those rooms which in the past she'd arranged so beautifully. Without her, the place fell apart: no one picked up Hugh's schoolbag or wiped up his cake crumbs or drew the curtains across the windows; no one turned on the lamps she had placed around the rooms to give off their welcoming glow; everything was bleak in the glare from the main light. This ought to have made her guilty, but she only thought crossly that it wasn't so difficult after all to make the place look nice. Why didn't anyone else take the trouble to do it? Perhaps they didn't care, or didn't notice. Roger meanwhile had been in touch with Abingdon. He was going to drive Hugh up to the school one weekend, take a look around. If they decided to go ahead, then Phyllis would have to set about buying his uniform and all the things he needed. Hugh seemed set on the idea of school, although Phyllis thought he had no idea what it would actually be like. She warned him that he wouldn't be able to take his collections with him.

— I know that, he said. — I'm not a baby. I just don't want anyone touching them when I'm away. No one's allowed in my room, under any circumstances: and that means you too, Mother.

— Mandy will have to go in there to dust.

— She doesn't count.

Phyllis began planning for an occasion when she and Nicky could spend a whole night together. She wrote to her elderly father in Leamington Spa, who didn't like using the telephone, suggesting a visit before Christmas. If she left Otterley one afternoon and didn't arrive at Leamington till the following morning, she thought, no one would notice.

———

Then one Wednesday in late October, before she'd heard back from her father, when she arrived at the Everglade — bearing all her joyous expectation so foolishly, and the eager offering of herself — Nicky wasn't in, and his door was locked. There was only a note drawing-pinned to it: *Out to lunch with my mother.* Suddenly it was too stupid that they'd prepared no system for communication, so that he could have warned her. Downstairs in the Everglade's entrance hall there was a telephone in a little cabinet of polished wood, with the door hanging off its hinges, and Nicky had said that people used it; if she'd given him her number, he could have called her. If she'd had the number for the cabinet phone she too could have called it in an emergency, surely someone would have answered it and got a message to him. They hadn't bothered to prepare for complications: superstitiously perhaps, or as if their Wednesdays were charmed, so that nothing could go wrong. This moment, anyway, was a breach in consciousness, through which came rushing all the recognitions they had pushed aside.

Phyllis didn't cry: she very rarely cried. Her sisters used to cry a lot, when they were teenagers; their eyes still filled up easily with tears even now, over lunch, if they were talking about their children or about the past or their dead mother — although they were stately grown-up women, so sensible and humorous. They laughed at themselves as they wiped tears away. Phyllis had resolved, however, when she was quite small, not to give in to weeping: she'd rather deflect attention from any distress she felt. So she only stood hesitating for a few minutes outside Nicky's door, rocking on her feet from the blow, sick with disappointment, resting one gloved fist against the painted wood. He had left her no clue as to what she should do next. Wait for him? But if she did, then he might turn up with Jean Knight in tow. Anyhow, his door was locked; she couldn't just stand out here in the corridor for hours, where everyone passing would see her. She ought to go to the Tate and look at the Constables, of which she had only a dim memory: she thought they would be consoling and airy, green, but couldn't make herself care. She only wanted to see Nicky. The idea of waiting another week was anguishing: any movement forward was blocked, she was like an animal in a trap. And what if in a week his door was locked again?

The top landing under the wide Everglade skylight ran round in a semicircular gallery, so that you could look over into the dizzying stairwell or up into clouds that seemed intimately close and dirty grey, through the glass panes that hadn't been cleaned for decades. Any noise drawn upwards in the stairwell resonated like sound effects in a film: Phyllis heard the explosive smash downstairs of the heavy double entrance doors of teak and glass, swinging back on their brass hinges, then footsteps ascending. She was pinned there listening, like a film victim; Nicky's room opened off one of the corridors which curved away from the landing. With a pang she realised that she didn't know how his footsteps sounded, hadn't ever really heard them: but surely not like this, so definite – didn't he wear old plimsolls, falling apart? And surely he wouldn't be plodding so deliberately slowly, but hurrying up the stairs two at a time, eagerly hoping to find her, full of his apologies. On the other hand, the steps came on to the very top, and then set out towards her along his corridor.

It was the young woman whose books she'd knocked down on

another occasion; Phyllis stood back against the door, to let her pass. This time she seemed more striking: taller, darker-skinned in the shadows, commanding in her nurse's uniform under a navy gaberdine cape, heavy satchel dragging down one shoulder. The shapes of her face and head were sculptural, cheekbones sloping almost from her temples; her forehead was very high, hairline set far back, matt black hair strained into a bun. When she came close Phyllis could smell that she was sweating from the climb, and from whatever long hours of labour she'd left behind her – sweat mingled sternly with a whiff of antiseptic. Her own perfumed sweetness seemed a travesty by contrast.

— Nicky's out, she explained herself defensively. — I can't get in.

The other woman stopped, unsmiling, to read the note. — So you're not his mother, she said.

In her extremity Phyllis didn't care. — Obviously.

— I thought not.

And as if she were too tired to talk more, the nurse continued along the corridor. She must have noticed Phyllis coming and going, then, from Nicky's room; Phyllis understood with a shock that this stranger, whom she'd been ready to condescend to and encourage, had ideas about her, and unflattering ones. Because she'd thought of Nicky's world as licentious and chaotic in contrast to her own, it hadn't occurred to her that anyone here might judge her. Exposed and shamed, she reacted with hostility to the nurse's uniform. Certain authority figures – teachers, nurses, even the officious woman in the post office who paid her Family Allowance – had always brought out a frivolous defiance in Phyllis; in the scale against them she'd counted on her pretty looks and quick wits and all the easy assurance of her class, just as she'd done long ago at school, maddening her teachers. And what a fool she appeared, marooned here in her nice clothes because Nicky, who was just about young enough to be her son, had dropped her to go out with his actual mother. Phyllis was on the point of departing. She would leave Nicky a note scribbled underneath his own, neutral enough so that anyone could safely read it. Of course she longed to protest: *How could you? I can't forgive you.* On the other hand she was abject, in case he stopped wanting her. *Sorry I missed you. Next week.* No name, no question mark. She searched for a pencil in her handbag.

The nurse had her keys ready, meanwhile, to open a door further along the corridor, on the other side – thank goodness at least that she wasn't next door, couldn't have heard anything. They had made love as if they believed that they were in the middle of nowhere. — You going to wait all day for him? she said. — I don't advise it. Better come in and have tea. I'm putting the kettle on now.

Phyllis didn't really want tea, or advice, or anything more to do with this nurse who belonged to an unknown world. But she couldn't go on waiting out here, and it was agony to leave the Everglade altogether when Nicky might come back for her. So she asked for the nurse's room number, then jotted it on the bottom of Nicky's note, using the miniature pencil from the spine of her pocket diary. — This is very kind of you, she gushed in her best social manner. — It's just a misunderstanding, so that we missed each other. I'm Phyllis by the way. Nice to meet you. You're an angel.

The nurse's stiff back, holding open the door for her, repudiated this way of talking; she replied that she was Barbara Jones. Phyllis held back from giving her own surname, although it seemed unlikely that Barbara Jones's life would ever cross with any Fischers. Barbara's room had the same sloping attic walls as Nicky's, but was smaller and got less light – though it did have a whole window to itself, a plain casement looking down into an interior courtyard far below, where tenants had thrown their rubbish. Pigeons flew past in the courtyard in formation, turning so that the light seemed to flash out brilliantly from their undersides, and Phyllis exclaimed at them; Barbara said they were a pest, carrying diseases. They belonged to a man who kept them in a loft on the roof. Looming on a coat hanger, hooked on a nail on one wall like a third presence between the two women, was a uniform matching the one Barbara wore underneath her cape: an old-fashioned long navy dress like a nun's, with an ironed, starched white apron and white linen cap. The severe dress, reaching to mid-calf on Barbara, suited her spare frame. Stooping to make tea, she was all shoulders and knees, her big feet narrow like boats in black stockings and lace-up shoes. Under the kettle the flames of the gas ring burned blue, with a rushing noise.

She said she was from Grenada. — I left when the quota came from England, asking West Indian girls to help out the NHS. It was an opportunity.

— Do you love your work? Phyllis asked enthusiastically, making an effort.

Barbara said no, she didn't love it. She'd wanted to be a doctor, but nursing was what she'd got. It was hard. — Some of those older sisters are monsters, especially with the coloured girls. You make up the sheets with the fold not quite on centre on the mattress, they have you strip it down, start again in front of everyone looking at you. No walking through a door ahead of anyone more senior, even by one grade, they tear you down.

She'd been on duty all night, she explained, on a ward in St Mary's in Paddington, then in the morning had gone to the library to study: she had to pass exams, practical and written, to become a staff nurse.

— Then you can become a monster in your turn.

She laughed without looking up. — We'll see about that.

This dedication of a whole life, ticked away on the watch safety-pinned to Barbara's breast pocket, seemed a reproach to Phyllis, looking around her at the room so bare of consolations: two squat armchairs covered in green moquette, tea and a biscuit barrel, the unlit gas fire, hot-water bottle hanging from another nail, single bed with its blanket of knitted squares. A table was piled up with textbooks, all their spines aligned. Barbara ought to have been dreary, yet Phyllis couldn't draw her stare away from the conker-brown skin of her forearms, chalk-dry at the elbows, as she spooned out the tea, poured on the boiling water. A milk bottle was kept in a bucket of cold water in the sink, which must also be where she washed the dishes and her clothes, as well as herself.

— This is an amazing place, Phyllis said. — The Everglade.

— You seen the WC? I have to share it with six, one of them isn't clean. Can't wait for it all to come down. I'm only here because it's cheap.

— For what to come down?

— You don't know? All this area's coming down, thank God. Making way for the new road, the Westway.

— Oh, I didn't know.

Phyllis had imagined life at the Everglade stretching on into the future, just as it was. She resented Barbara's rejoicing in its doom, mouth set in that hard line of disapproval: she *was* like the woman at the post office. The tea she made was strong, though, and was even served in china cups; Phyllis ate a biscuit, a Jammie Dodger, when Barbara offered it, because she was hungry for something sweet. Usually she hardly ate on the days she saw Nicky – it was easy to go without if she was with him, and now more than ever she wanted to keep her figure trim. Grenada must be lovely, she said. She had lived in Cairo for years, she knew how grey and dreary England could seem, with its eternal rain.

Barbara said she didn't suppose Grenada was anything like Cairo. — I was brought up very strictly. My family would be shocked if they knew I lived in any place like this. My uncle's a church minister, they think I'm still in the student hostel. I'd like to be somewhere more civilised.

Phyllis had imagined that London must seem so glamorous to foreigners. — Yet you're more at home here than I am, she said encouragingly. — I don't know this part of the city. Everything's new to me.

— I wish I didn't know it. I went to Oxford once, that's not too bad. Or Stratford-upon-Avon, I wouldn't mind living there.

Phyllis said that perhaps when she'd passed her exams, she could apply to hospitals in these places: though she couldn't imagine Barbara fitting in at Oxford. When she'd finished her tea she knew she ought to leave; the exhausted nurse must be longing to be alone, take off her uniform, draw the curtains across against the light, sleep – her eyes were yellowed and bloodshot. And yet Phyllis was overwhelmed by an impulse to tell this stranger everything. She hadn't spoken to anyone about her affair: she'd never been intimate in that way with any women friends, and talking to her sisters was out of the question. When she asked Barbara whether she knew Nicky – she called him *my friend Nicholas* – Barbara's glance slid away from her.

— I hardly know him, she said. — He's a friend with my friend Sam Harris, my cousin from home, a musician. At least I think they do some business together. How would I know a man like that?

— But like what? What is Nicholas like?

She shrugged, dismissive. — Educated, speaks nicely, but doesn't work in any proper job or wear a good suit. How does he pay the rent? I wonder. Why go around looking like a poor man? Why not get work, live somewhere better?

— He's a writer, he is working. It takes time to get started.

— Well, maybe so. It's true I'm too serious, everybody says so.

In the low armchair Barbara sat back, ungainly, her knees thrust up, long calves slanting to one side, nursing the warmth of the teacup against her chest; Phyllis was perched – a silly bright-plumaged bird, she felt herself – on the edge of the other chair. — You might as well know that I'm in love with Nicky, she carried on, making a rueful face as if this were all material for a comedy, lightly scandalous. — And that I'm married to someone else too, with two children. But I love Nicky. I've never loved anyone before, not like this. I don't even know why I'm telling you: I don't know you. And I haven't told anyone else. Of course you'll despise me for it. Ridiculous, isn't it? I suppose you think it's just absolute self-indulgence. He's closer to your age than he is to mine.

Barbara looked away from her, making a clicking, disdainful noise with her tongue. — A grown woman. You should have more sense.

— And yet here we are, it's happened. He loves me too.

— Break off with him. What about your children?

— I can't.

— Are you a Christian?

Phyllis said yes, but not a very good one, obviously; Barbara said she should pray, and read her Bible. Phyllis didn't really think the Bible would help much. From Religious Studies lessons at school she remembered David and Goliath, Jacob with all those flocks and wives, Judith cutting off the head of Holofernes. Yet perhaps there was something for her in the idea of the church, if only she could find her way through to it. Something to steady her and make her see what she was doing, how to stop it if she had to stop. *I lift mine eyes to the hills*, she remembered vaguely. She thought that she ought to go home, and stood up from her chair; she couldn't stay any longer in this puritanical, mean room.

— It's not my business anyway, Barbara coldly said.

Making her exit, Phyllis was ungracious, forgot even to thank her for the tea.

Meanwhile Nicky was enjoying lunch with his mother at their usual place, the University Women's Club: Brussels sprout soup and breaded escalope of veal. Jean had brought a few items of china up from Cressing, to take to be repaired; on an impulse afterwards she'd decided to call on her son, and he'd agreed to come out for lunch because he couldn't bear to see her disappointment if he sent her away. Thank goodness she hadn't arrived an hour or two later! Opening his door to find her standing there, her face full of anxious pleasure at surprising him, for a discomfiting instant – because he expected Phyllis – he'd seen his own mother in a different light, dressed up smartly for town in her navy suit and frilled blouse, in powder and lipstick, pearl earrings peeking under her hat, mac over her arm. But his mother was old, with a dowdy, faded prettiness.

She wasn't really conventional, however, under the conforming surface of her life. Jean had been amused, taking him into her stuffy club in his disreputable clothes: although in his room she'd at least persuaded him to comb his hair, put on the blazer Phyllis had rescued for him, wear a tie – which she had to fasten for him, while he lifted his chin obediently like a schoolboy. All the time she was fussing Nicky had been desperate for them to leave, in case Phyllis appeared. Quizzically Jean appraised him, tugging his lapels into shape. — If they throw us out of the club, she said, — we'll go for spaghetti somewhere. And I'll resign, I'll tell them you're the bright hope of future generations.

In his childhood, before boarding school, his mother had been his co-conspirator like this, unworldly and eccentric, ironic: she had covered for him if he broke things, invented illnesses to excuse him from the nightmare of other children's birthday parties, helped him to cheat if his homework was difficult. She'd never intruded, though, into his games or schemes for greatness, respecting his childish privacy with her scrupulous shyness. Long past the hour when he was supposed to be asleep, Jean had read aloud to him; if his father was at home and called sternly upstairs she was flustered, torn out of their story, not knowing for a moment where she was. Nicky had adored in those early days her startled look – gauche and tall with pale freckles and frizzy mousy hair: yet he'd understood even then, from something in his father's manner, that her beauty wasn't worth much, as currency in the outside world. Nowadays her unruly hair had been permed into extinction, coloured a dull brown, pinned back from her temples in tight rolls – drawing attention to her skull, which was delicately shaped.

His tie, talismanic, did the trick at the club, there wasn't any trouble; apart from the waiter, he was the only man in the threadbare, high-ceilinged dining room, with its virginal posy beside every typed menu. This concentrated his sense of his own male qualities, the blasphemy and mockery. Ladies at the other tables, mostly in pairs, perhaps classicists or ancient survivors from suffragette days, murmured as if they were in a library; they had decided opinions and were used to commanding the waiter, yet their soft plain faces and bodies were unguarded and helpless, as if for years they'd not looked in a mirror with any interest or hope. How different Phyllis was! Nicky worried about missing her visit – but he'd left her a note, and trusted her to understand. Phyllis was resourceful: she would go shopping instead. The idea of the frivolity of her shopping gratified him. The two of them were balanced together as opposites, he thought, each expert in their entirely different domains. Jean asked whether he was thinking of paying the Fischers another visit. — Apparently they liked you very much.

When Nicky said he was bored by Roger Fischer's Foreign Office talk, she drooped in disappointment. — But he's so very bright. I was sure you two would have something to say, what a shame.

Perhaps it was all a mistake, my silly idea. But Phyllis is fun, isn't she? I heard there was some disaster with your shirt – did you spill something?

— I behaved like an idiot, naturally. Came over as aggressively Marxist and ate like a boor.

— I expect you were charming. Roger's probably a bit of a Marxist himself. He's very left, you know, for a man in his position. He sees through things.

Nicky refilled their glasses from the bottle of Sauternes. — And how did you get on at the repairers? What was broken? What on earth are you doing all day, by yourself in Cressing? Aren't you going off your head with only the dog and Mrs Chick for company?

She told him he'd no idea how much time her privileged idleness took up. Everything that worked broke down sooner or later: even Mrs Chick the housekeeper was temperamental, and suffered with her sciatica. Jean was forever conferring with odd-job men, or hiring girls for cleaning and never sacking them, however lazy or hostile or pregnant they turned out to be. — And reading and gardening, she added vaguely. She laughed when in the middle of her account of a smashed tea set, Nicky yawned hugely without covering his mouth, raising his arms behind his head and stretching out his legs, attracting a muted attention from other tables. — It's a good sign really, she said, — that you're not interested in china! I'd hate it if you were. You're such a revolutionary, I suppose you dream of grinding china tea sets underfoot.

— Yes, and carrying Mrs Chick's head aloft on a pike.

— It will be my head carried aloft, darling. Mrs Chick will be among the vindicated classes, taking over the best bedroom and drinking all the port – not that there is any port. It's only me who's vapid and parasitic, with no part to play in a brighter future. I mean it. I do believe in a brighter future, and don't really see what I have to offer it.

— I wish I believed in it.

— I feel it coming: of course it frightens me no end. I'm so mixed up with everything wrong in the present. But isn't a bright future de rigueur for revolutionaries?

— Along with tearing down the houses of the upper classes. But I'm not a revolutionary: disabused by temperament, can't work up enough enthusiasm.

— Your father thinks Cressing should be torn down too, for different reasons.

They didn't discuss what they both knew: that whenever Jean wasn't at the Knights' London flat, in Woburn Square, Peter Knight moved in his mistress: a handsome, upholstered woman with brassy hair, whom he'd used to see whenever he flew home on business from Teheran – she was the ex-wife of a junior colleague. Jean sent precautionary telegrams, forewarning her husband of any London visits. Cressing was a perpetual drain upon their finances, Peter complained, in its leaky, dilapidated state. He wished Jean would sell it. Why didn't they buy somewhere in the Dordogne in France instead, where the summers could be counted on? Jean had told Nicky once that Peter liked Cressing to begin with, long ago when they first met. She must also have been describing his father's attitude to her. — I think it moved him in those days, she said. — The romance and seclusion and everything, the whole quixotic history. When he was less confident, not successful yet, more easily impressed.

Cressing was a rambling overgrown villa rather than a stately home, built in the Suffolk countryside in the early nineteenth century by Jean's great-grandfather, an amateur astronomer. There had been a more venerable and beautiful house in the family once, but that had gone to an older son who'd sold it, and it was demolished in the nineties. Cressing had an observatory in a turret, and stood on a low hill overlooking beech and oak woods which her great-grandfather and grandfather had planted. Jean had grown up there, a solitary bookish child, and her imagination was rooted in the place. His mother was still a girl, really, Nicky thought. She hadn't ever wakened from her enchanted sleep. Probably she didn't think much of Phyllis, under the cover of her condescension. Phyllis wasn't an intellectual by any means, outwardly she was only a bourgeois housewife, with all the unexamined ideas of her class and upbringing. And yet she was endlessly a surprise to Nicky. It seemed to him that she led the way into the future his mother talked about, not through ideas, but in her own warm body. He was carried along in the wake of her recklessness and careless freedom, washed through with a tide of recollections of her and longings, as he'd never been in any love affair before. The tenderness and sweetness in their relations disconcerted him; he had been sure he had a barren soul, incapable of such feelings. It suited him, too, that she came to him only once a week, like a lover in a book. He didn't have to adapt his whole life around her, and could get on with writing and building his contacts, in journalism and publishing.

———

When Phyllis arrived home that Wednesday, she could hardly climb the stairs to her bedroom to take off her coat and change her shoes, and she shrank from the sight of herself in the mirror. How could she live through the following hours and days, dreading that when she arrived next time at the Everglade there would only be another note, or no note and Nicky's door locked against her, no word from him ever again? His mother, appalled, would have got the truth out of him and made him see Phyllis's depravity, corrupting her child. Or Barbara Jones would have visited his room to remonstrate with him, offer him her own youth instead. By the time the children got back from school, Phyllis was tied into her apron, in fresh lipstick, her distress so extreme that she could only force it down under the surface of the passing minutes, like drowning something struggling for its life. She seemed to perform an imitation of herself, going easily through all the motions, relieved that she had cooking and washing dishes to preoccupy her. Then she had to get Hugh into bed, look over Colette's uniform for the next day, iron the creases out of her skirt with a damp cloth. Perhaps she could live out the rest of her life like this, smiling and unresponsive as a doll: embracing her husband and asking solicitously after his work, taking up the knitting she'd neglected recently. It might even be restful, after the end of her passionate deception: except that each time a living thought reared up she had to submerge it again, gasping for her own breath. — Are you all right, old thing? Roger kindly asked her.

And then the next morning, just as Phyllis was sitting down to drink Nescafé with Mandy Verey, the telephone rang in the hall and hurriedly she excused herself, pulling the kitchen door shut behind her, not caring what Mandy thought. — Yes? she said in a low voice into the receiver, half crouched over it, forgetting her usual telephone manner, hair falling forward over her face. — Yes?

— Phyl? It's me.

— I know. I knew it was you, as soon as the phone rang.

— I'm so sorry about yesterday. She arrived unexpectedly, I couldn't put her off.

— Where are you calling from? From that cabinet in the Everglade? Did you get the number from Directory Enquiries?

— From my mother. She's keen I should get in touch with you again. I mean, with you both, you and your husband, and obviously not under exactly these circumstances. I didn't tell her I'd been getting in touch with you every week. Getting in touch with you completely, in the fullest meaning of the word. Actually touching you.

— I'm so glad you've been in touch.

— I'm so glad too. In fact I'm so glad that I need to touch you again, quite soon. Can you come back? Can you come sooner than next week? I need you, Phyl.

— I need you too.

— Today? Tomorrow?

These words spoken aloud were outrageous in the decorous stillness of the hall, where dust motes hung in pillars of light from the window on the stairs. Phyllis was aware of Mandy in the kitchen – although surely she couldn't hear anything, not with the door closed. Nicholas was pressing her in urgent tones – and she had believed she'd never hear from him again. She shifted rapturously in her cramped position, gripping the receiver.

— I'll manage somehow, she said. — Yes, tomorrow. I'll cancel things.

— Not Church Education Group? I dread jeopardising your immortal soul.

— Friday Club. It's a sort of lunch club, we have topics for discussion.

— I'll make up for Friday Club, I promise. I have a whole list of topics. We can work through them.

When she went to his room the next day Phyllis thought that there was a new grown-up seriousness between them, as if a first, childish phase of their affair had ended with that terrible lunch-time. In the hush after lovemaking they made arrangements for contacting each other, if ever they had to change their plans for meeting. She told Nicky that she'd had tea with his neighbour Barbara while she waited for him. — Barbara? Which one's that?

— Sam Harris's cousin, the nurse. She disapproves of you because you don't have a proper job.

He seemed to recognise her description vaguely, remembered Sam had said he had a cousin in the Everglade. — He has cousins all over: everyone who gets off the boat train at Waterloo claims to be related to him. I rent this room from Sam, he's my landlord, he owns several apartments here: he's looking to make a killing because they're buying up everything to make room for the Westway. You'll like Sam. I'll take you sometime to hear him play the piano. He's really good.

She thought that he meant calypso, but apparently Sam played Chopin too, he had studied at the Royal Academy. Phyllis felt after this meeting with Nicky that she had crossed a line, like being on board a ship where there were certain ceremonies for when you crossed the Equator. It wasn't only that Nicky spoke as if they might go out together and she could meet his friends, gain entry to a whole new world of social relations. It was that she knew nothing about this world of his. Everything she'd ever known had been nothing: she might as well scrape away all the things she'd taken for granted all her life, to begin again. She seemed to watch herself undressing, in that room of Nicky's with no accretions of furniture or domesticity, dropping the pieces of her clothing one by one onto the bare floorboards, leaving her old self behind, climbing into his bed, weightless and transparent as a naked soul in an old painting.

Phyllis's father wrote from Leamington, saying he'd be pleased to have her visit before Christmas. When she had tea one afternoon with her sisters, they handed over presents and cards for her to take down for him and Marcia Deller; Mrs Deller was supposed to be their father's housekeeper, but there was clearly more to it than that. The three sisters, in their diffident, tactful way, shared a concern about what might be going on in Leamington, through a coded system of glances and ironies. They would never condemn their father: how could they, when they thought of his loneliness? But they couldn't help themselves disliking Mrs Deller, with her hostile pink-powdered face, the hard helmet of her dyed black hair, her spoiled Pekinese: Jane called her Cruella de Vil. They owned up to their resentment of the changes Marcia had made to their mother's arrangements in the house: replacing old faded velvets and brocades with Dralon upholstery, selling off antiques – *that rickety old thing!* – and replacing a bookcase, full of beloved old novels, with a TV set inside a Tudor-style oak cabinet, which had little doors to open when you wanted to watch. — Aren't we so hideously superior! Jane said. They were such snobs, weren't they? Disapproving of how Mrs Deller cooked, with packet soups and instant mashed potato. Yet they couldn't deny that their father seemed happy enough – though he had seemed to share their mother's tastes, for all those long years until she died.

— And what will we do, Anne had once said musingly, — if he leaves everything to Cruella?

Jane was decisive, as if she'd thought through the possibility already, from all angles. — He probably will. And we won't do anything. After all, we don't really approve of inherited wealth, do we? Anyway, we had that money from Mummy. It's enough.

— I suppose it's enough, Anne said. — I'd have liked to buy a cottage in Suffolk for my retirement. But you're right, it's enough. Never mind.

Phyllis told Roger she'd catch the train to Leamington on Thursday afternoon, he wasn't to worry, she'd call him Friday evening. Mandy would be collecting Hugh from school, giving him tea. She told her father she'd arrive at lunchtime on Friday: so she and Nicky could have the whole of Thursday night together. On Thursday afternoon she brought her suitcase to his room, and they made love while it grew dark. Phyllis thought she could hear the rushing of wind in the plane trees outside, above the noise of the city traffic. She got up from the bed eventually to wash, crossing the floor in a blue light from the round window, like crossing a stage set for a play, taking her sponge bag and towel into the bathroom next door. While she washed in cold water at the sink a man rattled at the door handle, asking urgently, impatiently who was in there. *Won't be a moment!* Phyllis sang out, hearing herself so fatally nicely spoken, out of place. She feared that when she opened the door the man would be waiting, staring at the cotton dressing gown which barely covered her, angrily questioning her right to be there – but he'd gone. In Nicky's room she switched on his desk lamp, set out on his desk her hairbrush and jar of cold cream, her scent bottle; the floorboards were gritty with dirt under her bare feet. Nicky had fallen asleep, with his back turned to her. She felt displaced and frightened for a moment.

Then he took her out to eat in a bohemian place, its entrance tucked down in a basement area. The restaurant was crowded into two small rooms, noisy with talk, thick with cigarette smoke and the smells of food, dimly lit by candles stuck in wine bottles on every table. Phyllis thought that perhaps Anne, who was an artist and had an unknown life apart from her sisters, came to places like this. A fat old Austrian woman in a lace-trimmed apron, Helga, presided behind a glass cabinet filled with pastries; she greeted guests by name, and knew Nicky. Phyllis was aware of Helga's mild scrutiny, assessing her relation to him, as they squeezed into their seats at a tiny corner table. — I'm dressed so wrongly, she apologised. She had put on her good dress in a silk print, black on olive green, with a flattering neckline, little tie thrown back across her shoulder, but the women in here weren't wearing couture clothes. Their drifting, flowery fabrics made her look old-fashioned, and she saw that elegance wasn't a thing any longer. In their crushed velvets and maxiskirts and Indian silver jewellery, heavily made-up, they were like temple goddesses; a girl all in black, with dead-straight waist-length red hair, kept on her black beret all through her meal, and one woman had a nodding ostrich feather stuck in her bandeau. Some of the men were as exotic as the women, with long hair, in flared satin trousers low on their hips, silk shirts and embroidered waistcoats; others wore suits, with only their ties loosened.

It was glamorous, but not in any way Phyllis was familiar with; everyone looked as if they had interesting lives, as artists or musicians or psychoanalysts. She was proud of Nicky because he was at home here, not even registering its stylishness, which impressed her, only taking it for granted. He knew people, they waved at him – one, he told her, wrote about politics and was very brainy, in the Communist Party; one was in a band she'd never heard of. Nicky didn't stand out as younger than the rest: even the older ones were trying to look as if they belonged to his improvised, uncertain phase of youth. No wonder he'd been bored when he came to Otterley for dinner. Here in his own environment he had that indifferent assurance which came to men if they were clever and had read a lot, had been to university. Phyllis was about to ask if Nicky's friend Sam came to this restaurant, then looked around and noticed that almost all the faces were white – which was a surprise and somehow disappointing, in relation to the population on the street outside.

She couldn't help herself being afraid of the girl in the black beret and other attractive girls in the restaurant, with their sullen unsmiling faces and long hair swinging, slanting black-painted eyes. Their gaze was sated and flattened, as if they'd plumbed the depths of experience, experimenting no doubt with sex – and drugs too. How long could she keep Nicky from those girls? It was a new experience, spending time with him when they weren't in bed together. When they'd ordered their food, Phyllis asked tentatively about his writing, and Nicky said he was working now for a magazine that had been started up recently, by a couple of guys in Long Acre with a typewriter. — Tom McGrath, this crazy Scots playwright, was living somewhere in the middle of Wales and they just sent him a telegram. *Come to London, you're editing a new paper.* And that was it. The point is it connects us to what's happening in Amsterdam and Paris and New York. I'm covering film and the visual arts, plus anything else I want to write about. Then the printers call Tom up, they're foaming at the mouth with indignation. *We can't print this filthy rag. We've got decent women working here.*

— And is it filthy?

— For Chrissake. It's war that's filthy, not some harmless magazine. There's a lot in it against the war, inevitably. And they're campaigning to change the licensing laws, have the pubs open all night, that sort of thing. It's full of *politics is pig shit*. Which I don't find particularly filthy. Because basically, as a statement it's not elegant but it's true.

— I suppose it's true, Phyllis doubtfully said. — But what about the National Health Service, for instance? That's a good thing, isn't it? And that comes from politics.

— Old women in curlers clutching their bottles of free medicine. It doesn't exactly change consciousness, does it? Keeps the factory workers healthy, so they can work for longer. It doesn't actually change the way people live together, or see one another.

— If you were very poor, though, darling, and needed a doctor for your child.

Nicky said yes, that went without saying, and Phyllis thought he was annoyed because she'd brought up the subject of children, which didn't interest him. She asked him about the films he'd reviewed instead – she belonged to a club in Otterley which showed foreign films. They bought a bottle of wine, and then when that was gone drank cognac; the food was rather greasy and heavy, Austrian-style. — I'm paying, she said, sotto voce, wondering if he'd be insulted. Roger would never have let a woman pay. — I'll give you the money so you can settle it yourself.

— It's all right, you know. My mother gives me money.

Phyllis was startled to hear this; she hadn't asked herself how he ate and paid his bills, had thought vaguely that he must make enough from his writing. — I don't want you paying for me with her money, she said. And Nicky shrugged, he was easy, he didn't care; she passed him pound notes from her purse. She had visited the bank especially, telling Roger she was taking out money for Christmas shopping.

On their way back to the Everglade, Nicky drew Phyllis against him in the cold night, inside the heavy greatcoat with military brass buttons which he'd bought, apparently, for a shilling in an old-clothes shop. It smelled of naphthalene from mothballs, and the rough fibres in the collar chafed in the cold night against her cheek. They kissed until they could hardly stand up, there in the public street: what did it matter, what anyone thought? Beyond where they were kissing there was only an uneven wasteland stretching away in the moonlight, part of the swathe of demolition for the road that was coming through, low walls and mounds where there must have been houses once, stunted bushes, the fluttering ends of advertisements pasted on wooden hoardings. In Nicky's room, they hardly had time to get their coats off before he was on top of her on the bed, she was pulling off her knickers: he was still wearing his shoes and she was in her stockings, his trousers and underpants were somewhere down around his knees. There must be stains on her nice dress, she thought after they'd finished, with their cries of such certainty – only this mattered, there was nothing else! The dress would be ruined. They were breathless and collapsed, amazed, laughing at themselves, kissing at each other in a daze of congratulation. Then Nicky stood up to take his clothes off properly, hobbling awkwardly with his trousers at half mast.

— Do you really think that politics is pig shit? Phyllis said.

She could only have used that word *shit* in the dark, she had never spoken it aloud before. — Do you think that what my husband does is pig shit too?

Switching on the office desk lamp which he kept on a crate beside the bed, Nicky said it was an odd moment to bring up the subject of her husband.

— But tell me.

He was taking off his trousers, hopping on one foot, peeling off his socks, his penis still buoyant and slick from their lovemaking. — Phyl, I don't want to think about politics right now, at this moment.

— I know. But I know you don't believe in what he does.

She got up from the bed, raising her arms to undo the zip of her dress and then stepping out of it, leaving it crumpled on the floor. Suddenly they couldn't touch each other.

— Of course I don't believe in it, Nicky said. — What he does is obscene. Don't you know it, really? There's a lie at the bottom of our civilisation. Men like your husband, for all their decency and wisdom and experience, don't address the lie. In fact in their own way they help to maintain it.

— What is the lie, though? Do you mean money?

— Worse than that. Deeper. Like those wise men on the television news: pretending to be grown-ups, pretending they know what they're talking about. Mangled bloody secrets inside the reasonable words. Nothing that seems normal and reasonable really is. Men in suits, like your husband, sit around calmly in meetings, deciding whether it's necessary to drop bombs on villagers and children. Which is an obscenity much worse than pig shit.

Phyllis stood in her nylon slip, her voice was shaky. — But you have to be realistic. There have always been wars, and people who make trouble. You couldn't just let them all take over.

— People who make trouble! Jesus, woman! Has it seriously not occurred to you that it's us who make most of the trouble? And do most of the taking over?

— But is that true? she said.

He climbed into bed and held the sheets open for her, inviting her to climb in beside him. — Come on in, Phyl, he said coaxingly. — Let's not quarrel now, it's too late for quarrelling.

— Roger would never do anything he believed was unjust.

— Maybe he truly believes that the trouble's all made by someone else. Maybe he really thinks he's one of the grown-ups.

— He has standards, she said, hearing how ridiculous she sounded. Roger would think she was ridiculous. — He would stand up against tyranny.

— I'm sure he would, Nicky said drily. — If he ever noticed it was happening, and that the tyrant was him.

Phyllis thought that she couldn't possibly sleep, not now. She wanted to argue against what Nicky was saying, and yet couldn't help herself making a connection between her own feelings for the two men, and their different politics. Hadn't there always been something rotten and untrue in her sexual life with her husband? She said that she had to go and wash, and then when she came back from the bathroom Nicky was asleep. So she sat up alone in her slip, on the hard wooden chair at his desk, her body rigid and numb with cold while her mind adjusted to this new perspective, thinking along paths which she had hidden from herself, obscure and overgrown. It was important to feel the cold air striking on her shoulders; if she got into bed now beside Nicky, her new perceptions might dissolve into mere happiness, which was not enough. She was remembering how, while she watched the television news, her awareness would flick back and forth between the steadying, regretful voice of the broadcaster, and grubby unclear snatches of actual film from the war in Vietnam: soldiers wading waist-deep in fast river water or struggling through jungle foliage, cowering villagers lamenting in their language – accusing, gesturing at awful heaps of rags. She'd pushed those film snatches away, as if they were fragments from a dream. Always she'd taken refuge, cowardly, in the safe, sane voice of the man in charge, trusting that he knew that what you saw was bearable. You didn't need to worry, it was admissible within the frame of your reality. But what if that man lied? What if those snatches were from another more terrible reality, equal with your own? Or more real, even. What then?

— How can you bear it? she said to Nicky, climbing in beside him eventually. — I can't bear it.

— Jesus Christ, you crazy woman. Your feet are fucking freezing.

— But how can you, though? If everything is a lie.

She must change everything, she said; change her way of seeing, and the way she lived. Nicky laughed dozily out of the comfort of his sleep, and it was a great relief to her. The warmth in his cave of sheets and blankets was like fire, he welcomed her inside.

Phyllis had hardly given any thought to her stay at Leamington. Her thoughts had stopped short at Nicky's room and her night spent in his bed, like a clock stopping for a death and refusing to tell any more time afterwards. In the morning when they woke up together they were happy; Nicky switched on an electric fire because the room was cold, he made her tea and toast in bed – then when she had to leave to get her train, everything seemed too abruptly broken off. It was raining and on the train she couldn't see for more than a few yards beyond the steamed-up windows in her compartment, couldn't shake off her eerily suspended state. At Leamington she had to queue under her umbrella for a taxi.

Her father had bought Rosemount after the war, when he and his wife were middle-aged and Jane and Anne had already left home. Phyllis could remember the fur coats piled on her mother's bed when they'd hosted cocktail parties there, the windows warm with electric light at dusk, the musky strong scent women used to wear. The house had a pretty curved front, pillared portico and sweep of gravelled drive; a white-painted spiked chain was looped around the flower beds, which were flaring now in sodden autumn colours, hydrangeas rotting on their stems. Marcia Deller had planted a marching line of raw young conifers, sinister in the drizzle, along the edge of the drive on either side. She came and stood in the front doorway with the dog in her arms, while Phyllis paid off her taxi. The two women were civil to each other, but their enmity wasn't far below the surface. The mask of Marcia's make-up was fierce and her blue-black hair stood up stiffly from her square forehead. In greeting, Phyllis rubbed at the Pekinese's nose with a gloved hand, thinking that at least she and the dog disliked each other frankly.

— You were lucky there wasn't a strike on the railways, Marcia said.

— Oh, why? Have they threatened one?

— There's been so much disruption recently. The unions think they run this country.

— Well, we arrived on time, Phyllis said, although this wasn't quite true. — Where's Daddy?

— Sir John's in the sun lounge. But I think he's dozing.

The noise of the rain was loud in the lean-to, and its glass panes seemed melted into water, smudging the view of the garden: blackened stems and seed heads, age-spotted bronze leaves. The old man looked deathly, in a cane chair with a rug over his knees, with his eyes shut, head drooped to present his age-spotted bald pate; yet when he was aware of company, he jerked into life again. Even in his eighties John Knott wasn't bad-looking: affable, slight and not tall, with evasive cloudy blue eyes, traces of corn-colour remaining in the white hair. — Daddy, what nasty weather! Phyllis kissed him quickly. — How are you? I feel like a drowned water rat.

She half expected, as she stood fluffing her hair and shaking out her skirt, that her father would pierce through her façade with his sharp look, guessing what she came from; he had had affairs with some of those women who came to the cocktail parties. But he'd been out of the sexual running for too long now, his gaze was turned too far inwards, he was only interested in how much she'd paid for her taxi. — You have to watch out for those chaps, he grumbled; they should have sent Marcia to pick her up. Marcia protested that driving was impossible, the council were forever digging up all the roads. The council workers were so shoddy, she said, nothing was ever finished properly. Phyllis noticed that there were new antimacassars over the backs of all the armchairs in the sun lounge – and bizarrely, in one corner, a little clothes rail hung with things drying in front of the oil heater, a woman's flesh-coloured brassieres and suspender belts, stockings. Marcia whisked up the clothes rail and carried it away out of the room with an apologetic noise, as if she were mortified, but Phyllis was sure she'd intended it to be seen, flaunting her intimacy with Phyllis's father.

Upstairs, all the furniture had been moved around in her old bedroom. The view from her window was dejected: beyond the garden with its pond – pocked with raindrops between the lily pads, and its fountain switched off – were the deserted courts of the tennis club, dripping tall elms and a copper beech, and beyond that the back end of the encroaching town, blank red-brick side wall of a manufacturer's, number 17 bus labouring up the hill. Phyllis shoved certain alien knick-knacks out of sight in a drawer – a china swan filled with a red satin pincushion, a jewellery box in the shape of a Swiss log cabin; when she'd unpacked her case she brought her Christmas presents downstairs. Between them, she and her sisters had chosen a pale cashmere pullover and a book of Cartier-Bresson photographs, a silk scarf from Liberty's, French soap and chocolates. Phyllis was hoping that unwrapping these treats would work as a peace offering, smoothing out any unpleasantness, but Marcia insisted coyly that they had to wait until Christmas. — Mustn't unwrap our presents yet, naughty! They have to go under the tree, until Santa comes!

Phyllis had to suppress an impulse of violence. — Can't I take the dog out before lunch? she asked in desperation. — I need fresh air, and I don't mind the rain.

— But he's such a little fusspot, Marcia said chidingly, lifting Tang-tang up to her face, waggling his paw and shaking her head, frowning as if she were telling him off, although obviously it was Phyllis she scolded. — He hates to get his coat wet.

So she had to sit listening to their discussion of a pair of shoes Marcia had to take back to the shop, or problems with the new immersion heater, or with the boy who was supposed to deliver the *Telegraph* each day. Phyllis had the same sensation as on the train, when she couldn't see beyond the misted-up windows: as though her life had paused while she awaited some significant news. Her father's opinions and interests had shrunk from what they once were; he had been a man of the world, at least. He had made money, and a knighthood, from a company selling metal-framed windows; there had been a brutality in the gloss of his success, he'd known where to get his suits made, how to get the best table in a restaurant. Politics had bored him stiff. Now all that carelessness was gone. — We read about everything going on in London, he said with salacious disapproval, over their lunch of tuna bake and tinned sweetcorn. — We see it on TV.

She and Roger lived very quietly, Phyllis reassured him. But she couldn't help adding that she'd been to Ladbroke Grove recently, on an errand. — That opened my eyes, it's a whole different world. Did you ever know that part of London? A place called the Everglade? It's a marvellous old art deco building, very run-down now.

— What kind of errand?

— I had to return something, to a friend.

— Funny place to have friends.

Her father didn't know the Everglade, how could he? She had only wanted to say its name aloud. Then he deplored the conditions in parts of London, which ought to be cleaned up, he said: it was usually the fault of the kind of people living there. — If they're poor, though? Phyllis remonstrated. Some kinds of people, Marcia said, didn't know how to live decently. Why did they have so many children, if they couldn't look after them? Marcia was an enthusiast for Enoch Powell. Then Phyllis claimed, just to shut her up, that one of her friends was coloured, a nurse who sacrificed herself caring for the sick. She was hot and ashamed of herself, making this claim when she hardly knew Barbara Jones, hadn't even liked her. Barbara wasn't sacrificing herself anyway, she was just trying to earn a living. In the afternoon, when, in spite of the roadworks, Marcia drove into town, Phyllis accompanied her, claiming she had her own shopping to do. In fact she only wanted to get out of the house. An uneasy truce held between the two women in the humming plum-coloured Mercedes, its gear changes so fluently effortless, until they parted in the car park. Phyllis hurried down familiar streets under her umbrella, in the opposite direction to Marcia, not caring where she went, and found herself outside the big nineteenth-century city church – which wasn't where she and her sisters had ever worshipped with their mother. They'd preferred, for aesthetic reasons, an ancient church in one of the villages nearby.

Dropping her umbrella in the porch, Phyllis went inside; after the torn grey light and perpetual splash of tyres in the road, entering the church's echoing quiet was a balm. The place was cavernous, built in the boundless confidence of a different era; someone out of sight was doing the flowers in the choir. Phyllis smelled the pungency of cut foliage, heard the snip of scissors and scrape of a china vase on stone. In here, at last perhaps she'd be able to think. She wanted to fall on her knees, but was afraid of the embarrassment of anyone seeing her: there were so many nice women in Leamington who'd been friends of her mother. Awkwardly she stooped down in one of the pews, closed her eyes, leaned her head on her hands clasped together, made a great effort of contemplation. What if her way of life was obscene, as Nicky believed?

Phyllis had always, since she was a child, been able to conjure up an idea of God if she tried hard enough. Not as a benign patriarch, personally interested in her; more like a concentration of clarity, a patch of white light like a magnesium flare, hovering somewhere outside her. If she focused on that clarity, she seemed to be able to see things impartially and justly from the outside, free from the clamour of her self. It was a kind of relinquishment, a divine easing. But now when she most needed it, she struggled to bring God into being: she felt her own pulse beating, the blood running in her veins. The church for all its blessed quiet felt like a dead end, a sham: its exemplary craftsmanship – soaring stone pillars and carved pew ends, patterned tiled floor – was tamed and bland, product of the materialistic Victorian age. On the other hand, if God only visited where his churches were old and in good taste, he couldn't really be God. Hearing the firm footsteps of the flower-snipper approaching, Phyllis shrank into her place. I have to change my life, she thought. I can't go on. Yet it's quite impossible to change it. She saw how fatally Roger and the children and her home – the whole domestic edifice of their life together – held her fixed inside their shape, so that she couldn't change her own life without bringing everyone else's down around her.

That evening she went out to the phone box to call Roger. — I never heard of anything so silly, Marcia said. — When there's a perfectly good telephone here.

But Phyllis hated the idea of talking while Marcia listened in the next room. Also she was glad to get out; her father and Marcia had their central heating turned up so high, and the television was too loud. It had stopped raining, but the night air was pungent from the soaked gardens, pavements were slick with leaves. The call box was on an empty stretch of road alongside the tennis courts; she felt its seclusion so intensely that it was almost a surprise to hear Roger's familiar voice in the receiver. She asked what he'd been up to at work. — Oh, you know, meetings and drinks receptions, he said. — World affairs winding down as usual for Christmas.

— So nothing too horrible.

— Horrible like what? Those drinks receptions can be pretty ghastly.

— Like ordering bombings or . . . I don't know!

— My dear Phyl, what do you imagine my responsibilities consist of? You have a very exaggerated idea of my importance. I can assure you I've not ordered any bombings, not today nor ever. Whatever got into your head to make you worry about that?

— I know that I sound silly, Phyllis said. — Take no notice of me.

She shifted the heavy receiver against her shoulder, stared down at the pale blobs of her shoes in the dank phone-box light. Her feet were freezing; rainwater dripped onto the roof, from shrubs over-grown above a wall. Her breath was turning to steam against the glass panes; she wrote Nicky's name in it like a teenager and then rubbed it out, making her glove dirty. It was characteristic of Roger's telephone manner that he was silent for long moments, just as he was in face-to-face conversation, while he thought gravely of the right response. — No, it's my mistake, he said, — not listening seriously to your question. If you really want to know what I've been doing, I've spent some time recently prepar-ing a paper for the minister to take to the UN, on security and cooperation in the Middle East.

— I see. Thank you. That sounds like a good thing.

— Well, let's hope it's an accurate enough assessment. It would be hubris to imagine persuading anyone to act in their own ra-tional self-interest. But at least we get into the future with our eyes open.

— And that's the best to hope for?

He paused again, weighing her words. — I probably come down on the side of not hoping for too much. It's a botched old civilisation, you know. Rather imperfect.

Phyllis felt Roger's perspective, for the moment, regain its sway over her. He appeared such a pillar of enlightenment and kind-ness, after her conversations with her father and Marcia. On her way back to Rosemount from the phone box, his old civilisation seemed to crouch around her in the dark, as if she were blundering among broken monuments in the Roman Forum, rather than past the bus shelter, and the tennis club where she'd gone to teenage dances. She smelled its composted ancient rottenness, felt its gravel prodding under the thin sole of her shoe, knew the futility of imagining anything different, anything less terrible or bitter. Marcia's conifers were a row of crucifixions. And yet Nicky proposed so carelessly to turn all this inside out, expose its secrets, make mock of them. Was he really so clever? Perhaps its secrets had better be kept.

When she returned from Leamington to Otterley, she made up her mind to break things off with him. There was no need to write to him at once, or visit for a last afternoon. She had warned him anyway that over Christmas she wouldn't have much opportunity to see him – and he'd said that he'd be spending a few days with his parents at Cressing. She put the idea of her lover away from her, numbly, as if he had never existed.

She and Roger were getting ready one evening for a party at the home of neighbours in the cul-de-sac: standing bare-legged in his shirt, he held out his sleeves to her for cufflinks. She had put on her dress already: not the olive silk print, but a maroon crepe dress she'd made herself last year, with a cowl neck. The olive silk had gone to the cleaners, not her usual cleaners, and they'd made a good job of it – but Phyllis shoved past it in sick haste if she caught sight of it on the rail, among her other clothes. The maroon dress was flattering but demure. She imagined herself circulating at the party, charming but not flirtatious, eyes lowered, her smile reserved and patient. *What a nice woman Phyllis Fischer is.*

And the wives would ask one another if they'd finished their Christmas shopping yet. *Are you having turkey? Alan won't eat turkey: his family kept geese when he was a child. It's such a dry meat anyway, isn't it?*

But that was not fair, only some of the women would be dull. Phyllis could seek out her friends, the ones with irony, who came to the Friday discussion group and were much better fun. *Darling, the word festive makes me reach for the gin bottle. We went out to see this mind-altering French film and he literally fell asleep in the seat beside me. If Christmas isn't over soon I'm going to kill the children, it'll be in all the papers.* Roger kissed the top of her head as she bent over his cuffs. Fumbling to thread the links through the thick layers of cloth she was exasperated, swore. — I think I need reading glasses. Or is everything just getting dimmer? Let's not go to the damn party.

— We could cry off. Or I could find a shirt with buttons, it's only the Holmeses. But I thought you were looking forward to it.

She dropped his wrist. — There you are, all done. But we could play truant, just drive off in all our finery with a bottle of Scotch, watch the stars from under a blanket in the countryside somewhere. Colette won't be back until after midnight.

Hugh was at a friend's house, Colette had gone on a class trip to the theatre with her English teacher, to see *Antony and Cleopatra.* Roger said doubtfully, putting on his trousers, that they might be cold, watching the stars.

— I know, you're right, she said.

— But we needn't go.

— We have to, though, we promised. You're right.

In his dinner jacket, Roger seemed more completely the man

Phyllis was married to. It wasn't that she disliked his body, her familiar enough friend: he was sturdily built, with a thick torso, no
spare fat on him – skin sallow and tough, wiry black body hair.
Yet when they were naked they couldn't quite look at each other
without compromise: their glances skidded away obliquely. They
were always polite, even when they quarrelled. There was no point
in picnicking under the night sky with Roger because it could go
nowhere new, could only be a pretence of romance. The idea of
their swapping intimate confessions was cloying; she'd never even
asked him about other lovers, or his first love. She was standing,
now, close enough to the window to feel the thrill of cold coming
off the glass, looking out into a pure blue darkness, burned
through by a few white chips of stars; trees were silhouetted
against it, their bare twigs and branches combed out like hair. In
one corner of her attention she was aware of the Holmes's lounge
windows, diamond-paned, brash with coloured lights and looped
with streamers, the party's noise already brewing, puny in these
wide chambers of the night. Love longing seized her, searing and
sentimental as a popular song, so that for a moment she couldn't
speak.

It was all settled about Hugh going to school; he would start
after Christmas, she had gone into town with him to buy what he
needed. She kept at a safe distance an image of her little son, ill at
ease in the outfitters' changing room, his brightness drowned in
the stiff uniform he must grow into. Her husband's will was set on
it. Although he was subtle, all Roger's intelligence led him down
inexorably to certain fixed points, from which he could not be
deflected; some fatalism was instilled in his character, by his heredity or his upbringing. She turned around from the window to

go out with him; when she'd finished with her lipstick and scent at the dressing table, they went downstairs together. There was a lot to be said for these companionable married exchanges: low-voiced and sensible, friendly, worn into their groove, each partner attuned through long familiarity to the needs of the other. Was it worth wearing their coats, just to cross the road? Phyllis thought she'd wear hers after all, because it was chilly. Should they leave the hall light on? She wet on her tongue one corner of Roger's handkerchief, to wipe off an ink smudge on his cheek – he'd been changing the ribbon on the typewriter in his study. He approved her earrings when she had a moment of doubt, peering in the hall-stand mirror. *These, or my coral ones? Those suit you,* he said. *They go with your dress.*

About an hour later, Phyllis was talking to someone at the party, in the midst of all the hubbub of voices and laughter. He was perfectly nice, some friend of Brian Holmes, with warm brown eyes and speckled hair, a puppyish sociability, bulky and at ease in his creased dinner jacket, one of those men whose expression communicates keenly how much they want to get to know you, until it turns out they only want to talk about themselves. Or in this case, in a lightly comical vein, about camping holidays he'd taken with his family, how these days in a tent you could replicate all the conveniences of home, even down to a portable plastic-lined canvas washing-up bowl on a stand. And how the facilities in campsites in Brittany were improving. — I know you're imagining the whole nightmare of French toilets, he said, as if he really wanted to persuade her. — That fearsome old stinking hole in the ground. We've all been there. But the French know that's got to change, if they want to attract the tourists.

— Excuse me, Phyllis said then, smiling and putting her hand on his forearm, as if she only asked him to wait for a moment while she went into the next room to refill her glass. Perhaps that was all she meant to do at first. But just as she entered the hall, Maggie Holmes was opening the front door for another couple arriving with cries of greeting and anticipation; Phyllis pulled out her coat quickly from under a heap on the newel post and shrugged it over her shoulders, slipped past these new arrivals and escaped out into the night, still smiling, explaining vaguely to Maggie that she'd forgotten something. And perhaps if she'd had a door key she'd simply have crossed the cul-de-sac and let herself in her own front door at home, got an early night, pleaded one of her headaches in the morning. But Roger had the key in his pocket. Phyllis hunted in her bag but couldn't find one, and she couldn't bear to go back into the party. So she pencilled a message for Roger on a page torn out from her diary, posted it through the letter box. Her 1967 diary was at the end of its usefulness anyway. She had pound notes and some change in her purse, and her chequebook.

Don't look for me, she wrote. *Just need to get away for a few days.*

And she hurried down Hillfield Road to the station, where she was in plenty of time to catch the last train into town. If Nicky wasn't in she could find a room for the night, in a hotel. She really had no idea then, that she wasn't coming back.

FOUR

Colette found the note. Letting herself in the front door with her own key, she stepped on the folded piece of paper, and recognised even before she picked it up a pink page torn from the diary she'd given her mother last Christmas. How odd. Her parents had left the lamp turned on in the hall, everything was as usual, obviously they weren't home yet from their party – their coats were still missing from the hall-stand. The chilly porch smelled of wet doormat and muddy wellingtons; she lingered in it with her back against the closed front door, looking into the hall through the panes of patterned, coloured glass, waiting for the agitation from her evening to begin to subside – the play, the coach trip with the other girls, Mrs Bernhardt. Stubbornly, not wanting to be snubbed, she had kept aloof from her teacher at the theatre, not making any effort to sit by her or speak to her, only hanging around within earshot at the intervals, so that she could hear Mrs Bernhardt's opinions on the play, and know what she was supposed to think about it. The girls were allowed to wear their own clothes and had been planning their outfits for days, but even inside the theatre Colette had insisted on keeping on her green school mac over her pink dress.

She had learned that the play was a masterpiece. Mrs B.,

rattling the ice in her gin and tonic, had spoken with excitement, gabbling and swallowing her words as she sometimes did, not looking at any of them directly, as if she was addressing someone else superior and not these foolish girls crowding around her. — It's a play for grown-ups, not a romance, she had said. Colette had flinched at how the teacher exposed herself in this risky new context, with her exalted emotion and lifted, dazzled face: some of those girls questioning her eagerly were very likely only studying her mannerisms so they could imitate her later. On the way home, however, it was Colette who found herself showing off impulsively, just as if she were drunk, although in fact she had barely sipped from the half-bottle of Famous Grouse which was being passed around in the seats towards the back of the coach. She lifted her face and squeezed up her eyes, copying Mrs Bernhardt's husky, drawling voice. *I hope this performance isn't wasted on you girls. I hope you can appreciate the magnificent representation of a mature passion. There's so much about passion that you can't possibly understand, at your age; but do ask, because of course I'm very familiar with it myself.*

This showing off had gone down well. The other girls had snorted with suppressed laughter, and when she carried on, developing and exaggerating her caricature – *a body ripened by the sun of the middle years* – they'd pretended to feel sick. She had kept a watchful eye on Mrs B.'s chignon, far off at the front of the coach, her head twisted away from all of them, staring out into the night, not attentive to their clowning. The others begged Colette to tell them more about mature passion; the hysteria of the whole occasion had lifted everyone out of their normal selves like a wave. For the first time she could imagine a role for herself among her peers at school: the unsparing, clever, contemptuous one, always keeping a few steps ahead, so no one could be sure how much of her irony was meant for them.

Impatiently at home she unfolded the pink paper note, and knew instantly, viscerally, her mother's sloppy, looping handwriting. At least in these few words there was no room for any of the misspellings which so exasperated Colette in her shopping lists: tomato with an *e* on the end, caramel with a double *l*. *Don't look for me. Just need to get away for a few days.* But who was the note intended for? Surely their father was with Phyllis at the party? Colette dropped it back onto the mat as if it were poisonous. Could it be left for her? Its message seemed unseemly and improbable, didn't make any sense: she shucked off its claim upon her. Now there was a muddy shoe print on the carelessly folded paper. It lay there just as if she had come in and, stepping on it, had not seen it, was blithely unaware that it existed.

In her bedroom she sat up reading in bed in her nightdress, waiting for the sounds of her parents coming home. They would be squiffy, fumbling with a key in the latch, laughing together subduedly; or perhaps they'd be relieved to get away after a dull party, their voices flat and friendly, depleted. Her mother would come upstairs with her high heels in her hand, her father would pour a last nightcap in his study; Colette might poke her head out of her bedroom door, to ask *what was it like?* All that brilliance her mother had worked so hard to assemble before she went out, at her dressing table and in front of the cheval glass, would by this time be dissolved and blurred. Swaying and unfocused, her mascara smeared and shoulders slumped, she would say that the party was a bore really, just the same old people. But quite fun.

Instead Roger came in on his own. His daughter switched out

her light, when she heard him unlocking the door downstairs, and put her glasses on the bedside table. She listened, excruciated, sitting up stiffly against her pillows, to his finding the note on the mat, pausing to unfold and read it, then coming upstairs to look for his wife in the bedroom. After that there was a considering silence – Colette imagined – before he set out to search for Phyllis all round the house, although he must have known by then that he wouldn't find her. He hesitated outside Colette's door, but didn't turn the handle; he may have believed she was asleep. Or he may have guessed that she wasn't, been aware of her breathing too rigidly and consciously on the far side of the door, intuited that she too had read the note and was sitting listening to him, upright and alert in the dark. Colette and her father had always been attuned to each other with an acute sympathy, but in these new circumstances he seemed translated out of her reach. She couldn't imagine what Phyllis's note could mean to him, or what he knew about it; she was ashamed now that she'd read it and then pretended not to see it, and wished she could climb back inside her old innocence.

– Your mother's gone away for a few days, Roger said to his children the next morning at breakfast. Hugh had stayed the night at his friend Neil's house; he'd called in at home to drop off his toothbrush and pyjamas. He wasn't supposed to drink tea, but there he was with a mug of it in front of him on the table, and he was pretending to like it, stirring in spoonfuls of sugar. Breakfast was already different without Phyllis. There was no bacon and egg, only toast and cereal.

Hugh was astonished, outraged. — But it's Christmas! She

can't go away. And it's the last day of my old school. The last day for ever. She's supposed to have made cakes for the party.

— Not everything revolves around you, Colette said darkly.

Roger reassured him about the cakes: they were waiting in a Tupperware box.

Last night's strangeness, when Colette woke up this morning, had seemed too improbable to survive into daylight; she'd ventured barefoot into her parents' room as soon as she heard her father go downstairs, feeling certain that everything would be back to normal, her mother's party clothes dumped on a chair, her pillow screwed up as usual into lumps, bedclothes thrown back on one side of the bed in her careless gesture, the smell of frying bacon from downstairs. Then the signs of her father's lonely night – his shoes arranged side by side, his clothes folded too neatly like a monk's in a cell, the bedclothes so minimally disturbed – had felt like things Colette wasn't meant to see, so she'd retreated hurriedly. Roger said that Phyllis been called down to Grandpa Knott's. Perhaps this was the truth: but then why write *Don't look for me?* Colette began to doubt that she'd really seen any pink note.

— She was already there last week, Hugh objected.

The look he shot at his father was piercing and purely righteous, but it met a returning force, opaque and weighty, in the adult gaze. — Please finish your crusts, Hugh. Mandy will be here this afternoon to make tea.

Colette's school closed before lunch for the holiday, and all four hundred girls had to queue to shake hands with the headmistress standing outside her room, each one individually – it was a school tradition. Some of the older, unmarried teachers, grimly merciless in their classrooms, would hover skittishly, exchanging banter in high spirits, around the line of girls snaking along the ground-floor corridor in Old House. The geography teacher called the physics teacher by her first name, then blushed and corrected herself, darting looks because the girls must be thrilled by any glimpse of their teachers' private selves. It was at these moments of camaraderie that Colette hated the school most: when the teachers let down their guard, as if their ritual of intimidation and punishment were only a performance. Mrs Bernhardt, she observed, wouldn't have anything to do with it. She hurried up Main staircase with her face turned away, mouth pursed sardonically, back bent over a pile of books. Linda Chubb murmured that Mrs B. was dying for a smoke in the staffroom. It was quite a scandal that she smoked. Often you could smell cigarettes on her when she came into class.

Colette was waiting in the queue with Linda and Susan Smithfield, who'd been on the coach with her the night before: they claimed to be sick with dreadful hangovers. They looked at Colette warily, unsure if her brilliance last night had been a fluke – perhaps today she would be insignificant again, contaminating them if they were too friendly. Her status among her classmates could go either way; Linda and Susan were in the crowd of popular girls. Susan was scrawny and lithe, good at netball, with sex appeal and a husky voice like a boy's; Linda was pampered and disdainful, wings of smooth dark hair and a puppy-dog face, brown beseeching eyes. She'd had a boyfriend with a car, and chucked him because she was sick of his WHT, *wandering hand trouble*. This had impressed everyone, with its adult dignity.

— God, you'll never guess what happened, Colette said, — when I got home last night.

She hadn't known she was going to say anything until the words were out.

— What happened?

— I found this *note*!

She put on a troubled expression, which was at the same time eagerly gossiping and confiding. — I think my mother must be having an *affair.*

Linda flinched dramatically. — God, Fish! You're not serious?

— What did the note say?

She explained how she'd recognised a page torn out of Phyllis's diary, picked up the note from the doormat to read it. — Then this morning at breakfast my father said she'd gone to visit our grandpa. My bratty little brother was asking all these embarrassing questions: I kept my trap shut.

— Your little brother's *sweet*, protested Linda reflexively.

— But why, if she'd gone there, would she say *Don't look for me?* And anyway, she visited our grandpa only last week.

Anything would do, to hold off their tedium of waiting; the queue shuffled forward along the corridor. The two girls put on pitying faces, calculating whether or not to believe Colette, shocked by her letting them into the vulnerable private recesses of her home life. Most girls hardly spoke about their parents, except in the most nondescript general terms. — I expect she's really at your grandpa's, Linda said sceptically. — It's just a misunderstanding.

— I hope so, of course.

— Beastly, though, if it's true! commiserated Susan.

Linda widened her eyes. — I'd be so sorry for your father. Imagine how he must feel.

Colette saw the potential for wrong-footing and intriguing them, if she took the opposite view; it would be less mawkish than playing the abandoned daughter and depending on their sympathy. The sophistication of these girls was only skin-deep, underneath it they were stuffily conventional. — It may be an amazing affair, though. You know, irresistible like in *Antony and Cleopatra*. 'Let Rome in Tiber melt . . .' She may be madly in love.

— It's all right in a play, Susan said gruffly. — But not when it's your actual mother.

— They may be amazing in bed together.

Linda squealed and leaped away from her; a teacher called to ask why she was out of line. — How can you? she hissed, puppy face screwed up fastidiously. — And anyhow, do you have any idea who's the lover boy?

Colette hinted that she had one or two ideas, although this wasn't true. Until she used the word 'affair' just now, she hadn't really gone anywhere beyond an aura of danger and disruption attached to the note. Susan suggested they could ring up Colette in the holidays, to find out what happened. — When we've said our bye-byes to Topsy, you can tell us your phone number, Fish. I'll write it on my hand.

Roger told Mandy Verey the story about Phyllis being unexpectedly called down to her father's: Colette was starting to believe it must be true. Then Mandy began coming into the house for a few hours every day; she brought shopping, washed up and tidied, prepared supper and left it for them in the fridge. Her presence made things seem more normal. Mandy was calm and large, monumental, with even, golden skin and silky fair hair tucked behind her small ears; when she asked how their grandfather was getting on, Colette said he was much better, thank you. She hung around while Mandy was in the kitchen, enjoying her competence as she pounded out piles of neatly aligned, clean-scented clothes at the ironing board, or batted fishcakes between floury hands. Mandy's husband, Don, was a postman, and they had three children; sometimes the youngest had to come over with Mandy to the house, and got in her way as she worked, clinging to her knees and whining, asking to go home. — Take her out from under my feet and play with her, Col, there's a love, Mandy asked. And although Colette didn't like children, she got out the wax crayons and colouring book, and set about wooing the unlovable little girl whose downy, snotty, flat face was closed against her and hostile. It was important to Colette, for some reason, to prove to Mandy that she had this womanly skill of childminding.

Colette was left in charge of Hugh all the rest of the day. Under normal circumstances they'd have fought together, but they managed to achieve a truce in the time that remained before Christmas. Both presumed, without saying it explicitly, that their mother must come back for Christmas Day. In the mornings Hugh sorted through his collections, looking up butterflies in a book and then listing them under various headings: Common, Quite Common, Rare, Very Rare. He didn't have anything yet under Rare, and the only Very Rare butterfly was a swallowtail he'd bought that summer from a mail-order catalogue – it had arrived in a cardboard box. Colette skulked in her room, trying on her mother's make-up; then she hunted all over the house for Phyllis's note – in the hallstand, and the bureau in the sitting room, in her father's bedside table and in his desk in the study. One of his desk drawers was always locked. In the afternoons they fetched out old board games they used to play, Monopoly and Cluedo, even Snakes and Ladders. Some impulse made them draw the curtains across the windows early and switch on the lights in the sitting room, where they set out their games on the hearthrug in front of the oil heater, lying full length to play. After supper when their father was home they could hear him using the telephone in his study, and presumed he was pursuing the mystery of their mother's disappearance.

When Roger stayed late in town one evening, for a work party, Colette went into the study to call her grandfather's house in Leamington. Marcia answered the telephone and Colette put on a hoarse voice, asked to speak to Phyllis.

— Who is that? Marcia said. — Is that Colette?

Colette cleared her throat. — Yes.

— Well it's no good calling here, dear. Phyllis isn't here. We've already had your father ringing us, and Jane. Sir John gets agitated, it isn't good for him.

— Oh that's all right then, thanks, Colette said, doing her best to sound blithely indifferent. — I knew she wasn't, really. Just checking.

Although she tried to replace the receiver without its making any pinging noise, Hugh heard it, and came creeping downstairs in his pyjamas; when he asked who she was talking to, she said it was just some girls from school. Hugh hung about in the study thoughtfully, picking up the hole punch and then the cigarette lighter from their father's desk, zooming them through the air making aeroplane noises. Usually the children weren't allowed in this room, which seemed set apart from the rest of the house, a male domain where their mother mustn't encroach. Set out on the massive roll-top desk, which came from Roger's dead father in Guildford, were his typewriter and steel desk calendar, ashtray and ink bottle and paper clips in a tobacco tin; box files ranged on the shelf behind it were labelled in his writing – Tax, Insurance, Rates, Bank. Colette looked to see if any letter of her father's had been pressed onto the blotting pad, so that she could read it backwards. — On Christmas Eve, Hugh wondered, — should we hang up our stockings as usual? Because I know it's our mother who brings the presents really. I don't believe in Father Christmas or the reindeer or anything. I don't want to waste time hanging up my stocking, if there's going to be nothing in it.

— It's a good job you've grown out of that baby stuff, if you're going off to school.

— I want to go, I hate it here.

There was something maddening to Colette in her brother's shock of blond hair and clean strong limbs, his impervious pure childishness in those white pyjamas decorated with pictures of rockets and tractors. What would happen at school, to all his privacy and certainty? — Anyhow, I don't believe she's at Grandpa's, Hugh said. — I sort of know where she is.

— No you don't. How could you possibly know?

— Because I saw something – and she smelled funny, a dirty smell.

— What do you mean, smelled funny? And what did you see?

— I saw her kissing someone, in the bathroom. It wasn't Daddy.

Colette laughed. — Well, that's not very likely, is it? You just had a dream.

— It wasn't a dream. I saw it.

— Who was it that she kissed?

— I don't know. Someone. I couldn't see him, he was inside the bathroom. I just saw her, like this.

And he made a ridiculous pecking, submissive motion with his head.

— Don't be silly, Hugh, Colette said tolerantly. — It was only a dream.

When the children woke up on Christmas morning their stockings weren't empty, but the contents were all wrong. Usually there was a guinea in an envelope – a pound note and a shilling – tucked into the toe, from Grandpa Knott, and then a tangerine, then bubble bath. A few of the presents they did get were things their mother might have chosen for them before she went away, but these were muddled in with other unlikely items: gobstoppers and sherbet fountains, a supermarket pack of plastic soldiers, toy make-up set. Hugh didn't come into his sister's room in the early morning. He opened his stocking alone, putting all its contents neatly aside on his bedside table without comment, not even eating the chocolate.

For Christmas dinner they went over to Guildford as they always did: fixed traditions belonging to that house were usually part of the happiness of the day. As the dinner table's centrepiece, faded plastic reindeer pulled a sleigh laden with crackers; coloured pictures of snowmen and Christmas trees, whose glitter had long ago lost its shine, perhaps even in their father's own childhood, had to be in their fixed places on the walls, with their paper ruffs unfolded, representing snow. Their grandmother's cake was bitter and black, its icing hard as rock, stained by the marzipan. No one but Phyllis could make the angel chimes work. With her deft fingers she was the one who knew how to put them together: without her the cherubs with their trumpets wouldn't turn the right way in the candle's heat, or strike the bell.

Roger must have told his mother and sister the story about her having gone to Grandpa Knott's; Marnie asked after Sir John in a certain tone, because she was a republican and didn't believe in titles. Colette felt her father's rapid glance at her; he should have known that he could trust her. She answered, as calmly as if she'd spoken to her mother that morning on the telephone, that Grandpa Knott was recovering well, and Phyllis was sorry to miss Christmas with them all. It was hateful to think of Marnie's false face of regretful sympathy if she ever found Phyllis out in any weakness, or believed that she'd let Roger down. When they were home again in Otterley that evening, Roger asked the children to come into the sitting room, where he lit the heater and turned on the lamps, trying his best to make it cosy. He'd tied on their mother's apron and made sandwiches with the turkey Marnie had given him to bring home, and warmed up her hard mince pies, but the children weren't hungry. There was something demeaning in the sight of their father involved in these domestic details. He made Colette think of a lumbering bear on a chain, with his deliberate slow movements and bowed heavy head.

— I've heard from your mother, he said. — I wanted you to know.

— I knew she wasn't at Grandpa's, Colette said quickly, because she couldn't bear being caught out in any mistake.

Hugh was prickly with resentment. — So where is she?

— I thought at first that she must be in Leamington. But when I telephoned, they knew nothing about it. Now she's sent a note, and asks us to bear with not knowing where she is, not yet. She's taking a break from family life. I think it's all been a bit too much for her lately. She needs a break from us. I don't blame her.

— I do, Hugh sternly said. — I do blame her.

— But how is she managing without all her things? She doesn't even have her toothbrush.

— I expect she's bought herself a new toothbrush, Roger said. — She left in a hurry, and didn't have time to pack. I appreciate that it's all very difficult, from your point of view – and mine too, it goes without saying. But I suggest that we all keep an open mind. And also that we keep this to ourselves, at least for the moment. I've spoken to her sisters, because I thought they might know something. But there's no need for anyone else to know that she isn't staying over at Rosemount. She just needs time to sort herself out.

— I don't care about her sorting herself out, Hugh said. — I don't even want her to come back.

When Roger put a kindly hand on his son's shoulder, Hugh shrank under its weight.

— What did she say in this note? Colette insisted. — Exactly what words did she use? Can't I read it?

He said no, it was private, and addressed to him; she guessed that probably he only meant the note she'd originally found, the pink one. Miserably they chewed their way through one turkey sandwich each, wrapped up the rest in greaseproof paper for the next day; then Roger went into the study. A muffling blanket of

desolation descended on the house, wrapping up all of them sep-
arately with their own thoughts – even while Colette and Hugh
sat side by side on the sofa, both laughing at the same jokes on
the television. Colette held herself stiffly, not slumping, wondering how to escape from her weakness and dependency inside
her family. Perhaps this was the right moment to try slimming,
and leave off her glasses. Phyllis had always wanted her to get
contact lenses, and for as long as her mother was at home, Colette had refused to contemplate it. Now she was free.

Hugh asked if he should tell their father about the bathroom
thing.

— What bathroom thing?

— You know. *Kissing.*

— Oh, that. No, because it wasn't real.

Hugh insisted that it was real. But he didn't say anything to
Roger.

Roger took them out for a drive on Boxing Day, although it
rained. They stopped at a country pub and he went inside for a
pint of beer, brought out ginger ale and crisps for them to eat in
the car; because Colette had been reading Phyllis's dieting books,
she gave her crisps to Hugh. In the evening they played Newmar-
ket at the card table, with a dummy hand. When Roger said a
couple of days later that he had to go into the office for a few
hours, Colette thought that he simply couldn't stand another moment of their considerate constraint in the house together; and it
was a relief to the children when he set out with his briefcase to
catch the train. They called out to each other loudly around the

rooms, clattering up and down the stairs. Colette unwound a paper clip and poked it into the keyhole of the locked drawer in her father's desk, but couldn't coax it open. She had the same hectic feeling of surplus energy that she used to get when she was a child playing outside, closer and closer to the river, farther away from the watchful house; although the weather was too miserable now for them to actually go out. From an upstairs window she and Hugh saw one of the Chidgely girls – not Anthea but her older sister – walking mournfully among the flower beds in their garden, without her coat, in the rain; then Anthea, framed in her pale plaits, appeared at the back door, delegated presumably to persuade her to come inside. — I hate you all and I don't care if I die, they heard the older girl say. Colette and Hugh sank out of sight inside the window, gaping at each other, then collapsing into delighted mockery, furtive in case the Chidgelys heard.

Colette began reading *L'Étranger* in French, using her dictionary; it was set for the A level next year. She wasn't sure what was happening in the story, but the book's stylish brevity, and its jagged unsparing sentences, exuded a chic spirit of refusal. When Linda Chubb and Susan Smithfield telephoned in the afternoon, she insisted on speaking to them in French. — *Je suis en train de lire* L'Étranger. *Je l'aime beaucoup.*

— You what? Shut up, you idiot.

— *Pourquoi? Toi aussi, Linda, tu comprends le français.*

Colette could hear from the dank echo around their voices that they had called her from a phone box, no doubt so that they could be out of parental earshot. She imagined them jostling in the narrow space, grabbing at the receiver, both of them trying to listen at the same time.

— Is there any news? asked Susan in a solemn voice.

— No sign of my mother, if that's what you mean. Apparently she's written another note, but my father won't tell us anything, he keeps it in a locked drawer in his desk. I've tried to prise the drawer open, but I can't. Anyhow, he's gone into work today.

— God, poor you. And perhaps he isn't really at work, perhaps he's walking the streets, looking for her.

— I don't actually think that she's gone on the streets. Or not yet, anyway.

She enjoyed their intakes of breath, scandalised giggles. — Oh, *don't*, Colette!

— The atmosphere here is certainly pretty weird. *Écoutez, les filles.* I was planning on getting contact lenses. What do you think? A good idea? I might as well do *something* to pass the motherless time.

— They can get lost inside your eye, Linda said reprovingly.

— No they can't, Susan said. — Don't be a twit, my brother wears them. Why don't we meet up, Fish?

Colette said she couldn't at the moment, she was supposed to be looking after Hugh. With studied casualness Susan explained that she'd meant they could meet in the evening, at the Queens Head. — We go in the back bar. Won't your father be home by then? You can just say you're coming out to visit one of us. Obviously don't say where.

Colette hadn't known that these girls went to the Queens Head: she was startled and impressed. She guessed that it was Susan who'd first had the cold-blooded nerve to go into a pub, because she really was blunt and outspoken like a boy. Last summer Colette had caught sight of her once out of school, dressed in khaki shorts tied around the waist with a length of garden twine – not negligently, but in a statement of style wholly her own. Because she was a brilliant goal attack – with her streaky blonde hair, squinting light eyes, and that frowning, impatient authority when she held the ball poised on her shoulder, looking around for someone to pass to – you couldn't point to anything ridiculous in the outfit, she carried it off. The idea of a meeting at the Queens Head filled Colette's horizon at once, making her sick with nerves. She'd been intending to go to the pub very soon, it was a necessary initiation: only not under the critical scrutiny of these girls. — How many calories is beer?

— Fish, are you dieting?

She told them that she was changing everything, her entire life.

Walking down to the Queens Head, Colette didn't care about the transgression against parents or teachers, or the law for that matter – only dreaded exposure to the superior sophistication of her peers. The trick, she knew, was to imagine yourself doing the audacious, courageous thing and then follow through in external reality, without even thinking, the picture you'd created: approaching the door of the pub and crossing its threshold as if you went in there every day. And then at last she was immersed in that thick air, fragrant with beer and cigarette smoke, which had rolled enticingly onto the street whenever she passed any pub door; a rumble of youthful noise came from the back bar, which must be down this passage, past the quiet nooks and snugs panelled in brown wood just as she'd always imagined, the encouraging glitter of bottles and lemons and crisp packets reflected in mirror glass, the old men following her with their eyes. It helped that she'd left off her specs. Everything was indefinite in the dim light.

Linda and Susan were sitting round a table with a boy who must be Susan's brother because he was sinewy like her, with the same abrupt gestures. The Smithfields had mugs of beer in front of them and Linda was drinking something yellow, with a cherry on a cocktail stick. All three looked self-conscious, weighed down by their awareness of being the youngest in the crowded bar, although no one took any notice of them – they sipped at their drinks as if they'd run out of things to say. When they caught sight of Colette they were amazed by her transformation. From her mother's wardrobe she'd borrowed a black velvet jacket and Liberty print shirt, which she wore with her own jeans; she'd made up her eyes thickly with black pencil and blue eyeshadow, and sprayed on L'Air du Temps perfume. When she picked up a heavy handful of the beads and chains which Phyllis kept looped across the dressing-table mirror, she'd only meant to choose one, but then outrageously put on all of them at once. It wasn't a possibility for her, she seemed to see, to be merely like other girls, or to fit in. All that time she was getting ready, she'd felt that she was preparing and adorning a grotesque figure quite outside herself, like a fetish doll or a pantomime dame. Certainly she wasn't trying to make herself *attractive* – her mother's all-important word.

Colette sat down between Linda and the boy, whom Susan introduced as Jeremy, her kid brother. — He wanted to come, and promised not to embarrass me. We're supposed to be at orchestra practice.

— Our violins are under the table, Jeremy added.

Colette had never before been in a room packed with so many people who interested her: slouchy boys with long hair and black polo-neck sweaters, girls in PVC macs and white patent boots, smoking and talking to one another with urgent animation. — I raided the safe, she announced triumphantly. — Or actually, my brother's piggy bank. I've got money! More custard for Linda.

— It's not custard, ignoramus, it's a snowball, it's delish. Wearing all that junk round your neck, I'm surprised you can hold up your head.

— You're referring to the contents of my mother's jewellery box.

— Those aren't real jewels!

— If you don't believe me, next time I'll come in the tiara.

They were relieved to be making more noise, laughing as if they belonged here. And it was miraculous, Colette discovered, how a few mouthfuls of innocuous-tasting beer could unmoor you from the familiar solidities, loosen you to take giant steps forward into new experience. She revealed hidden reserves of knowingness and scepticism, surprising even herself; she was far more mocking – about the august institution of the school, about their classmates – than she had been on the coach when she imitated Mrs B. In the recesses of her awareness she knew that the others were reserving judgement, waiting to see whether she was the wrong sort, not their type at all; yet she hardly cared, in that smouldering, smoky light of the pub's present. They discussed which of their teachers must be lesbians, and she shared, rashly, some of the private nicknames she had for other girls – Lavvy, The Crisp, Light Bulb. She might indeed turn out to be the wrong sort. She could feel the allure of that.

In her state of elation even Susan's brother became interesting, with his earnest blinking and scabbed elbows, warty fingers. Jeremy didn't seem to be funny or clever but his mere maleness gave him some authority in their all-female company. Colette decided to make him notice her; it was probably the first time that a girl had paid any attention to him, apart from his sisters. He was voluble for a while about contact lenses, and then when they got on to favourite subjects at school, announced that he hated Eng Lit. — Fish is brilliant at it, Linda suggested slyly. — She could give you extra tuition, help you get better marks.

— I doubt if she could, Jeremy said with vehemence. — Because I hate books.

Colette pressed her knee against Jeremy's under the table, accidentally at first, then persevering with it; when he stared unhappily into his beer, she was surprised. Wasn't he supposed to enjoy this? They had been warned at school, though always in veiled language, about the irresistible and overpowering onrush of male desire, which girls must be careful not to trigger. Jeremy tried to move along the bench from where he was jammed in between her and Linda; when he'd finished his second half-pint, he looked significantly across the table at his sister, wondering if they ought to be getting back. — I warned you, didn't I? Susan scolded him furiously. — If you came out with me, you had to stay as long as I wanted. Worse luck, I'm not allowed to let you go home on your own.

When finally they parted outside the pub, the Smithfields swinging their violins, Colette threw her arms around Jeremy to kiss him, pretending to be drunker than she was; he shied away from her and wiped his cheek with his fist, even Susan looked uneasy. But it didn't matter by that time anyway, because towards the end of the evening, on her way back from the ladies' toilet, Colette had had to push past a group of drinkers standing up, and one of them had said he liked her beads. She'd been able to use her joke about the tiara again, as if she'd just thought of it freshly, so that she seemed to be witty and relaxed, though in truth she'd hardly dared look up to see the boy who'd spoken. Was he even a boy, in fact; wasn't he actually a grown man? He was certainly older than she was, far older than Jeremy Smithfield. And he'd seemed swathed – in her snatched glance at his stubbled jaw, beak nose, tinted shades, battered leather jacket – in a haze of experience, which enchanted and dazzled her.

It wasn't the joking words which mattered most, as Colette played their dialogue over and over in her mind's eye afterwards, at home. What undid her was the memory of his tone – sultry, snaky, insinuating – and his look. Using her mother's beads as his justification, flaunting his own shamelessness, he had stared while he spoke at the heavy breasts which she had up to that moment so hated and resented: he knew that she knew he was staring, and challenged her to pretend she didn't like it. In the moments of this exchange taking place, it had seemed wholly inevitable, a rightful tribute; in retrospect, she was amazed. Could that girl, whose breasts were the object of a man's interest, be the same child that she'd been yesterday, and whose bedroom this was? The room was painted white, there was a pink silk counterpane on her bed, the shade on her bedside light was made of pleated pink silk. She looked around at the children's books on her shelves – the folders of schoolwork, white china horses, the musical box dead Grandma Knott had given her, pebbles from a childhood beach – as if they were suddenly strange to her, and piquant, because she had outgrown them all at once.

Roger guessed, when he heard Colette blundering in the front door and tripping over the bottom stair, that she'd been drinking with her friends. He shrank from confronting her; he didn't really care what she'd been doing, and sat very still in his study, hoping that she wouldn't come in and discover him there, obliging him to take action, step into the role of the concerned and responsible parent. Anyhow, he'd been drinking too, only he wasn't drunk. The more whisky he drank, sitting on his own in his study in the evenings, the colder his mind seemed to become. He thought dispassionately about his daughter, admitting that her clumsiness and plainness as she'd changed in adolescence had dismayed him; he'd loved her so uncomplicatedly as a little girl. She had inherited his looks – heavy head, glossy thick eyebrows, drooping spaniel eyes and strong jaw – which didn't matter in a man, but were bad luck for her. A clever girl like Colette, so solidly built and graceless, with no idea how to dissimulate her impatience or charm anyone, couldn't hope to make the transition into adulthood easily. He foresaw volatile years ahead, which wouldn't necessarily have to do with her mother's taking off, although that didn't help. It was always difficult for a plain girl with a good-looking mother.

As for the boy, it was a good thing he was going off to school, poor kid. Perhaps by the time Hugh came home at the end of term, Phyllis would be back. If she did change her mind and want to return, then Roger had decided to go along with it; no doubt they could reassemble, given time, an arrangement as good as what had gone before. He had been shocked by his own coolness and flatness, deciding this, packing fresh tobacco from his pouch into his pipe, bedding it down with his thumb. His heart was not broken, without Phyllis; she had not been the companion of his heart. He would miss how pleasantly she had kept his home, that was all, he thought, with his new coldness. And he felt the humiliation of her leaving him, and the deep inconvenience; he loathed the idea of explaining his situation to anyone. On the other hand, he also didn't care what anyone thought. Although Phyllis was outwardly so vivacious and flirtatious, she had never been passionate, he considered now: or at least, not with him. But then his own most intense experience of physical passion – when he was very young, long before he'd met Phyl – had been with someone who might have seemed outwardly, to any boor observing her, merely dull and good, not vivacious or flirtatious at all.

He had telephoned Phyllis's sisters, whom he liked very much – it occurred to him that he might like them better than he liked her. — There was something, Jane had said, the more forthright of the two. — When you telephoned, I *knew*, before you spoke. The last few times we saw her: she was tugging at the leash.

— Leash?

— Oh, Rog, I didn't mean you were the leash! I meant – you know! Life! Because Phyl always was – years ago, when we were young and she was even younger – the restless one. Only I thought she'd traded it in, her wanderlust.

— Traded it in?

— Now don't pick me up on every word I use. But give her time.

Anne had mentioned something, then regretted it. *I wondered what was going on.* That weekend when Phyllis was supposed to be visiting their father, some friend of hers had thought they'd seen her in a restaurant in Notting Hill, a dive where all the artists went. Roger would not ask: was she with anyone? Anne had hurried on, in any case, to say that if there was anyone with her, then the friend hadn't recognised him. If it was a *him.*

Roger didn't need to take out Phyllis's new note, which had arrived at the office today, from the locked drawer in his desk; with his facility for quickly absorbing the contents of a communiqué, he could remember all she'd written. *Nothing I've done is sound or sensible in the long run. But then in the long run we're all dead, aren't we? Perhaps I'll live to regret it, sometimes I think I will.* And she had written *when I think of the children* and then stopped, crossing these words out over and over, with angry black crosses. When he turned the paper over – lined foolscap paper, torn from a pad – he could read easily what she'd meant to obliterate. That was the only moment he'd actually felt the violent spasm of resentment against her, that he supposed a cuckolded husband was meant to feel; if she'd really meant him not to read those words, then she should have had the sense to start again, on a clean sheet. She recognised at least that she had no right any longer, she had forfeited the right, to display as any part of her femininity such sentimental thoughts about her children – so it was disingenuous, then, to leave even their trace. In fact the whole letter was awkward: gushing, misspelled, lacking in tact or any practical information, full of a spurious inconsequent kind of philosophising, talking about *changing her life, seeing everything differently.* Plain manila envelope, no return address, central London postmark.

But Roger knew there was a man, although Phyllis never named him. And he had simply, blankly, no idea who it might be, no candidate to slot into the vacant space – nor could her sisters think of anyone. Phyllis in her letter never came out with it frankly, she wrote instead all those things about her spirit, and freedom. And yet he knew. You could smell the sex coming off the page.

Nicky went to spend three days with his mother at Cressing over Christmas, and Phyllis was left alone in his room. She reassured him that she would be fine, and he must go. — Look at all these books! I'll be able to catch up on all the reading I've never had time for.

— I did promise her, Nicky said. — Before I knew that you were coming. Fuck all the Christmas shit, but I don't like to think of her there all by herself.

— Won't your father be there?

— Not likely. More probably holed up with his girlfriend in Woburn Square.

They were lying very close together, facing each other, in Nicky's bed, and Phyllis's eyes were closed; he was stroking across her face intently with slow fingers, and she thought that he was learning to read her, like learning Braille. She didn't care if he saw all the faint flaws and lines of ageing in her skin. In fact she wanted him to see them, wanted the whole truth of herself to be seen – as if she turned herself inside out for him. The pleasure woken in her by the touch of his fingertips was so intense that it obliterated everything else. What could it matter if they were parted for three days? Without him she would simply go into a trance of waiting, suspended until he returned.

— You never told me he has a girlfriend.

— It isn't interesting. She's more or less a fascist, truly thinks the Labour government are all communists and should be shot. Also she flirts with me, when he goes out of the room.

— How old is she?

— Older than you, Nicky said, with a carelessness which might have been tactful. — Very highly polished, wears those stiff dresses made of something metallic, covered in big leaves and flowers. You know, like Louis XIV might wear in a painting or something.

— Brocade.

— That's it, brocade. She looks a bit like Louis XIV, now I come to think of it. Got the same mean eyes.

— Wears the same wig, Phyllis suggested.

Nicky thought that this was funny. — Built the same palace at Versailles.

— Had the same head cut off.

He kissed the corner of her mouth tenderly. — That was Louis XVI.

Early in the morning on Christmas Eve, Nicky went to get the train to Ipswich, where his mother would pick him up. In her sleep it felt luxurious to Phyllis at first, to have the narrow bed to herself. Dozing, facing the wall, she could imagine that Nicky was still in the room behind her – he had left her sleeping in the bed sometimes, in this last week, when he got up to sit reading or writing at his desk. It was a freezing winter's day – pale sunlight glimmered on the white paint, and when she sat up eventually she could see the bare twigs of the plane trees through the window, lead-pencil strokes against an icy sky. Shuddering with cold, she got up to switch on the electric fire and boil the kettle, then climbed back inside the blankets to drink her tea, wrapped in an old shirt of Nicky's, suffused in his smell. On that first day she was almost glad he'd gone. Her emotion when she was with him, in the week since she'd run away from the Holmes's party, had been too overwhelming. Now, while she was alone, she could begin her new life.

She resisted the desire to fold Nicky's clothes into the chest of drawers, or put away his books on the shelves built out of pine planks and bricks; she mustn't spoil her new happiness, she thought, by falling back into these patterns, cleaning up and organising things, arranging the furniture more attractively. In her old life she'd been only half alive: too busy perfecting the appearance of her self and her home for others to admire. Now she was taking her first faltering steps away from that falsehood. Already there was an outpost of her belongings on one of Nicky's shelves: she'd had to go foraging in Peter Jones, buying make-up and underwear and a hairbrush, a pullover and wool skirt because she couldn't wear her cowl neck all the time, a flowery sponge bag for transporting her wash things into the shared bathroom. To pay for these things she'd used money from the bank account where she kept what she'd inherited from her mother – she wouldn't take anything that was Roger's.

She washed in the bathroom and dressed and tidied the bed, then went out to the grocer's on the corner, where she bought a pint of milk and a bottle of sherry, as well as cheese and ham – and a wilting bunch of cut flowers at half-price, from a greengrocer who was closing early. There was no vase for the flowers, but at home in the bathroom she rinsed out sour milk from the old milk bottle and put them in that, then made more tea and ate two biscuits. They had been out for spaghetti the night before, so she wasn't hungry; as the day wore on she liked the sensation of hollowness and faint light-headedness that came from starving herself. For a while in the afternoon she slept again.

When the light began to go she switched on the Anglepoise lamp, poured herself a glass of sherry, then went through Nicky's LPs and played Bob Dylan on his Black Box portable record player. She'd known who Dylan was, she and Roger had joked about his rough voice – *poor fellow, he can't sing* – but she'd never attended to these songs before, or anything like them. Roger had taken her to classical concerts, or when she was at home alone she'd listened to whatever was on the radio, pop or dance bands. Now the intimacy of this new music pierced and enveloped her. She might never have found out, if she hadn't met Nicky – if she hadn't sought him out, and followed him here, leaving everything behind – that this new shape of being existed: the glamour of it and its seductive invitation, careless and mocking and free. Nicky and Bob Dylan mingled together in her mind. She thought that she was in love with this voice, these words.

Phyllis played the two records in the double album over and over, especially 'Sad Eyed Lady of the Lowlands', which seemed to speak to her intensely, as if she were herself the sad-eyed Lady. Nicky had other Dylan LPs too, but this one was enough for now, it was almost too much. She drank more sherry and danced in her stockinged feet like a girl, in the dim light in the bare room, which was deliciously warm by this time from the electric fire; she was filled up with the music's beauty and its emotion, with her new full life and her own deep, interesting story. It didn't matter if this had come to her too late, when she was already forty. There was only this moment, this joy now.

She woke in the dark on Christmas Day, and remembered her husband and children – although of course she'd never forgotten them, only pressed awareness of them back from her conscious thought. And now, this wasn't so much a thought as a sensation; some infection had invaded her while she slept, taken over her heavy limbs and feverish brain. The force of the daily normality of her family returned to her like the current in a deep river, so much stronger than any dream of hers. How had she believed that she could go against it? She imagined herself kneeling in front of Roger, begging his forgiveness. She thought that she should set out for Otterley, right now. There would be no trains or buses today: but surely if she started to walk now, she could get there in a few hours. She imagined herself toiling, doing penance, through the bleak suburbs on Christmas morning. And probably, anyway, she could find a taxi. Yet she didn't stir from her place in the bed, where she was cold even under all the blankets.

Switching on the lamp, she watched the minutes passing on Nicky's alarm clock. If you go now, she told herself, you will still be in time. But she didn't move. Or if you go now, or even now – but she lay watching all these deadlines pass, as if her illness were a spell of paralysis. They would have opened their presents by now; by now they would have set out for the house in Guildford. When eventually she did get up she couldn't turn on the electric fire, because there was no more change for the meter. She sat frozen at Nicky's desk, wearing his shirt and dressing gown, to write a letter to Roger, tearing pages from a pad of file paper. She could have typed the letter, but this raw scrawl with messy crossings-out was a better match for her self-disgust. Making an effort to communicate what she had believed the night before, her words only seemed inert and dead; when she thought that she ought to send messages to the children, she had no idea what to say, and was nauseous with shame. She went back to bed and slept again. In the afternoon she got up and dressed and found a stamp in her purse, went out to post the letter.

It was a relief to be in the deserted streets, pretending to be purposeful. She went on for miles, trying to warm up and at the same time outwalk the pain of her thoughts, until her feet ached – she only had the flimsy shoes that she'd worn to the Holmes's. There were taxis crawling in the streets, looking for business. I could still go home, she thought. She pictured herself stopping one of the taxis, pictured Roger and the children arriving back from Guildford to find her waiting for them. But she didn't act. Nicky hadn't even told her when he would be back from Cressing – it might be tomorrow or the next day, or the one after that. She hadn't wanted to press him, because in this new world they mustn't make claims, or possess each other. He was free to do as he liked.

Climbing up again inside the coiled spring of the staircase in the Everglade, the idea of returning inside his room was anguishing. Aware of noise and music on the third-floor landing, Phyllis stopped to listen, then followed to where it came from behind one of the closed doors: impulsively she knocked. She put on her old looks, flirting and appealing, for the man who opened it. At least she had made up her face and brushed her hair before she went out.

— I'm alone on Christmas Day and feeling blue, she pleaded apologetically. — Can I sit in your party for five minutes?

He didn't seem surprised, and invited her in, slung a heavy arm across her shoulders proprietorially; his name was Paul, he said. He was stocky and small, with a lined, ugly, expressive face, check shirtsleeves rolled up to his elbows, forearms thick with black hair. This room was different to Nicky's attic – high-ceilinged, gracious, shabby, with foxed mirrors above the mantelpiece and torn floor-length purple curtains, not drawn against the gathering dark outside. It was crowded with people, she and Paul had to raise their voices to make themselves heard above the din. This wasn't his place, he told her when she asked. He lived on the fourth floor. This was Raúl's.

— And what do you do? Phyllis asked politely.

All she really wanted was a drink, she didn't want to talk.

— What do I do? What do you mean, what do I do?

— I mean, for a living.

He screwed up his eyes against the smoke from his cigarette, as if her question were comically absurd. — And what do you do *for a living*, Phyl?

— Oh well, nothing. Nothing much. I can type and do book-keeping. But I'm at a sort of transition in my life.

He exhaled exaggeratedly. — All the women I meet are at transitions in their lives.

— Are we so tedious? Phyllis asked.

— Well, you are when you're always changing. We like you the way you are. Don't change and have ideas! I hate ideas!

— You mean you hate ideas when women have them.

— Something like that, he laughed. She thought that Paul wasn't really charmed by her, only hanging on in the hope she might sleep with him later. When he brought her a plastic cup of something sweet and strong, with rum in it, she told him she'd moved to the Everglade to live with someone she was in love with. — Oh, really? he said without much interest. — And where's he?

— Well, tonight he's with his mother.

This sounded funny, and lightened the atmosphere between them. He introduced her to Liz, who offered a limp, damp hand; apparently she was a poet. Paul said she was one of the ones who had ideas, and Liz said, *Fuck you, Paul.* She was angular and hostile, resolutely unfeminine, in thick-rimmed glasses, tight tartan slacks, a gauzy scarf tied round messy dark hair; she sat on a high stool with her legs crossed and smoked cigarettes rolled in black paper. Paul melted away into the crowd, Phyllis sat on cushions on the floor next to Liz, who didn't condescend to drop a word down from the heights of her stool. And every so often Phyllis went over to the big table where the punchbowl was, to refill her cup. It was just a big Mason Cash mixing bowl, like the one she used for cakes in Otterley, with a soup ladle in it.

— What does Paul do? she asked someone.

They were surprised that she didn't know – he was a sculptor, quite famous.

— How interesting, she said.

— You should see his bronze birds and animals. Miraculous, so vividly alive.

She didn't know what kind of people these were and didn't care, didn't know what she was doing here. They were passing round something to smoke which she supposed was pot, and she tried it. White faces and black were mixed up together at the party, some people were dancing, she danced for a while with somebody, to smoky jazz. Then a woman she didn't recognise, in a flowered dress, was bending over her. — This is Nicholas's friend, the woman said, and Phyllis realised that it was Barbara Jones. It must have been Barbara who helped her get back to her room later – in the morning she couldn't remember it. She woke up with a bad hangover, and had to be sick into a bucket she found in the bathroom. Barbara knocked on the door at some point, on her way to work, making sure she was OK. This time Phyllis recognised her easily, dressed in her nurse's uniform.

When Nicky first arrived at Cressing, he thought his mother must be packing up to sell, the place was in such a mess. Mrs Chick had gone for the holiday, apparently, to her sister's in Saxmundham. Chairs were upended on tables, tea chests were half filled with items packed in straw, bundles of magazines were tied in string; the contents of cupboards were spread out on newspaper and there was no room to eat on the dining table, which was piled up with dinner services and heaps of table linen and knife boxes. Who could ever have needed so many plates to eat from, so many silver fish forks, wine coolers, chafing dishes? Since Jean had moved back to Cressing she hadn't done any entertaining. — I'm just sorting things out, she said to Nicky vaguely, assuring him that she had no plans to move. After a while he understood that, rather than packing, she was unpacking what had been stored while there were tenants in the house – and also that some of these cupboards had been pulled out months ago. If he ever saw her at work on the disorder, she was only tinkering, picking up items from one place and putting them down in another. Nothing was decided, nothing was thrown away. The dog ran everywhere with dirty paws. Nicky asked Jean for an ivory egg he'd found on a low table in the library, because Phyllis might like it; inside the egg carved without a join, another egg was carved just as intricately. The house was full of knick-knacks like this, brought back from ancestral travels to far-off places. He said he wanted to give it to someone as a present; contemplating it on her palm, Jean was regretful. — If you'd asked me for anything apart from this, she said. — But it's precious, a fond memory. I keep it close, you see, whenever I'm reading in here.

No wonder his father hated it in this house; no wonder his mother was at a loss in the ordered plush comfort of Woburn Square. Nicky saw with a pang how, left alone, Jean might develop into a true eccentric, now that she was released from her duties as a company wife among the expats abroad. Yet her intelligence seemed as quick as ever; she kept up with the news on the wireless, and had stocked the kitchen capably with food and drink for their Christmas together, decorating a little tree she'd had cut in the woods, wrapping up presents to put beneath it – books for him, and a jumper. For their Christmas dinner she roasted a duck, which was his favourite. In the afternoon on Boxing Day she lit a wood fire in the library, which – along with the dog, stretched before the fire ecstatically — made his asthma worse. Then she stood measuring ephedrine with a dropper, out of its bottle into his pink rubber pump, just as she'd done when he was a child. Outside, the rain was steady, tapping among the glossy leaves in the shrubbery, which grew close up against the library windows; in the library corridor it dripped into a preserving pan. Long over-grown bleached grass in the lawns was flattened, the stone urns and balustrade on the terrace were stained dark with wet. Winter woods, massed on the low horizon all around, blotted up what was left of the light; Jean plugged in a single standard lamp with a fringed shade between two armchairs drawn up to the fire. — I'm watching the electricity bill, she said. — I have to be so careful with money.

— But my father has such heaps of it.

— Yes, but he doesn't like to spend it on Cressing.

— I hate his meanness.

She wouldn't own up to resenting his father, only hinted at it, yet Nicky knew that she liked him to take her side. To take his mind off his wheezing, she read aloud to him as she used to do, Marvell and Donne and *Vanity Fair*; fire was reflected in the glass fronts of the walnut bookcases, and the dusty busts of great think-ers, punctuating the tops of the cases at intervals, receded in the dusk. Sitting straight-backed in her chair, Jean held up her book in front of her face as she'd been taught as a schoolgirl, peering closely at the page because she was short-sighted and the light bulb was dim. She was dressed in shapeless old clothes — a dirty Arran fisherman's jumper, pleated wool skirt, ugly suede bootees which zipped at the side, lined with sheepskin. On the other hand, her voice as she read was elegantly assured, the voice of her class, educated and clearly enunciated, with a drawling edge of satire. These days, perhaps her accent was a bit much. Nicky had been conscious of damping down, at university, whatever gave his class away in his own tones.

He might almost have confided in his mother. For one foolish moment as the light went on that winter's afternoon, it seemed possible to share his news: of a fully grown married woman arrived to live with him, knocking at his door in the deep of night until she woke him, bringing nothing with her, not even a toothbrush, leaving her whole life behind. And not weeping but laughing at her own reckless behaviour, astonished at herself: she'd held his face between her cold palms, and searched it in the faint light with her look, seeming to marvel at the reality of him as if she'd feared, hastening towards him through the dark, that he might not exist. He'd got up naked out of his bed and his sleep to open the door, and the smell of the freezing night was in her coat. It would be a relief to express the whole riotous comedy of all this to someone – that the world really was turned upside down, anybody could do anything. But Jean was a friend of the Fischers', and would surely feel obliged, if she knew, to talk to Phyllis's husband. Nicky shied away from bourgeois complications, they could wait. After all, nobody owned Phyllis.

And anyway, he couldn't talk about this – about sex – to his mother, of all people; of course not. He loved Phyllis, he supposed he did. He adored her, but his mother didn't need to know that, she wouldn't understand. He was besotted with the days he'd spent with her in his room since that night she arrived, hardly

venturing out except to buy the food she cooked on his Baby Bell-
ing stove – and once to Franco's, for spaghetti. His room, with
Phyllis in it, had become all of a sudden fantastically, gloriously
crowded with the grappling, groaning, deliciously lascivious excess of their lovemaking: how could anything else matter? He was
in thrall to her delicate sandy prettiness, small hands and feet, the
sand-coloured tips of her small breasts, her fun and her husky
laugh – and her nervous guilt sometimes, which he had to coax like
a wild thing. And not only that, she supported his work. While he
was at his desk she slept, or kept quiet, or turned over the pages in
a book – though without taking anything much in, he thought.

He was working well, people wanted more of his writing. He
handed over his copy to one magazine whose rackety offices were
up a narrow staircase above a café in Soho, and to another in an
elegant Georgian premises in Bloomsbury; he knew how to vary
his tone from informed and controlled to opinionated and slangy.
He was commissioning work now, too, from other writers, and
had an idea – if only he could borrow the money from somewhere –
to put together a small press, publishing cutting-edge short books
and pamphlets, catching the new ideas while they were still fresh.
There were people around on the scene who had money and were
giving it away. Perhaps he could even persuade his father to part
with some; that would be gratifying, a nice irony.

He and Phyllis had neither of them spoken about any future,
nor even turned their faces in its direction. If once or twice perhaps, in this last week, he'd entertained a perverse momentary
longing for his old empty solitude, then it was ungracious of him,
and was only in order to take in wholly, and properly savour, the
new superabundance of this grown-up happiness of fucking. Not

until he was on his way to Ipswich in the train, and his mother was going to meet him at the station, had he really intuited, alone in his compartment, an alternative perspective on his situation – like a tickling icy draught from the window, which wouldn't quite slide shut. He loved Phyllis. Shifting on the prickly moquette, uncomfortable in the heat pumped out under the seats behind his knees, he was restless with his memories of the pleasure that she gave, with her rare sensuous intuition. But really, he thought after a while, what would he do with her as time went on? She wasn't a girl, but a grown woman: she would need a proper home, and couldn't stay in his room permanently. How would they live, when her mother's money had run out? He wasn't even earning enough yet to support himself.

Phyllis had given up everything for him. But he hadn't asked her to do it: and he remembered then those dangerous childhood games in the playground, where if they made you swear to something, you kept your fingers crossed behind your back. There were other women in the world. He was newly awakened to all this abundance of contact with women: one had wrapped for him with soft hands, in a corner shop, a bottle of gin to take home to his mother; another one, brown-skinned, checking his ticket in the station, touched at his wrist with crimson fingernails. Each of these women was subtly folded, it appeared to him now, around her secret erotic life. Even at Cressing there was Cathie, Mrs Chick's niece, who cleaned for his mother and wasn't pretty but uneasy and sullen, with bowed shoulders and a heavy stomach, fat breasts overspilling her bra under a tight-fitting jumper. If he tried to speak to Cathie she only mumbled, glancing around as if she contemplated flight. When he caught sight of her, however, on her knees on Christmas Eve afternoon, scrubbing the kitchen floor with her backside in the air, he'd known that she knew what he saw, and that she despised him for it, lifting her rear nonetheless towards him slyly. He didn't choose these thoughts. They only arose in him, in spite of himself.

FIVE

Dear Jean,

I don't suppose you will have heard — although the channels along which gossip flows are tentacular, so one never knows — of the odd twist of fate that's befallen me, humiliating and a little absurd. And yet because you and I have always been in tune, I find myself imagining your ideas about it as if you had heard. So I might as well tell you anyway — and you'll have to forgive me for unburdening myself and, you might feel, burdening you — that Phyl has left me. Just before Christmas — it's only a few weeks and she may be back, for all I know, by Easter. From my perspective, it's been rather more like something out of a comic opera than Anna Karenina. *All very sudden and sensational, with no preamble — in fact not much post-amble either. A coup de foudre — and presumably, as far as Phyl's concerned, something like rough justice. Do you remember that old ballad children learn at school, where the Lady runs off with the Raggle-Taggle Gypsies? In a note, Phyl most definitely suggested that she'd seen through something false in our 'way of life' together. No doubt the Lady, leaving her feather bed behind, said something to her Lord along those lines.*

In this scenario, at any rate, I seem to play, alas, an unenviable role. Talking of Anna Karenina, *I've been checking my ears every so often in the mirror in the hallstand, because if I remember rightly, Tolstoy gave an unflattering pair of them to the deceived husband, and I know I felt ungenerously at the time of reading that those ears, or horns, were very richly deserved. But you will have read* AK *more recently than I have, you can correct me if I've misremembered it. I imagine you these days shut up against the world and the weather, working your way absorbedly for the umpteenth time through all the classics, in the library at Cressing, which is where you belong. It's a happy thought.*

Anyway, Phyl has gone, and I don't know where, and as yet — bizarrely — I don't even know with whom. Perhaps the most disconcerting thing, dear Jean, is how I'm chagrined and embarrassed and even at times outraged, but not heartbroken. Of course there are the children to worry about. Hugh, thank goodness, has gone off to Abingdon, where I know they'll look after him; Colette is more of a problem. Her marks in class have fallen off, her teachers are concerned, and she's hanging around with a bad set of girls. At home — when she's at home, and not out goodness knows where — she cooks up messes which make me fat and give me indigestion, but which I have to pretend to enjoy.

I hope you don't mind my writing. It's a long while since we met up. Five years, since you and I had lunch? Much longer, a lifetime ago, since I came with Phyl that once to Cressing. Two lifetimes since you were kind to me, and meant so much, in the middle of my war. All my best wishes anyway, to you and Peter, and of course the boy.

Roger

———

Phyllis rang one morning when Mandy Verey was cleaning in the house, to ask if she could call in to pick up some clothes, and a few personal items – obviously not anything belonging to Roger. Warily, Mandy responded that she'd have to ask Mr Fischer first.

— Yes, of course, I completely understand. May I ring you again?

— I'm here most mornings for a couple of hours.

Mandy felt the awkwardness of the situation: standing in the hall, talking stiffly like this to her old employer, fending her off from coming to her own house. It was strange that she was at work here almost every day, going through the routines Phyllis had established: washing up at her sink with its frilled curtains, watering her African violets on the window sill, putting on the dining table the same brand of polish Phyllis had decreed. Mandy hadn't changed anything around in the kitchen to suit her, although she and Colette were the only ones using it: making changes wasn't part of her job. Roger had told her that Phyllis had gone away for a while and might not be coming back; reading between the lines, Mandy was scandalised and intrigued and upset, although she went on with her work as if nothing had happened. She didn't tell her husband for a long time that Phyllis had left; she had always defended the Fischers when Don spoke against them. Indignantly, though, after their telephone conversation, she thought that Phyllis hadn't even once asked after her own children. It had always been clear that Phyllis favoured the boy over Colette: and now he'd been sent away to school, poor mite. Mandy didn't know how they could send them away.

Roger said that of course it was all right for Phyllis to pick up her things, she could take what she wanted. Mandy had thought he might insist on being present when Phyllis came. He rested his two fists on the desk, standing in his study, staring down at some of the important papers she never touched when she was dusting. He and Mandy were uncomfortably shy when they had to discuss anything. — Will you ask her if she'll give me a forwarding address? was all he said.

So Mandy let Phyllis into the house one morning when no one else was home.

— Oh Mand, isn't this awful? she said in the doorway, with tears springing in her eyes. It seemed as if she wanted to explain more. But what was there that could be explained? Phyllis didn't look any different — or perhaps that wasn't quite true. She'd always got herself up nicely, very groomed, even first thing in the morning, in her housecoat. Now, although she still had her dainty prettiness, she was dishevelled. Her hair was longer, growing out from its cut, and she wore less make-up, there was some different vagueness in her expression. Mandy knew how old Phyllis was – it was a risk, at her age, letting yourself go. And naturally her demeanour towards Mandy had changed. She'd always been friendly, but used to have a superior veneer, the faint impatience of the one in charge. There couldn't be anything like that between them now.

While Phyllis was upstairs, Mandy stood around in the shadows in the hall, listening to her hurrying backwards and forwards in the bedroom, opening drawers and the wardrobe doors; she felt as if she were keeping a lookout, though she didn't know whether it was on Roger's behalf, or Phyllis's. She was aware that a man was waiting for Phyllis, in a car parked on the road outside, and went quietly to peer at him through the porch window. He was dark and thickset, in some kind of rough donkey jacket like a workman, smoking with the window wound down in a battered Ford Anglia, resting his forearm on it, staring straight ahead of him through the windscreen. Mandy tried to imagine giving herself over into those strong arms. Phyllis carried a couple of cases downstairs. — Tell Roger I've only taken the oldest suitcases, she said, then went into the sitting room to fetch her sewing box, and a few things that had belonged to her mother.

Mandy held the front door open, while Phyllis struggled out with the suitcases. When she asked about a forwarding address, she knew that Phyllis wouldn't give it to her – she shook her head quickly, and said she wasn't ready for that yet. Donkey-jacket was watching them from the car, then got out to open up the boot for the cases. Noticing how Mandy glanced at him, Phyllis exclaimed in sudden amusement. — That's not him, Mand!

— Isn't it?

She was replete and secretive, smiling brilliantly. — Oh no! I couldn't have left Roger for anyone like that.

— Like what?

Dizzily, laughing, she shook her head. — I mean, so stumpy and grumpy.

Against her will, Mandy laughed too – because he *was* stumpy.

— Mine's beautiful, Phyllis whispered into Mandy's ear.

This was more like the old days, when they'd confessed their dissatisfactions with their men, joking over coffee together in the kitchen. — This one's just a friend, Phyllis reassured her. — He's Paul, a sculptor. Actually he's rather a genius, makes the most amazing birds and animals. What's more to my purposes this morning, he has a car. Though it's such a junk heap, isn't it? It was difficult persuading him to get out of bed so early. Usually he sleeps till the afternoon, then works all night.

She seemed to be showing off, about mixing with the kind of people who could live like that. Mandy went inside before they drove away, she didn't want to know too much about Phyllis's new friends. When she looked around in the sitting room, she saw that one of the photo albums wasn't put back in its right place on the shelf, Phyllis must have been foraging among the family photos. Mandy flipped through the album and found three or four gaps, places where a picture had been slipped out from its corners, or where the black paper was torn, if the pictures had been glued. Quickly she closed the album up, feeling this was none of her business – all this weight of the happy family past, shut up inside their photographs.

No one had told Colette that her mother was coming, but when she got home from school she saw at once that Phyllis's summer mac and straw hat were missing from the hallstand, and imagined she could smell traces of her perfume. Dropping her satchel in the hall, she hurried up to her parents' bedroom: its new emptiness glared, abandoned coat hangers jangling when she opened the wardrobe door. Her mother's vanished presence was a hallucination, agitating the still air of home; she had taken jewellery and make-up too, from the dressing table, and underwear from the chest of drawers.

Sitting down in her school coat on the stool in front of the depleted dressing table, Colette scowled at her reflection in the three-winged mirror, making a haughty face, sucking in her cheeks and lifting her chin, turning her head to see herself from different angles. Her cheekbones and the line of her strong jaw were sharpened because she had lost weight, existing on Ryvita and cottage cheese while she cooked dishes for her father in the evening from a cordon bleu recipe book, performing the devoted daughter, leaving shopping lists each week for Mandy Verey. She was managing with contact lenses, and had left off her glasses; also she had taken to wearing make-up to school, which got her into trouble but she didn't care. Nothing could transform her, however, into her good-looking mother; she had only the brooding force of her consciousness, which stared back at her. It was as if her mother's ghost flitted in the room behind her, choosing which things to take away with her, to wherever it was she went.

— You can tell me, Colette had pleaded with Roger. — I'm not a baby.

Her father flinched these days, if she spilled over with her emotion. He assured her that he didn't know where Phyllis was, and would tell her as soon as he found out anything. When Colette tried in her imagination to supply, as her mother's lover, any man from her parents' acquaintance, none of them were remotely plausible. Going through the drawers in the dressing table, she wondered whether Phyllis might not have left something behind for her today, as a sign – to make up for Christmas, or as an encouragement to hang on and wait, until there could be further communication. She *ought* to have left something: just a new fountain pen, say, or some nice talcum powder with a puff. Colette could visualise this item so distinctly – wrapped in its pretty paper, tied with a ribbon, sitting on the desk in her bedroom where she did her homework – that when she went to look and there was nothing, she actually felt nonplussed and cheated. She hunted around in the cupboards and under her pillow, in case Phyllis had hidden it, for a surprise – she might not have wanted Roger to know that she'd left anything.

Then Colette checked to see whether her mother had gone into Hugh's room, and knew that she hadn't, because before he left he had fastened a thread around the doorknob, to detect whether anyone intruded. Carefully she unwound the thread, and went to stand inside her brother's sanctum. In the cold late light of the spring afternoon, Hugh's absence lay on all his possessions like dust: the paper carrier bags full of cigar boxes, his stamp album open at the page for Malta. The room was full of his childhood, broken off abruptly, left as if he meant to resume just where he'd left it, when he came back from school. The narrow bed was neatly made up, clean white sheets tucked in tightly – Mandy had noticed the thread too, and unwound and rewound it. Mandy knew all about Hugh's little games and his rules. My mother couldn't bear to come in here, Colette thought.

As soon as Phyllis got back to the Everglade she knew that she should have left Colette a note, or some sort of a sign. It wasn't that she'd forgotten through indifference or cruelty. She'd hardly known what she was doing, the whole time she was back inside her old home. The place had felt both like a dream, and also banal. While she'd been away, its spaces in her imagination had begun to seem mythic and impossible – but as soon as her feet were actually on the stairs, it was all so shrunken, disappointing, known. There were the same worn patches on the stair carpet, where the thread showed through. She had imagined this familiar old life ending when she left it behind, but it had run on more or less unchanged alongside her new one, as if she could step back inside it at any moment. Only a few small details were different: Mandy Verey always arranged the furniture at right angles to the walls, setting the cushions along the sofa in a row, like the audience in a cinema – and of course there weren't flowers put out anywhere. Also Hugh was away at school, which changed everything. The sameness of the old place sickened her.

Her stupid suitcases seemed an intrusion, now, in Nicky's room. And then she had to get rid of Paul, who was scratchy and cross from helping her carry them up five flights of stairs, and probably still hung on to some idea that she would sleep with him. This wasn't a compliment, he hoped it about every woman who was even remotely attractive. Nicky was out, he was investigating an alternative kind of university they were setting up through the Bertrand Russell Peace Foundation, for a piece he was writing; amazing things were happening, he said. Phyllis shoved the cases in a corner and didn't want to open them up, couldn't remember why she'd ever thought she needed all those foolish things, which belonged to how she was before. She lay on the bed with her knees pulled up to her chest, face to the wall. There wasn't any point, she told herself, in thinking about the children. No reparation could be made for what she'd done. Yet this suffering didn't resemble thought, it was more like an attack of migraine in her chest or her stomach, and couldn't be evaded, she had to wait for it to pass. The only thing to hang on to was that she must truly change, to give meaning to her betrayal. She had to believe that what Nicky awakened in her had sprung out of life itself.

Burying the photographs of her children deep underneath her things at the bottom of the suitcase, she tried to put them out of her mind. She was growing her hair long, and liked to walk on the boards of Nicky's room in her bare feet, playing her favourite LPs, standing in the warmth where spring sunshine came through the window. Or she and Nicky went together to Hyde Park and lay on their backs in the grass side by side, not touching, looking up at the pale new leaves shaken out in the trees, crumpled where they'd been tightly stashed inside the sheaths of their buds. When one of his magazines paid Nicky in pot as well as cash – its finances, he said, were kept afloat by clever drug dealing – Phyllis smoked it with him, and sometimes smoked it when he wasn't there, learning to roll joints until she was better at it than he was. She gave up on gin because it was too expensive, and bought sherry instead from a little shop run by an old Spanish couple, who would refill your bottle out of a barrel. Cross-legged in her loose faded sundress, with bare dirty feet, hair falling forward into her face, she sat with an album cover across her lap for a flat surface, rolling up deftly. Nicky liked her dirty feet and kissed them, he said they turned him on. He used these hippy expressions, *turn me on*, *drop out*, *get high* – but teasingly, as if he kept them inside inverted commas; for Phyllis the words were a threshold, she passed across them into new realms of experience. When she thought of the stiffness and falsity of her old self she was suffocated: always putting on that smiling grimace to please somebody, and rattling on with her artificial sociable talk. Now she was smiling less. The muscles of her face relaxed, she was returned more inside her own mind, at peace there, not constantly projecting outwards. She thought that she must look more like those girls she had envied the first time they went to eat at Helga's – not charming or performing but mysterious, withheld.

Nicky had given her a book about the history of Africa, and she was trying to read it. The book was amazing and compelling and at the same time hard going; she never used to read non-fiction, so her mind wasn't trained to its discipline. Often when she was moved or horrified by something she learned, and lifted her eyes from the page to take it in, her thoughts would begin to wander. She had to remember to look down again, and read on. Painfully, she was taking apart her picture of the world, putting it back together differently. Everything was much more terrible than she had allowed herself to see, even in those years when they had lived in Cairo. What happened in history was not just fate, or a series of accidents, it was mostly the wickedness of capitalism and the West. Sometimes when Nicky came in from writing in the library he found her agitated, filled up by what she'd learned. Reading was not enough, she wanted to act to change things. — Couldn't we go there? And try to help?

In the spirit of her new life she believed they could do anything. He laughed at her, not unkindly. — Go where? And help in what way exactly?

— I don't know. I wish I was a nurse or something useful.

Nicky said this was only the latest scourge inflicted by First World privilege, the Third World flooded with well-meaning liberal Europeans and Americans, trying to get their share of righteousness. — The new African states will find their way, the last thing they need is us, he said. He suggested that Phyllis read Julius Nyerere's *Uhuru Na Umoja*, and Doris Lessing's *This Was the Old Chief's Country* – she had no difficulty concentrating on the short stories. These struck at her imagination with devastating force, and she was washed through with outrage, and with shame because she made so much of her own bourgeois guilts and traumas. When Nicky said he'd been part of the protests outside the Rhodesian Embassy against Ian Smith's Unilateral Declaration of Independence, she wished fiercely that she'd been there too. — I remember discussing it with Roger, of course we disapproved. But it didn't occur to me to do anything. I didn't think it had anything to do with me.

— I don't suppose that our protests kept Smith awake at night.

Phyllis imagined all the accumulated wrongs of the South as a great mass, unbalanced against the unjust privilege of the few in the North. How could this imbalance not be broken, sooner or later, and their privilege overwhelmed? Sometimes she was afraid of this change coming, and protective for the Western world which was the only one she knew – then she was ashamed of her fear. In the meantime, she thought, it was better at least to live simply, in one room, without too many possessions, which only weighed you down. Or two rooms, perhaps. Nicky might get tired of her if she was always under his feet, preventing him from working. Phyllis was in negotiation with Barbara Jones's cousin Sam: he'd advised her to take out a hundred per cent mortgage on a couple of flats in a Victorian house only five minutes' walk from the Everglade. The rent from one flat would pay the mortgage and she could live in the other – which consisted of one big room on the first floor, along with a tiny kitchenette. She could cook there, and Nicky could eat and sleep with her, go back to his own room if he wanted to work in the day. She'd offered to do Sam's typing for him too, to earn some money.

Phyllis's new interest in Africa complicated her relations with Barbara. When she tried to tell her what she was reading, it didn't go down well. — I don't come from Africa, you know, Barbara said coldly. — Everybody thinks that. Girls at work believe I lived up a tree or something.

— But you do come from there originally. I mean, your ancestors did.

Barbara shrugged as if this didn't interest her, or was vaguely insulting. Her fellow students at the nursing college, she went on indignantly, had asked her to wear a grass skirt in their panto-mime. — They think everyone in my home is lazy, spends their days fishing in the creek, with a string tied round their toe. But my aunt is headmistress in a girls' school!

On the ward, she said, the coloured nurses were given the worst jobs, stripping the soiled sheets, emptying bedpans. Phyllis was sure she should complain, but Barbara said there was no point, it only made things worse. The other nurses were decent enough girls, she said, which perhaps meant that she thought Phyllis wasn't decent. And if Phyllis scoffed at the strict hierarchies at the hospital, where even in the dining room staff sat in their ranks, then Barbara defended them, said they were necessary for discipline.

Phyllis couldn't help feeling proud of having a coloured woman for her friend. It was a new thing for her, and sometimes she mud-dled up Barbara in her mind with an idea of all the wronged victims of colonialism. Yet this new conscientiousness overlooked the particular reality of Barbara, who was often abrasive and moody, and pushed away Phyllis's offering of friendship. When Phyllis cooked supper in the evenings for Nicky – he poked through it warily with his fork, in case she'd smuggled in something he didn't like – she saved some for Barbara at the end of her shift, because some nights Barbara was too tired to cook, kept herself going on biscuits and toast and cocoa. Phyllis sat with her in her room while she ate, in the light from the gas fire, and boiled the kettle for tea. It was good to give Nicky some privacy, anyway. And Barbara was so exhausted that she submitted to Phyllis's slipping off the shoes from her aching feet, massaging them in her lap, putting Radox in a bowl of hot water so that Barbara could soak them when she'd peeled off her stockings. She told sardonic stories of the mistakes certain doctors made, and how she had to keep her mouth shut, she had learned her lesson over speaking out. Phyllis remembered that Barbara told her once how she'd wanted to be a doctor herself.

— Did I say that? Well, no chance of it ever.

— Nursing must be very rewarding, though. To feel you're doing good, helping sick people get better.

Frowning, bent forward in her chair, Barbara paddled her feet in the hot water. — I don't even like sick people! I don't care about their sickness.

— Then why want to be a doctor in the first place?

— I wanted to be one of those ones in a lab, researching. At school I was always top in chemistry, physics, biology. But they said, you've got to be either a nurse or a teacher, you can't ever make your way as a doctor. I'm not even a good nurse. The patients don't like me. But you have to always smile and make nice.

I don't want to end up in psychiatric or geriatric like the other coloured girls, just because no one else will do it.

Phyllis took in properly, for the first time, how difficult it must be for a wide-ranging mind to submit to this narrow path of discipline, working until you could hardly stand, taking orders from doctors and senior nurses who were sometimes wrong, performing the same mundane tasks over and over for patients who weren't always grateful – probably some were prejudiced and hateful. No wonder Barbara defended it all so bleakly. She's cleverer than I am, Phyllis thought with surprise. When she enquired about training, herself, to be a nurse, Barbara said she was too old. — No offence. It takes youthful strength. Past thirty you can't learn it.

Sam Harris was funny when he talked about Barbara; he pretended to be afraid of her and called her the vengeance angel, because she was so severe and tried to get him to come to church. Sam was compact and tidy, with slanted shallow-lidded eyes and light golden skin; he was always in a hurry on his way somewhere, preoccupied with his latest business project. As well as dealing in property, he ran a booking agency for rhythm and blues and jazz bands, and for pan drums, which were the latest craze – he got himself a slot on TV, playing the pans. Phyllis noticed that Sam changed his tone and his language subtly, depending on whom he was with. When he talked to her he was suave and regretful, flirting, his accent lilting and seductive; with the other men on the street, black or white, he spoke challengingly in broad dialect. *So what happening these days? It ain't have no prospects, boy.* The white men liked this talk, some of them copied it in their own speech.

— Do you trust Sam with your money? Nicky asked.

She was indignant. — Do you mean because he's black?

— I mean because he's a fixer and a hustler.

Phyllis reassured him that she had good instincts about people. — He's just making his way, she said. — Like everybody else.

She admired Sam's elegance and languid, melancholy style, was
delighted when she found out he owned a racehorse which he kept
somewhere in the north. And in fact the deal Sam got her was a
good one. If he took a cut on it, what did that matter? Her new
flat was in a street of tall rooming houses, between a Jewish school
and a bingo hall and a shop selling yam and plantain. An old
woman living downstairs from her was supposed to practise obeah
and give spiritual advice; next door there were Jews who'd come
as refugees in the war, and told her about race riots in the street
ten years ago. Sam found her a tenant for the second flat, a pasty-
faced white boy with ginger hair, bass player in a rock band. She
heard him bring home girls sometimes after his gigs, and when
she met him on the stairs he was usually stoned or high, mumbling and staring down at his feet, or unfocusedly over her shoulder. He'd worked in a local butcher's, apparently, before he got a
break with the band – but they weren't making any money. Phyllis saved leftover plates of food for him, too.

Her own room was airy, and its floor-length windows opened
onto a balcony which wasn't safe to stand on, though she could
grow pots of flowers there. She stripped off the wallpaper and
painted the walls white, ripped up the foul old carpet and bought
a striped dhurrie in the market. Also she found a big antique gilt
mirror put out for rubbish on the street, along with flimsy gold-
painted chairs, which someone said came from a dance studio. Her

bed was a mattress on the floor, covered in the daytime with a spread and bright Indian-print cushions; behind a screen at one end of the room was a kitchenette. Paul brought her a chandelier which he said was nicked from Porchester Hall. Then he asked if she would keep one of his sculptures for him, until he found a buyer. It was bronze, a mongrel dog twisted round on its haunches, biting for fleas above its tail. Paul stood watching Phyllis with his hands in his pockets while she crouched on her heels to look at it.

She couldn't take Paul quite seriously. He was good company, but he was full of vanity, because of his success as an artist – and there was something coldly perfunctory, too, in the way he flirted with her. In fact she suspected that he thought of her with disdain, as a bourgeois housewife. She wasn't attracted to him, with his flopping black hair and leathery, lined face, bright peering eyes. Paul had a chip on his shoulder, Phyllis told herself, about growing up on a council estate in the West Midlands – his father was a factory worker, and because of this background he exuded some force of contempt and mockery. His ragged thick jumper was unravelling at the cuffs, he smelled of cigarettes and old wool, sour sweat. Nicky didn't like him, he said that he was a shit, but a talented shit. He also said that Paul's kind of work was yesterday's news. No one was interested in imitations of nature now, however cleverly they were done.

Yet the dog was a marvel. It filled Phyllis's room with its inimitable living self; she wondered at its insolent life, so jeering and dirty, outrageous – lean scabby muzzle like a fox's, digging for fleas in tufts of greasy fur. It wasn't a realistic sculpture, an exact imitation of a real dog. She didn't know anything, really, about modern art, or how it was done. How could he have caught the animal movement, so momentary and spontaneous, in this rough splat of solid metal?

— Oh Paul, I love this little chap.

She was amazed and respectful. But of course she had said the wrong thing, and Paul took her words as insulting; no praise, in any case, would ever be enough. He kicked idly at one of her little gold chairs, knocking it over, and told her scornfully that the sculpture was a bitch and not a *chap*. When she looked more closely, under the tail, he said you couldn't tell from that. But the dog so thrilled Phyllis and moved her that she was able to get past Paul's vanity, and the question of whether he was likeable or not likeable – he had seen the frenzied, nuzzling little bitch so purely and completely. She didn't get any closer to Paul, or like him any better, but his sculpture was her companion in the flat as the spring and summer days passed, and she hoped it would be a while before he sold it. Even if she got up to pee in the night, she was aware in the darkness of the charged presence of the little dog. When Nicky insisted on calling it Fido and draping it with his scarf, or their friends used it as a hatstand, she knew they were trying to diminish its power, by turning it into a joke.

While Phyllis and Nicky were talking after sex one night, on her mattress on the floor, she told him the story of her bad experience in Cairo; she'd never spoken about it to anyone before. Nicky was lying on his back, smoking, with his arm around her, and she was washed up against his ribs, tasting the sweat and sex on his skin. She could see in the half-dark that his eyes were open, he was listening. — It was nothing really, she said. — It happened a long time ago.

— No, tell me.

— I was a silly girl, I was so naive. It was my fault.

Johnnie Maddox had torn her clothes, he'd half strangled her, dragging her by the hair and forcing himself onto her. On more than one occasion. — More than one occasion? Nicky queried. — It can't have been so bad, then.

— That's what he said. He said I must have a dirty mind, if I came back for more.

— Hypocritical cunt! he said sympathetically. — Typical hypocritical upper-class cunt.

— I don't know if he really was upper class. I think he just put it on.

— Typical hypocritical grammar-school cunt then.

— He said that I was unnatural, I wasn't like other women. But it wasn't true, it wasn't me that was unnatural. He damaged me, gave me a nasty infection. I was so ashamed, when I had to go to the doctor.

Stubbing out his cigarette, Nicky leaned over to kiss her face in the darkness, tickling her with his hair, his tarry breath. — Poor old love, poor little Phyl, he murmured kindly. He was also impartially interested. — And was there any pleasure in it for you? Because some men say that women like it.

— I don't know about other women, Phyllis said. Johnnie had drawn her in, and then once she'd shown that she was keen, his attitude changed and he began to hit her. For certain, from that point, there was only pain and fear. *See what you've done?* he'd said.

See how you've got me going, you dirty girl? When he called her a cab afterwards, she could hardly walk out to the lift: he lived on the fourth floor in a block of flats in Gezira. — It put me off sex for a long time. But it doesn't matter now.

Johnnie Maddox used to crop up in conversation with Roger for years afterwards, Phyllis said, because he was attached to one embassy or another in the Middle East. Roger knew that he'd been a friend of hers in Cairo, before they knew each other. Even the sound of his name used to make her sick, yet she'd only ever said to Roger that she'd *gone off* him. When she heard that he'd died, in a car accident in Lebanon, she'd felt relief, as well as a weird kind of emptiness. The funny thing was that she'd really liked Johnnie to begin with; she'd even imagined she was in love with him. He was clever and extrovert, big and fair with a ruddy face like a countryman, popular in the set of young men and girls she belonged to, a good dancer. There was something smouldering and suggestive in how he was with women – not crudely, but in a way that seemed full of promise. Phyllis had a secretarial job then at the British Embassy, and Johnnie was involved in negotiations over some road the Egyptians were building along the Nile, on embassy land. She'd been in a state of euphoria, flattered and excited, going out for dinner with him and for cakes at Groppi's.

— I wanted to go to bed with him. I knew he was experienced with women – I wasn't planning anything explicitly, but I thought it was bound to happen. And then afterwards I was bewildered, wondering what I'd done wrong. I was sure he wouldn't want to see me again. When he asked me out the next time, just as pleasantly as if nothing had ever occurred, I thought that I must have misunderstood. And I hoped that this time it would all be different.

— But why didn't you tell Roger, when you were married?

— We just didn't talk about those things.

— You were lying next to the guy every night!

— I suppose I was afraid he might think less of me, for going after that kind of man. Because Johnnie did have a reputation. I didn't want Roger to know that Johnnie Maddox had kicked me out of bed. I was rather in awe of Roger in those days. After all he was a war hero and everything.

— I can understand that. I mean, I'm in awe of him: I'm afraid of him.

She scrambled up on her elbow to look at him. — Are you? Seriously? Of Roger? But you hardly know him.

— Not that he'll call me out in public and horsewhip me or anything. That would be too infra dig. But I'm afraid of his judgement. The steady assessing look through the pipe smoke, weighing me up and finding me wanting.

Phyllis stroked his hair to console him. — You don't need to be afraid of Roger, silly boy. He's a kind man, and he liked you, he said so.

— He might like me less when he knows I've been fucking his wife.

— Well, of course, that's only natural. But I've seen through Roger's type now. All that weight of judgement: it's just nothing, darling, it's based on nothing. It's a sham, it's boring. I don't find you wanting, do I?

— It's not the same. You're a dangerous woman. You don't get to decide.

———

Colette arrived home one day to find her father in the sitting room with a stranger. — Colette, this is Jean Knight, he said. — I've known Jean for years.

— Oh, for ever, Jean agreed cheerfully. — Our acquaintance goes back into the mists of time.

— D'you remember that her son Nicholas came to have dinner with us last summer?

Colette eased her satchel from her shoulder, scowling warily from the doorway; she was in her school uniform although she hadn't actually been in school, she'd spent the afternoon in the park with Susan and Linda and their new friends from the Boys' High. Her father and Jean Knight were buoyant and giddy, she thought, in a way that might come from drinking; there were glasses on the coffee table in front of them, the whisky bottle was out. She did remember Nicholas Knight, and all the hysteria of that evening: her mother flirting insanely, then dragging them off in search of something lost in the Chidgelys' pond. It seemed to belong to an era long passed away. That pink dress! How could she ever have worn it?

— I don't remember, she coldly said.

— Why should you? Jean exclaimed. — I expect Nicky was boorish, and totally unmemorable.

— He wasn't boorish, Roger insisted. — He spoke with unusual directness. I enjoyed that.

— He has no idea how to make small talk – though I try to persuade him, it's what makes the world go round. I suppose men don't feel obliged to learn it, to the same extent. When I was your age, Colette, I was virtually mute: and now here I am, chattering away like an idiot. That's civilisation for you.

With her ironies and clipped enunciation, Jean Knight was surely not the kind of strange woman you needed to be afraid of, Colette reassured herself, when your mother had run off and left your father exposed. She was elderly and thin, with frizzy, faded permed hair, nondescript mauve dress, caramel-coloured stockings wrinkled at the ankle; her bony long face, bright with eagerness to please, reminded Colette of a scripture teacher they'd tormented in the first form. — It's so nice meeting you again, Jean said. — You won't remember the last time, when you were a delightful baby. So refreshing how babies just gurgle and grin, bypassing all the social angst.

— You're probably thinking of my brother. He was the delightful one.

— That baby was most definitely you. And what a sweetie! I remember you wore a little blue smocked dress, and had two teeth. But these reminiscences dragged out of the distant past are just excruciating for the young, I know it, and I do apologise. When you're a child you swear that never, ever, once you're grownup yourself, will you repeat all those appalling inanities to children, like *how you've grown*, and *I remember when*. I could ask you how school was today – another inanity, because there's no doubt school was a dreadful bore, it always is. I remember often thinking that I'd rather die than go through double maths and games even once more. Hyperbole: but when you're young what else is there? Hyperbole's usually closer, anyway, at any age, to the truth of things. Roger says you're terribly clever.

— School was fine, thank you.

Impressions from the park were still flashing around in Colette's awareness. On their backs in the grass in the chilly spring afternoon, they had passed round cigarettes and a packet of pink and white marshmallows – feeling more free to talk about themselves because they weren't watching one another but staring up into the great cityscape of the sky, its clouds as tall as monuments, a moody grey-blue slashed with brilliant light. To shock the others and make them laugh, Colette said that when she grew up she wanted to be a topless waitress in a nightclub. They had played on the swings and roundabout, in a nostalgic and sentimental parody of their childhood; the girls had lost themselves in an ecstasy of swinging, kicking out their legs and leaning far back with their hair hanging down, then at the top of their flight snapping forward, sending themselves the other way. They knew that on the upswing the boys saw their knickers and they didn't care, they exulted in it. It was the fashion to make your school skirt scandalously short, folding it over and over at the top into a soft tyre of cloth around your waist, showing the tops of your thighs from behind as you walked. Naturally, Colette had pulled hers down as she approached her home.

She was sure now, in a cold fury of exclusion, that her father and Jean were wishing she hadn't come in. They hadn't been expecting her, they'd forgotten her. And yet when Roger said that they were going out for dinner in town, so there was no need for her to cook tonight, Jean quickly invited her to join them. — We're going to Chez Solange, and we'd love to have you with us.

She said she couldn't come, she had her homework to do. — Oh, do get your homework out! We can all muck in together. Let's cheat! As long as it isn't chemistry, I wasn't any good at that – but perhaps you're good at it? And then you can come out to dinner.

— Jean's a gifted Latinist, Roger said encouragingly.

Colette insisted that she'd rather not, and was sure they were relieved; when they'd gone she was relieved too, having the house to herself. Skipping supper, eating dry crispbread, she didn't do her homework after all – in fact she'd more or less given up on homework, apart from English sometimes. For a while she tried on clothes and then got undressed for bed early, prowling upstairs and downstairs in the lurid evening light, barefoot, aware of her heavy limbs and her breasts, loose under her Bri-Nylon nightdress. Restlessness and nothingness devoured her, the air was charged and close. *This is an atrocious place,* she thought: her father's stale study, her brother's closed room, her mother's abandonment. To save herself she must get out somehow. Peering through the coloured panes in the tall window of frosted glass halfway up the staircase, she saw the first drops of rain stir in the neglected, overgrown shrubs which grew along the side of the house – only tickling to begin with, then falling fast and purposefully with a boiling noise, rattling on the dusty evergreens and beating them down. Long spears of rain showed pink through the red glass, against the purple foliage of the trees behind. In Hugh's bedroom, when the rainstorm was over, she made a note in his weather diary.

Hugh's housemaster had telephoned the other night from Abingdon, Colette had listened at the study door. She'd thought he must be ill, but Roger said afterwards that he was fine. He'd developed a touch of childhood asthma, that was all.

— Is that why they were calling?

She'd been aware of her father's making an effort of patience, sitting in front of his papers at that monster of a roll-top desk, as he considered what to tell her. Their companionship these days, left alone in the house without the others, had none of its old spontaneity. She could tell from the set of Roger's shoulders that he found something belligerent and unattractive in how she persisted in the doorway, waiting for an answer. His telephone calls were none of her business. *He's wondering whether to lie to me,* she'd thought. For one dreadful moment when he put his hands to his face, massaging the flesh under his eyes, she'd believed he was going to weep – only when he spoke his voice was perfectly controlled. The problem, apparently, was that Hugh was telling his schoolfriends and teachers that his mother had died. — They were phoning up to check, Roger said drily. — I was able to reassure them. They're going to talk to him. They're very understanding, under the circumstances. Anyway, he'll be home for the holiday soon.

Roger dropped Colette off in the mornings at the bottom of the hill which wound up to Otterley Girls' High. But sometimes as soon as his car was out of sight, she turned against the flow of green-clad girls plodding their way up, ignoring their surprised looks and envious, awed remarks as if those dull girls hardly existed, and set off for the station, at a certain point snatching off her horrible green felt hat and stowing it in her satchel. The hat began to have a ridge from front to back, like a warrior's helmet, where it was folded so often. She'd claimed in an interview with the headmistress, Miss Topham, that she was missing so much school because she'd been diagnosed with an unusual sleeping sickness; Topsy was a fool, Colette despised her, everyone knew the school was going to pot under her regime. But even Mrs Bernhardt had asked for a talk with Colette. There was a small, windowless, carpeted room beside the staffroom, with two easy chairs, where the teachers took girls to discuss delicate matters.

Colette would have been breathless with excitement only a few months ago, alone like this with Mrs B., confined with her so closely that she could smell the cigarette smoke on her clothes and the faint musky waft of her perfume; she was wearing a tweed suit in a pinkish brown, whose skirt must be shorter than she was used to because she kept tugging at it, wanting to pull it down over her tan-stockinged knees, pressed close together. Mrs B. was angular and slim, her limbs very finely made – she was skittish like a nervous thoroughbred. Old already: she must be getting on for fifty. But beautiful still in her decay, with her weariness and slight lisp and sagging, liver-coloured lower lip. Colette felt she knew in advance what her teacher was bound to say.

— You're a very intelligent girl, Colette.

— Am I?

— Oh, I think you know it.

— And why would you care?

The teacher braced herself, against the rudeness of the uncouth child. — I hate to see you throwing away your chances of a good education. Whatever you think now, in the years to come it will open doors for you, to a fuller life.

Colette thought about her teacher, but didn't ask: is this your fuller life? She kept her hands tucked under her thighs and her gaze mostly on the low ceiling, covered in yellowed polystyrene tiles, reluctant to meet Mrs Bernhardt's laden, pleading look. — I'm keeping up with the work, she said. — Ask me anything. I've read all the books. In history she just reads out to us from Trevelyan, and we make notes, then at home we're supposed to copy the notes up.

What's the point of that? I can read Trevelyan for myself – and more interesting books too. Trevelyan's out of date.

Mrs B.'s mouth twisted in cautious amusement, she knew at once which teacher this was. — Learning to be bored is a precious lesson in itself. But difficult to appreciate when you're young.

— And then you ignore me in English, Mrs Bernhardt.

— Colette, you're not an easy girl to teach. You have a confrontational manner, and you're greedy for attention.

This was news to her, she was surprised and interested. — Am I?

— I know you have problems at home. It can't be easy managing without your mother.

— I'm fine at home, Colette said. — It's school that's the problem.

The heated intimacy of this scene was dreamlike, because it so resembled fantasies she'd cherished in the past: the aloof teacher unbending from her pinnacle of sophistication and reaching out for Colette, to acknowledge and save her. But it had come too late. Colette didn't want any longer to be saved, she wanted to be free. She didn't want the life of the mind. In the Otterley station toilet she made up her face and changed her clothes. Often she put on dresses or skirts that her mother had left behind – but wore them differently, in a satirical spirit. She'd taken up the hems, sewing in crude big stitches in black thread; or she wore her school tie knotted around the waist as a belt. When she got to London Bridge she put her satchel and uniform in a left-luggage locker.

All she did in the city was walk around in the crowds, pretending to be absorbed and purposeful like everyone else. She went to browse in certain bookshops; in Carnaby Street she bought tinted sunglasses, underground magazines and cones of incense from stuffy little shops, also henna to dye her hair at home. Sometimes she screwed up her courage to ask for a glass of barley wine in a pub, then sat alone defiantly to drink, reading. Men tried to pick her up; in order to fend them off she developed the necessary curtness and hard, sour expression: no eye contact.

Mingled in among all the people she saw as she went around the streets, there were a few individuals who stood out as different to the rest, exceptional and desirable men and women. She grew adept at spotting them, to worship and imitate them. It was partly their clothes – they were dressed strikingly, in kaftans, or bright-coloured embroidered dresses sewn with mirrors, shabby unbuttoned military uniforms, leather trousers. Often the men had moustaches; they wore their hair long and flaunted their bodies and their looks in a way that was almost feminine – and yet their sexuality was more blatant and brazen than in the ordinary men around them, battened up stiffly inside their maleness, their suits and crew cuts. The women swaggered too, unsmiling and defiant, painted thickly with black eyeliner, wearing aggressively on their surface the sex appeal that was supposed to be hidden and subtly suggested. All these beautiful individuals were nonchalant and oblivious, as if they'd been initiated into some code that others couldn't break, and saw through the world around them, into something better. Colette felt the scorch of their power as unmistakably as if they'd been film stars, or aristocrats walking among the peasants, who were the ordinary dull people in the crowds. She longed to know these distinguished ones, to have them see her and reckon with her, include her in their lives.

———

She arranged to meet up in town one day with her aunt Anne; they had lunch in a vegetarian restaurant. Inside the family, Anne was thought of as the unconventional and bohemian one, and Colette had always adored her. — It's Phyllis's secretiveness I can't forgive, she said at once, when they were tucking into their bowls of shredded raw vegetable salad, covering her shy diffidence with her brusque manner. — If only she'd talked to us. Not because I'm necessarily any stickler for marriage. But to just take off like that, without letting anyone know. It's so frivolous and hurtful. So difficult for you and Hughie – and Roger too, though he's the starchy type and won't complain. I suppose that Phyl must have been very unhappy. But then why not discuss it inside the family? Tom and I could have recommended a good therapist.

— Do you think she was unhappy?

— Why else would she have left?

— Perhaps she fell in love.

— Love, at her age? Anne jabbed disparagingly in her bowl with her fork. — I mean, I know she's always been a flirt. But flirting isn't love. You don't give up on your family for it, do you?

Colette shrugged. — I don't know what anyone does. Nobody tells me.

She had marvelled for years at the mystery of her aunt's painting, in her studio at the top of the shabby tall house in Highbury – so absorbed and messy, the big incomprehensible abstracts, the painter so solemnly forgetful of herself. Her children were allowed in to watch if they sat quite still; if they whispered or fidgeted then Anne told them to go, without stopping work or even looking round, and invariably they obeyed. Anne had the same soft full mouth as Phyllis, but her jaw and brow were squarer and she made Colette think of an intelligent terrier, with her brown eyes so candidly wide open, and the greying stiff hair standing up in a wave from her forehead. She was wearing a man's loose white shirt over her substantial bosom. — Did you know that a friend of mine saw her? she said. — Only that was months ago, before Christmas, and might not mean anything. Here in London, in a restaurant, when she was supposed to be in Leamington with Daddy. I told Roger.

— He didn't tell me.

— Then I suppose I shouldn't have mentioned it. But on the other hand you're old enough not to be shut out.

Colette put her fork down, to protest. — I am shut out, though, Anne, from everything.

— It's a horrible age. I remember it: everyone treats you like a dunce and expects you to cope like an adult.

— Was my mother with anyone, when she was seen?

Anne admitted that her friend had believed Phyllis was having dinner with her grown-up son, not knowing she didn't have one: but then she'd only glanced at them, and hardly knew Phyllis. — This was all in the time before Phyl left home, so there was no reason to wonder about anything. There may still be no reason, that dinner may have been quite innocent. It was in a little place Tom and I used to go to. We liked the Viennese atmosphere, when we were still eating meat.

— That's interesting about the son. I suppose it's a clue.

— Jane would be furious if she knew I'd told you. We both think that Phyllis will come home as soon as she's tired of her adventure, whatever it is. She's never had much staying power, quickly loses interest. I wish she'd had more of a career, something to give her a purpose. Phyl was always perfectly clever, but couldn't make up her mind to anything. And so she stuck with office work, which wasn't at her level really. She was bound to give it up as soon as she married.

Colette was trying to develop a new way of looking at life, with more lightness, as if everything that seemed so substantial, like a school, or a home, or a marriage, was in fact only disposable and breakable. It was frightening, but also a relief. Phyllis used to joke about how Anne and her husband Tom had experimented with free love before they were married, and Colette saw now how they'd have set about it earnestly, in pursuit of an ideal. Perhaps it was better to be frivolous. And yet Anne's home had seemed deliciously chaotic to Colette, whenever she went to stay in the scruffy bare rooms of the terraced house, where her boy cousins slept in home-made bunks, and wore each other's faded and patched hand-me-downs. Anne's husband, Tom, didn't mind taking a subordinate role, making time for Anne to teach as well as paint; he helped out with the cooking and shopping and washing-up. One of their sons had been born with a mental handicap, and a lot of the jollity in that house revolved around Roly. They included him in everything although he couldn't really talk, and his movements were jerky and odd; Anne drew him, she said he had a beautiful head, like a little prince. Those boys played very wild games, but they knew how to stop and calm Roly, if he got too excited or emotional. *They ought to put them down at birth, it would be kinder for everyone,* Grandma Fischer had said about Roly once. *You and Adolf Hitler, Mother,* Roger had reproved her, and he said that they'd fought a war against those ideas. Colette had been so grateful then for her father's goodness, his force and certainty.

Roger went to fetch Hugh from school for the Easter holidays; Colette cooked a grand three-course dinner to welcome him home, which Hugh hardly touched – he stuffed cake instead – so that she ate too much and had to make herself sick later, in the privacy of the bathroom. She wasn't fooled by her brother's bright glaze of belonging and prowess, his chatter about school – what house he was in, and why it was the best house, and how he'd been picked for the first team at rugger. She knew him too well, it was as if he'd copied this style out of a book. Their father appeared to be satisfied though; they heard him on the telephone after dinner, telling someone enthusiastically that Hugh had taken to Abingdon like a duck to water. He seemed to be hurrying past this news, to get on to other subjects; while he was still talking he closed the study door, carrying the phone awkwardly in one hand, speaking low-voiced into the receiver tucked under his chin.

Hugh went up to his bedroom, snapping the thread wound around the door handle – perhaps he'd forgotten ever fastening it there. Following him inside, Colette half expected him to be furious with her because she'd been writing in his notebooks, but he seemed not to notice it or not to care, frowning around at his old belongings as if he was having difficulty recognising anything. He was taller, definitely, than when he'd left after Christmas, and his face seemed larger and shallower, his expression was different – some nuance was bleached out from it. Even the shock of his gold hair was paler, more subdued. Her odd little brother had become more ordinary. — So what's it really like? she asked confidingly, dropping onto his bed and pulling her legs up, with her arms around her knees. — I mean, obviously it's awful beyond imagining. I knew it would be. Tell me the worst.

— Buzz off, *big* sister, he said calmly, not looking at her, emphasising the *big*. — I have work to do.

— Work? That's so passé. I don't do any schoolwork these days.

— You've probably reached the limits of your natural capacity.

— No, my brilliant brain's outgrown anything school has to offer.

— That's because it's a girls' school, where you only get easypeasy stuff. Anyway, where are your specs?

Hugh waved his hands vaguely in front of her eyes, testing whether she was blind: she explained that she had contact lenses now.

— Yikes, don't they get lost round the back of your eye?

— Dear little brother, to think that we're paying so much for your education!

He jabbed at her meanly in the stomach with his fist, she hit back hard and then they tussled together on the bed, pummelling viciously, muffling their rustling, breathy struggle so that their father couldn't hear and didn't come in to tell them off. The fight restored a friendly enough equilibrium between them. And when it was over Colette was stricken suddenly with the loss of their old family life, and of their mother. An image came to her, dense with emotion as if it were a dream, of the four of them seated in their proper order in the old Morris Traveller:

Roger at the wheel, Phyllis beside him spouting cheerful enthusiasm, Hugh and Colette's younger selves bickering pleasurably
in the back seat. They were driving out for a picnic in the country, accompanied by Prince, their black Labrador – who'd had to
be put down, in fact, the year before last, because of kidney
disease. The reality of this scene was more overwhelming, for a
short moment, than any changes since. Then Hugh was standing again at his desk, with his back to Colette, turning the pages
of his stamp album thoughtfully. His father had bought him
packets of new stamps. She said she'd heard that he'd had difficulties settling in at school.

— What d'you mean, difficulties?

— For a start you've developed asthma.

— Oh, that. It was just the blankets. They gave me a puffer.

— And then you've been spreading stories, telling your chums
that your mother's dead. Isn't that a trifle weird?

She was afraid he might insist, like someone who was actually
mad, that their mother *was* dead; to her relief after a few moments
he said, still turning pages slowly, that at school you got a hard
time, if your mother was cheap. — She sent me a beastly birthday
card, he added carelessly.

— No, really? Show it to me.

— I threw it away, into the vat with the leftover dinners. They
feed that gunk to pigs, and then they slaughter the pigs and cook
them for our dinners, we chuck the dinners away because they're
foul, they go back into the vat for the new pigs, and so on. It's like
the rainfall cycle.

— But we could have studied the card. We could have got on
her trail!

— Do you still not know where she is? Hugh said scornfully. —
I swear to you, she's with the one she was snogging in the bathroom. I'm not interested in her anyhow.

— When was this snogging supposed to have taken place exactly? Not that I believe in it.

— You remember. That time when Barnes-Pryce lost his sandal
and his mother rang up.

The next evening, while Hugh was watching cartoons, Colette
went into her father's study and told him she knew why Mrs
Knight had come visiting him.

— And why do you think that is? Roger asked in a chilly, surprised voice.

He lifted his head with an effort from where it had been propped
on one elbow on his desk; he had been going through a pile of
typewritten papers with his pen in his good hand, and seemed to
return to her across great distances, from Arabia or Palestine.

— Because of her son, being with our mother. I suppose that
you two were making plans, to get them apart or something.

— Whatever are you talking about?

— Hugh saw them kissing, Mum and Nicholas Knight, that
evening when Milo Barnes-Pryce lost his sandal. He told me ages
ago, but I didn't say anything because I didn't believe him, and
anyway, I didn't know who he meant then. Only now I do.

Roger stared: she thought that he really might not know.
But then why had Jean Knight come to their house? Things
Colette had been imagining seemed crass and grotesque now
that she'd spoken them aloud, in the face of her father's sombre

decency – the brown blind pulled halfway down at his study window, the labelled folders on his shelf. Had she made a humiliating mistake? She flushed with shame, as if she'd exposed herself to him in her underwear, or he'd caught sight in the bin of one of her sanitary towels. — And then there's Aunt Anne's friend, she persisted. — Who saw her in a restaurant, with someone young enough to be her son, they said.

Roger laid down his pen and stood up, thrusting his chair back from the desk with a loud grating noise, like the release of something pent up; Colette flinched as if he might lift his hand to her and hit her, though he had never, ever done that in his life, and never would. — Is this possible?

— Didn't you know? It is him, isn't it?

— Is Anne behind this?

— Nobody's behind it! Only me.

— Have you spoken to Anne about it?

— I haven't spoken to anyone. I worked it out for myself, yesterday.

He looked at her as if he couldn't forgive her, she disgusted him. — Please refrain from working anything else out, Colette. You're out of your depth, you've no idea. And it's of the utmost importance that you don't repeat what you've just said to anyone. Not to anyone, is that clear?

Colette walked out of his study and into Hugh's room, where she stood crushed and hot-faced, hollow with indignation, riffling with her fingers through the box of stamp hinges, which at least were weightless and harmless as moth wings. Hugh hadn't begun to stick his new stamps in. Downstairs she could hear the cartoons: whack! thud! squeal! *I will never again,* she thought passionately to herself. She wasn't sure what it was that she wouldn't do, but she knew what she felt. *Not ever again.* A hard cold nugget inside her, certainty.

Roger rang Jean at Cressing the next day, before he left to catch his train, to ask if they could meet. Colette would be out all day, taking Hugh to the zoo, then to the cinema in the evening. Could Jean come into town to meet him after work, the same place as usual? Roger said he had things to tell her, which he couldn't discuss over the phone. Complications beyond anything they'd imagined.

— She wants to come back to you, Jean flatly said, as if this were only the news she'd been waiting for.

— It's worse than that. Don't try to guess.

She paused while he waited. — I'll try not to try.

— If this thing is true then I think we'll have to act, we'll have to take steps to stop something.

— Let's hope it's not true then, dear Roger, whatever it is. Because these days I do hate stopping things. It makes me too sad.

Behind Jean's voice Roger imagined, although he knew it was fanciful, that he could hear Cressing, which he'd only revisited that once, with Phyllis, since he was there in the war: its high ceilings muffled with damp plaster, ornate clocks whose ticking struck upon blackened oil paintings of dead game, birdsong in the woods. He seemed to see the moat: full of weed and stagnant and still, only insects skittering on its surface tension. In 1942 a few remaining evacuees, whose parents hadn't seemed eager to reclaim them, slept in the Cressing attic and swung across the moat on a rope inexpertly, skinny scabbed legs flailing, falling in from time to time. Roger felt Jean's intelligence active in the silence on the telephone line, obediently not unriddling the puzzle he'd handed her, but working to be always ahead of any difficulty, smoothing the path for comprehension; finding, if not the best way through, then at least the clearest view of how things really were. Even under the present circumstances, this companionship of their minds was a balm and a joy to him.

Phyllis went to Barbara first, with her new discovery. She lay on her back on the bed in Barbara's room one evening with her dress pulled up around her ribs and her tights pulled down from her waist, while her friend examined her abdomen. Barbara's gaze was far away, all her perception was in her concentrating long hands as they worked, the flat of her angularly jointed fingers pressing and probing, speculating. Her touch on Phyllis's skin was cool and heavy, impersonal, competent: it was a restful moment between them, each attending to something in the other that was not personality or history, race. Barbara measured with a tape Phyllis had fetched from her sewing box, then she checked in a book: about four months, she thought.

— I told myself my curse had stopped because of the shock, Phyllis explained, pulling down her dress and sitting up on the bed. — Because of the alteration in my life. But I was so full of dread, Barb, that it might be the change, I might be turning into an old woman. And now this instead! It's another chance at new life, it's amazing, I can't believe it. I must have got pregnant as soon as I left home, because I was so happy at last. Roger and I always had difficulty conceiving, so it never seriously occurred to me. When I was sick, I thought at first I had a bug I couldn't shake off, because of the shared toilets.

Barbara was washing her hands at the sink. — So what will you do?

— I won't do anything. I'm very happy.

— This isn't a good set-up to bring a baby into. How will you keep it clean? Does Nicholas know? Can you support it?

— No one knows, except for you. No need to tell him yet; I will, as soon as the time's right. And I'll find ways to make a living. Sam's pleased with my work, I can do some of that at home. I've heard about a place where they make pies, I might earn five pounds a week there if I could take the baby, or someone would look after him. I can't think of any better way to bring up a child than in a community like this, everybody getting along together, no one caring who you are or where you're from.

— That's how you think it is?

— Honestly, if I try to imagine going back inside the way I used to live, I'd feel as if someone tied a sack over my head. I couldn't bear to go back to that. Sending your children off to school, to be trained to conform and be part of the system, make money and get on in the world. And you don't need a fancy layette to have a baby. It's just more advertising. You can put him to sleep in a drawer, bath him in the sink.

— You think it's a boy, hey?

— I know it's a boy.

— Do you want tea, you foolish daft woman?

But Phyllis couldn't bear the smell of tea, she'd gone right off it, so they toasted the baby instead in a tot of rum. Phyllis wondered then whether Barbara didn't want a man herself. Wasn't that fellow Zeke interested? She'd seen the way he hung round after her, when they went to the Cue Club. Wouldn't she like to have a family and children? Barbara said maybe one day, but not now. There was no room in her life for a man alongside work and study, let alone a no-good loafer like Zeke. And she said that if she had a dream of the future anyway, it didn't involve men.

— So what do you dream about?

When she said that she imagined having an office all of her own, Phyllis laughed and told her she was incorrigible, she was the least poetic person Phyllis had ever met. But this wasn't just any ordinary office, Barbara insisted. She'd seen a photograph in a book, once, of somewhere like it. — It's a big old room in a grand building, like in the old part of the hospital, walls all panelled in polished wood. There's shelves up to the ceiling, filled with so many books, and a big desk with a typewriter, every surface piled with books and papers. My name is on a brass plate on the door. I'm working in there, I'm writing a paper on something. And at eleven o'clock, when I've got my head deep in my work, there comes a knock at the door and a maid brings in my coffee.

— Really, a maid!

— That's my dream.

Phyllis sighed, she said it showed how deep Barbara was – and she was so trivial and shallow. But she could tell that Barbara regretted speaking, as if she'd given herself away. — I think you ought to aim for it, she encouraged her. — You ought to aim to get that room.

— You don't know what you're saying. Some things can't happen.

And Barbara was abrupt and snappy afterwards if Phyllis tried to bring up the subject of her plans for her career. She refused to see any further ahead than passing her exams and getting on to the course to study for a third year, to qualify as a State Registered Nurse. Meanwhile, Phyllis was so happy, hugging the secret of her pregnancy to herself, her hidden treasure. She went along to a local doctor's surgery with her National Health card – luckily she'd picked it up when she went back to Otterley – and queued for an hour and a half in a waiting room heated with a gas fire, crowded with elderly working-class white women, West Indian girls, a toothless old Greek man, a handsome Pakistani in an embroidered cap, a couple of bored girls who looked like secretaries, worn-out mothers shouting at their children. The doctor was a tiny, squat, middle-aged Hungarian woman with dyed frizzed red hair, squeezed into a tight suit and high heels – Phyllis found out that she and her husband were Jews who'd come over before the war. Dr Papp booked Phyllis a bed in the maternity ward in a hospital in Marylebone, and gave her a letter of introduction to the antenatal clinic there. Phyllis remembered her loneliness and fear in her first two pregnancies, in the comfort and privileged quiet of a private nursing home. In those early weeks of her pregnancy in Ladbroke Grove she felt a genuine deep satisfaction in belonging, in the rightness and justice of muddling in – queuing patiently and waiting her turn, like all the other women. Whatever happens to me, she thought, whatever bad things I've done, at least I'll have this child.

SIX

Jean Knight should have left her husband years ago; for such a long time she'd loved another man. But that love had begun in all the chaos of war, when he came to her home on leave, as a family friend; they had to part when he went back to fight, first in Bosnia as liaison with the partisans, then in the assault on the Axis Winter Line in Italy. There hadn't seemed much chance that he'd come out of all that alive. And then after a while she'd had her baby son to think about too. Her husband was willing to bring up the child as his own; it had seemed only sane to stay inside the shelter of her marriage.

But when Jean looked back at her own past now she felt sickened, thinking of her cowardice and the failure of her imagination, in the aftermath of her love affair with Roger. She'd allowed herself to submit to an outward order as if it mattered; now that order itself was crumbling anyway, and all the sacrifices made to it turned out to have been a sham. She might as well have flaunted her affair and her love child: who would have cared? This passivity and excess of diffidence on her part – not on Roger's: she had burned the letters he'd written after the war, from Beirut, Jerusalem, Cairo, pressing her to leave Peter – could be traced, she saw, to her class and upbringing, and her own inability to transcend them. Somehow, from her traditions and education she'd not learned aristocratic shamelessness but instead a horrible rigid sweetness and inability to act without self-doubt, punishing herself. She imagined her Englishness and niceness now like a dull stale biscuit, clogging her mouth, preventing any sincere speech.

Well, she had paid for her mistake, staying in her marriage. If Peter was a bully, then that was her fault too: she'd given him the wrong advantage over her. In long hallucinatory afternoons under the mosquito net in her bedroom in Teheran, when Nicky was away at school, she had thought she might go mad. Parcels of books sent out from Hatchards and Foyles, so scrupulously rationed and reread, had meant too much: she'd lost herself inside them. In fact there had been a spell in a rest home in the hills, under a French nerve doctor. When she'd dreamed of the moat at Cressing, which figured so romantically in Roger's mythology, she dreamed of drowning in it; as she'd said to Roger's daughter, in the sudden shock of meeting her again – so poignantly lovably like him, in her sheer stolid persistence and wary tensed shoulders and dark head, that searching gaze – hyperbole usually came closest to what one really felt.

And meanwhile at all those BP receptions and embassy parties Jean was a grinning doll: nodding, apologising, broken. She had believed that she was not a real woman. The women she saw in the Persian countryside when they motored through it were real, turning away in disdain from the car, tall in their dark shawls like figures from Greek tragedy; her mosquito net sometimes, in her hallucinations, became a luxuriant chador in which she might conceal herself. She'd been devoured with shame by what the West was bringing to that country, despoiling its ancient dignity:

the shabby engineering of the coup against Mossadegh, the clap-trap Americanisation. But at least if you were a man out there you had something to do. She should have tried helping out at clinics and schools set up by the other company wives, but quailed at the false position, pretending to bestow good alongside extracting maximum profits from the country. Though surely doing nothing, only reading novels all day long, was the worst position of all.

Jean laughed when Roger told her that his wife's mystery lover might be their son Nicholas. They were sitting opposite each other as usual, in the lounge bar of an obscure pub in the streets behind Piccadilly, which had become *their place* over the weeks since Roger had written to her after Christmas. As soon as she got that first letter, she had telephoned him at his office to arrange to meet him and to talk: she thought she knew now, when it was too late, how to be shameless, careless, frank. They had the tiny lounge to themselves, with its cold tiled grate and framed cartoons from *Punch*, and in any lull in their conversation – sometimes their fingers touched across the sticky table – they could hear the rumble of working men's voices from the public bar, which seemed to shut them in together more intimately: flare of cockney wit, scraping of chairs, scratch of a match, jangle of the till.

— Is it funny? Roger said, wounded and solemn, when she laughed.

— It's not funny at all.

She quivered still, though, with the joke of it – no doubt this was partly nerves – like an irrepressible schoolgirl.

— Don't you shudder at it? Roger insisted. — It's a disgusting idea, malevolent — if it's even true in the first place. But something makes me think it's true: it all adds up. I hate it that Hughie had to see anything. Insanity on Phyllis's part. Blind malevolence, the worst kind, because she has no idea about who he is. Only for goodness' sake . . . she's old enough to be —

She stopped him, her hand on his sleeve. — Poor Phyllis, though.

— And what about Nicholas? What does it do to him? I'm so sorry for it.

Jean was sorry for it too, naturally; though she didn't pretend to know anything about her son's private life. She had thought there might be something going on at Christmas, when Nicholas was so impatient to get home from Cressing — how absent he'd seemed, skulking around the place, sated and amused, wheezing, glistening in his male assurance, ogling Cathie. Were you allowed to see those things in your own son? He was a scruffy dropout but he was also devastating: handsome, potent. And he had wanted the ivory egg that Roger had sent her long ago from Cairo, to give to somebody — perhaps to Phyllis, she thought now. — But the young men in general don't come out so badly from this sort of affair, do they? she said. — I mean, with older women. Apart from the particular complications in this case.

Roger wondered if she were reproaching him, and she said never, ever, not in a lifetime: she heaped up all the reproaches, always, on her own head. — It's only a shame though, it turns out, that you didn't confide in Phyllis. And it all comes from my stupid plan, for you and Nicholas to get to know each other. If I hadn't nagged him into going to Otterley, and badgered you into inviting him, they'd never have met.

— It was my plan equally, dear girl. I wanted it.

Their fingers traced a path on the table, while they spoke, past the puddles where he'd slopped his beer, and their glasses of whisky: when they joined hands, and he clasped hers in his whole-heartedly, the jolt was always electric, and she felt all their lost time in his withered palm. This was more or less all the touching they'd done so far, in their renewed acquaintance – plenty enough for happiness, Jean considered, at her advanced age. Roger had kissed her once when they parted outside Chez Solange, but on the forehead, chastely.

— Of course we don't know yet whether this story is true.

— It's too absurd not to be true, she said.

— If it is true, Roger said firmly, pressing her hand, — then we have to tell them. Or tell her, at any rate, so that she separates from him. Perhaps he doesn't need to know.

— But does anybody really need to know? I mean, apart from us. Can't we just keep it our secret, and leave them alone? A cosmic comedy: the gods can enjoy it. I've never told anyone apart from Peter, have you? And Peter wouldn't say anything.

Roger shook his head. — It's no good. If they stay together, then we can't.

He hadn't ever talked before, since they began meeting again, of their *staying together*. — But why not? Jean protested: dazzled by this new prospect. — If nobody else knows?

— I couldn't do it to Hugh – or Nicholas. Think of the gossip, and the burden of disgrace for them, if anything came out.

She brooded on it. — We have to think of the children, all the children. And yet. How could anyone ever find out, if we didn't tell?

— If we're together, we draw their attention to it.

— Yes, she said slowly. — Yes, I see that we do.

Roger sat hunched on his stool, like a man used to a more supportive and dignified chair; Jean's perception flickered back and forward, fascinated, between this heavily built middle-aged man with his folded sad face, dark jowls and habit of authority, and the lean youth he had once been. She wasn't disappointed: she'd have been disappointed if that boy with his intensity hadn't grown so substantial, and worldly. Whereas he must naturally be sorry, she thought, seeing how she had shrunk from what she once was and become an old woman. He was very kind, though, and wouldn't give her any glimpse of it. It wasn't as if she'd ever known Roger as untouched; when she first held him in her arms he'd been very young, but initiated already into all the horrors of hell. It had been a revelation to find that her own extreme innocence – not in sex, but in worldliness – was exactly the right match for the extremes in his experience. He had loved Jean's hatred of the war, and her dread of violence, although he wasn't in the least a pacifist himself. In those days he was a pessimistic socialist, who doubted the likelihood of human beings ever again, out of their abyss, contriving any halfway tolerable form to live by. His socialism was a kind of stubbornness, the last redoubt of a better idea which he wouldn't, for the sake of his sane survival, quite give up.

And he'd talked her round to his socialism, out of her own pessimistic conservatism, on those long wartime Suffolk walks, a quarter of a century ago, when Peter was away in London and they'd gone out all day and come home in the dusk, and had taken in certain hidden woodlands, where light was filtered through the fans of young beech leaves, onto the tan leaf mould and violets nestling among the tree roots. Jean had kept faith with Roger's vision of politics ever since. She'd been surrounded, all her life since she and he were last together, by people with the most appalling opinions: except for Nicholas, but then he didn't really talk to her, not any more – she heard the affectionate condescension in his voice. Of course you could like people whose opinions you didn't like. But still, she had been in some sense intellectually alone, abroad and at home, for all this time. And now – although she must be careful not to bore Roger, whose opinions were his daily bread and butter – she couldn't help herself wanting, as keenly as if it were passionate desire, to know *what he thought* about everything. What he thought, with its twists and turns and surprises, was a banquet to her. Because he had kept faith too, with his old vision – even if it was deep-buried now, inside the labyrinth of all the crusty, hoary, compromising accretions of peace, and power.

Now they talked round and round, in the pub off Piccadilly, this knot of their impossible situation. Roger proposed that he'd ask his sister-in-law Anne to visit wherever it was that Nicholas lived. Anne didn't need to know anything; if she found Phyllis, she could arrange a meeting with Roger. Jean shrank from these details, which seemed to her menacing and clumsy. She couldn't bear, under the circumstances, to see her son herself, or even speak to him, not yet – she didn't trust herself, for all she was advocating lying to everyone, not to spill over to him with some intimation of the truth. Fortunately Nicky hardly ever telephoned. If he did, she would tell Mrs Chick to say she was out, or had gone early to bed.

— Nicholas ought to go abroad, Roger said. — I could sort something out.

Alarmed, with an exaggerated idea of the reach of his authority, Jean almost for a moment imagined kidnapping and secret agents. — What kind of thing?

— A journalistic assignment, perhaps?

— Oh, I see.

— I've been keeping an eye on his stuff. It's rather good.

— *Have* you? Will you save things to show to me? He always promises to send me copies, then forgets.

Roger said that he had them collected together in his desk drawer at home; he would post them to her. Jean said that she'd treasure them. For a moment they were like proud parents anywhere.

Colette searched in the old address book on the telephone table in the hall, its pages crossed out and infilled and scribbled over, soft with use, some detached and out of order. Under *K* there were addresses – several abroad, two at home – for Jean and Peter Knight, who were the older generation. But Nicholas couldn't be living with them, if he was living with her mother. She was guided by some instinct of cunning she hadn't even known that she possessed: the book fell open in her hands to its pale blue back page, and there, among the upholsterers and electricians, pencilled very faintly in a corner, she found in Phyllis's writing, miniaturised as if it were in hiding: *N, 53 Everglade Bldngs, Walmer Rd, W10.*

One afternoon at the end of April, before Roger got home, and while Hugh was busy in his room, she set out with an A–Z in her shoulder bag, to see if she could find the place. Who knew if it was the right one? The address would probably turn out to be something innocuous. She'd prepared herself for any dramatic encounter, or none, in a very short skirt, with her school shirt and tie worn in parody under her mother's velvet blazer, to defy her; she'd painted thickly in black around her eyes, and backcombed her hair and sprayed it. It was a cloudy muggy day and a fine drizzle was blowing; on her way down to the station, buds were sticky on the shrubs in the gardens and daffodils blazed against the black earth, rain misted in the cobwebby mass of her hair. Other girls from school were on the station platform, with its flower beds and pretty fretwork roof, but she pretended not to see them. It was of the utmost importance never to look perturbed by anything. When the train arrived you must step onto it as if in a vague dream of competence, and on no account ever run for it if you were late, or push on as the doors were closing – unless you were with friends, when you could shriek at each other and scream about it. If you got on the wrong train you mustn't get off it again, for several stops. You must never look as if you didn't know where you were going.

W10 was a surprise, when she was finally in it – tracing her way without needing the A–Z, in the Underground and then through the streets whose sequence of names she'd memorised at home. Colette hadn't realised she had any mental picture of where she might find Phyllis, if she found her: out of open-mindedness, she'd left all detail blank. But why in a thousand years would her mother, with her charm and maddening elegance, want to live anywhere like this? It wasn't that Colette didn't like it: quite the contrary. Her imagination leaped at once in response to the frowning tall terraced houses blackened with soot and traffic fumes, the windows dark or boarded up, the broken pavements; but this wasn't Phyllis's terrain. Colette was afraid for her mother, and felt for the first time that what she had done might be sordid; perhaps it was her punishment to live here, without flowers or fashion boutiques. The grandeur of these buildings felt ancient, and modern fronts tacked on to some of the shops at street level looked out of place, were already cracked and shabby. Roads were greasy with rain, and the damp-smelling shops with dingy interiors sold vegetables she'd never seen before; brown-skinned men passing on the street didn't deign to notice her, and she saw a woman with a baby tied in a blanket on her back. One road ended abruptly, abutting onto nothingness – her A–Z was out of date. Out of the enclosing deep gulfs of the streets, she suddenly saw across a flattened chaotic wasteland of rubble to a gasometer far off on the other side, and thought this must be bomb damage from the war, until she realised it was planned demolition, cutting a long swathe through the area.

The streets in Otterley, by contrast with these, Colette thought, seemed so safe and smiling: benign to the point of extinction. And this intricacy and history and foreignness were what she thirsted for: seedy bars, a stumbling drunk, dirty numbered fanlights, efflorescence of electric bells, tracery of fire escapes. In such dim, hidden rooms things happened: and if you weren't afraid, you weren't alive. Colette had always believed that she'd finish school, and then go off to university to study something; even in these past weeks, in trouble for truanting, she hadn't seriously wavered from that plan. It didn't interest her, but had seemed a road stretching ahead down which she must inevitably plod, being intelligent. Now she saw that she could choose something differ-ent, if only she knew how. Young women passing her looked ex-actly as she wanted to look herself: dangerous and deadpan, in junk-shop clothes, cultivating fascinating inner lives – though she couldn't stare, because it was more important than ever, here, not to show that you were lost, or new.

She'd stopped believing by now that she could find her mother in this part of London. Arriving at Everglade Buildings, over-whelmed by its scale and seedy magnificence, she pushed in any-way through the tall doors of teak and glass and then climbed the stairs, encouraged by the dancing girls in a plaster frieze, allowing herself this one cowardice of not using the lift; the heavy door thudded back and forth on its hinges behind her. On each land-ing, getting hotter in the velvet jacket, she stopped to decipher the old faded painted numbers, and painted hands pointing to apartments in either direction along curving corridors. A woman, who turned out to be a man with long hair, clattered indifferently in loud boots downstairs past her; from out of sight on the third floor she heard yelling voices. Leaning over the balustrade on the fourth floor, an old lady in white gloves and a white straw hat observed her toiling up, then stood back to let her pass. The stair-well was airy and beautiful, smelling faintly of urine, filled with dim blue evening light. Colette couldn't turn around to look be-hind her, after the old lady matter-of-factly spoke. *Might as well cut your throat.*

From behind the door of number 53, on the top floor, came the sound of music and subdued voices, laughter; when she knocked no one seemed to hear her so she opened it anyway. It wasn't ex-actly a party; there was none of the artificial eager babble she knew from her parents' entertaining. Seven or eight people were sitting around smoking in a semicircle, one of them actually strumming on what she recognised as a lute: she thought they were like a painting of the gods, in their serenity. — I'm looking for Nicholas Knight, she said, stepping forward into the room.

— He's split. He isn't here. Who are you?

Their faces turned towards her in the poor light were alluring, characterful; a woman with her dark hair tied up in a leopard-print scarf, cross-legged on the bed, said that Colette was a pretty name. — My name's Liz. I wish I had a real writer's name like yours. There aren't any writers called Liz, are there? At least, there weren't until now. Now there's me.

Colette suggested Mrs Gaskell. — She doesn't exactly seem like a Liz, though.

— Oh, good God: she's read the nineteenth-century novel! And how do you know Master Nicky, Miss Colette? You don't look like his type. He hasn't despoiled you, has he? Have you come to confront him with the wages of his sin?

— Actually, do you also know someone called Phyllis?

— We do know Phyllis. If anyone really knows Phyllis. Why?

— Well, she's my mother.

They were all vaguely amazed. — No, you're kidding!

Someone whistled: a thickset wrinkled man in a purple shirt, black knitted tie loosened, collar unbuttoned, cigarette burning down between stubby fingers, tipping his drink back and forth in a glass. He was sitting on the only chair, leaning forward with his elbows on his knees; the others were on the floor, or on cushions. — I should have known, he said. — Because I went to her house, to pick up suitcases for her. I should have known it was the kind of house that has children in it. Stank of children. But it was too early in the morning for me, I wasn't noticing anything.

— That's my house.

— How old *is* Phyllis, anyway? Liz said. — Who knew that little wifey had children smuggled away somewhere? How many of you are there, for God's sake?

— Come on in and wait for her, said one of the other women. — She was here ten minutes ago, she'll be back. We don't know where she's gone.

— Does she live here?

— She doesn't exactly live here.

Liz widened her eyes. — But on the other hand she sometimes does, in a way. In a sexual way, that is. Are you shocked, Colette?

Colette said she'd worked this out for herself; nobody ever told her anything. — I even met Nicholas once, he came to dinner at our house. And then I hunted round at home and I just had this instinct: she'd written his address very small at the back of the phone book, where no one was supposed to see it. But I found it. And so I came here.

— Isn't she priceless? Liz looked around at the others. — Natural-born detective.

She patted a place on the bed, Colette sat down cross-legged beside her, the bedsprings shifted and squeaked. — Meet everyone: Paul, Jenny, Sam, Raúl, Maggie, Ezekiel, Robert. Sam's a musical genius, Raúl's queer, he's Brazilian. Robert's involved with the Free School or some such idealistic dream shop.

— Shit shop, said Paul, the thickset one in the chair.

— Robert comes from the country, you can see he's a country boy, pink cheeks, he's sweet. He really can't play the lute though.

Raúl isn't sweet, although he looks pretty. He's taken too many drugs, ruined his mind. Maggie was a debutante, she went to one of those balls where you meet the Queen, now she's just sleeping around. She really thinks people like me should be cleaning her boots and washing her knickers. But no such luck, Maggie!

— Fuck off, Maggie lazily said. She was the one who'd made Colette think of a painting, with a black ribbon tied round her forehead, sleek chestnut hair and a very white, straight parting.

— And what about me? said Paul. — Why don't you tell her who I am?

— Man, we don't even want her to know your name, the one called Sam protested. — You're bad news, seriously. This is Phyl's daughter, we got to look out for her.

— Paul's an old letch, Liz said. — We don't want him any-where near you.

— I'm also the only real fucking artist in this room, Paul said. — All the rest of you put together aren't worth the fucking shit on my shoe.

Colette couldn't work out when any of them were speaking se-riously. They seemed to insult each other and yet they had these calm, amused voices; their tension gripped and excited her, coil-ing under the surface. They were passing round something to smoke and she puffed at it too when it came her way, though she'd only smoked cigarettes before. — You think this is OK? Sam que-ried. — You don't think that her ma would get mad with us?

— What does her mother have to do with it? Remember she abandoned her children, to run away with her boyfriend. Leave the girl alone.

— I was just saying.

He shrugged expressively.

Colette reassured Sam she could look after herself. Raúl the Brazilian attended with religious seriousness to the rolling of the next joint; it grew too dark to see so they lit candles, and the shadows slipped around his long brown fingers, drooping moustache, long neck and jaw, prominent knots of cheekbone. Robert gave up the lute to Sam, who played Elizabethan music on it, and then something like the blues; the music deepened the mood in the room, made it tragic and yearning. Nothing lasted, everything must die, there was violence all around so you might as well snatch your pleasures now. Listening to him play, Colette knew why the others deferred to Sam in his good suit cut with sharp lapels, with his almond-shaped eyes and lazy glance, his mat of tight-curled black hair. His gift set him apart, although he seemed so mild and easy. She kept on puffing at the joint whenever it came round. When she asked them to tell her the name of this part of London, someone said it was the Grove and someone else said it was the Gate. — The Gate is white, Sam explained. — The Grove is black.

The others protested: it wasn't like that. Pink-cheeked Robert said he couldn't handle all these definitions. — Don't get into that game, man, don't get into politics: setting up one army to fight another.

Sam tucked his smile away, looking down at his fingers on the strings. — If I had an army, you think I'd be wasting my time showing you how to play this thing? You got to owe me, for what I'm giving you here.

— You have to admit, Rob, Liz commiserated. — You do look nice with the lute, but you can't play it.

When Maggie announced, on the subject of armies, that she hated all wars, Paul groaned and put his head in his hands. — Oh for Christ sake. The profundity.

— Well, I *am* profound.

— Her father's a colonel, Liz said. — That makes it mean more, apparently.

— Brigadier, as a matter of fact.

— She thinks she can get away with anything, Paul said, — just because she has tits like sugarplums.

Maggie blandly agreed that he was right, they were like sugarplums. She sat on her cushions with a straight back like a dancer, and her green velvet dress was cut very low in front; you could see the perfect small shape of her white breasts. Paul complained that she was flaunting them at him. Colette asked whether Liz really was a writer, and Liz gave her a lugubrious look, lighting a tiny black cigarette with a silver lighter. She could feel the pressure of Liz's knee in thick black tights against hers; it wasn't either companionable or sensual, more like a challenge, to see if Colette would back down. And she didn't, she pressed back. — Whatever you do, Liz said, — don't tell me you want to write.

— Oh no. At least, I don't think so.

— Thank Christ for that.

After a while Colette couldn't make out the actual words anyone was saying, only the gist of some long grievance, a feud between two lots of people, a theft of papers and a typewriter, something to do with a magazine, one group thinking the other had sold out, the whole operation had become too bourgeois. *Somebody put methedrine in his drink,* Maggie was explaining indignantly in the middle of some anecdote, and Colette laughed because it seemed funny that in

her clipped outrage Maggie sounded just like the head girl at Otterley High, complaining because the lower forms weren't wearing
their hats outside school. This made her remember her home, and
think that her father might be worrying about her. She stood up
precariously from the bed.

— She OK to be wandering roun' here by herself?

— Do you know where you're going, Colette?

— Where is Phyllis anyway? Why isn't she here?

She considered the lift but didn't trust herself: so she set out very
slowly down the stone staircase, whose lovely spiral seemed unsta-
ble under her feet this time, flying out dizzily ahead of her in the
near darkness – only a few of the bulbs in the lily-shaped glass
lamps on the staircase were working. The old lady had disap-
peared. Colette had got almost as far as the landing above the
ground floor when she was aware of a commotion above her, something tearing through the stillness outside her absorption in putting one foot in front of another.

— Oh wait, wait! Wait, Colette!

Her mother was flying down the stairs after her in a clatter of
heels, hand barely skimming the handrail. — Oh, I can't believe
this, Phyllis cried. — I can't believe you found me. How did you
do that? But you're so clever, I should have known. Wait for me,
darling.

She threw out her arms and Colette was enveloped in the mi-
asma of her mother's warmth and perfume, soft flesh: when she sat
down abruptly on the stairs, Phyllis sat beside her, holding on to
her.

— I should have known you'd find me, I should have trusted you. I'm so angry with them! Why didn't they tell me you'd come? I was only just along the corridor, sitting with my friend: I was testing her, she has exams to pass.

— What friend? Which exams?

— She's a nurse. What are you wearing? Isn't that my jacket? I wondered where it had got to. It looks great on you. You're so different, Colette, and so grown-up. But what a state you're in! What have they done to you? I'll have to take you home. Can you forgive me for not telling you? I didn't know how to tell you.

— I thought you lived here.

— I did live here at first, but I've got a place of my own now. It's not far. It's really too filthy here, nobody cleans the toilets. Nicky never washes the sheets, you wouldn't believe, he complains if ever I strip his bed to take them to the launderette. But I've got a nice little place, you'll love it, Col. We'd better call your father, to let him know you're safe. So you met Liz. I left the room partly because she was such a bitch tonight.

— Is she jealous of you with Nicky or something?

— Liz isn't interested in men, in that way. She's a . . . you know, prefers women. But she doesn't like me, thinks I'm vacuous and posh, she's always getting at me. Sam's lovely though, isn't he? Did you hear him play? Can you walk? Are you going to be sick?

— I don't think so.

— I can't believe they let you smoke that stuff.

— Do you smoke it?

— Yes, but I'm used to it. You mustn't tell anyone; we keep it hidden under the floorboards.

They made their way out from Everglade Buildings onto the

street, Phyllis hanging on to Colette's arm and steering her, watching her with tender concern, sometimes stroking her hair out of her eyes, encouraging her to keep going. *Not far now.* Colette grew steadier but had a sensation as if the night were criss-crossed with cobwebs brushing against her face. She allowed her mother to lead her and in this strange state accepted, as if it were part of a dream, that Phyllis knew where she was going, making her way with such assurance through these improbable streets. They stopped at a phone box on one corner, although the receiver dangled from its cord and the light was broken, the phone books had pages torn out of them. — Usually it's working, Phyllis reassured her, picking up the receiver to check. Colette slumped against the box outside: it was working, and of course her mother didn't need any phone book, but dialled her old number easily in the dark. When Roger answered she pushed in her sixpences and spoke in her familiar bright voice, blithe as if there'd never been any rift between them. — Oh no, she's fine, she can stay with me. I just didn't want you to worry. I can't talk now, Roger. I want to get her home. We can't discuss anything right now.

Waiting outside the phone box, Colette watched passers-by hurrying with their hats pulled down over their faces, a drunk girl shoved out from a café, then its lights extinguished, a knot of kids not in bed yet, huddled on the kerb, heads down between their skinny knees, absorbed, with subdued excited cries, in playing with something in the gutter. She imagined in her pot dream that she could hear her father's voice, though not his words, through the glass in the call-box door: a displeased heavy rumble on the far end of the line. The weight of Roger's authority and good sense was diminished here, less of a protection. While he was still rumbling Phyllis replaced the receiver and the machine swallowed her coins; she came back anxiously to Colette and kissed her. *We're nearly there.* She was wearing her old winter coat hanging open, with a print scarf wound limply round her neck; her hair was long, cut in a new fringe across her forehead, and her lashes were heavily mascaraed. This was a new look, to match her new surroundings.

They stopped at one of the houses in a wide, quieter street, with a long strip of trees and grass running down its centre; Phyllis unlocked the door and shepherded Colette inside. The stairwell was dingy but Phyllis's room on the first floor was impressive and stylish, once she'd switched on the lamps and lit a paraffin heater – high-ceilinged and bare, no carpet, no curtains at the floor-length windows. Propped against one wall, opposite a grand fireplace, was a huge gilt mirror, with a philodendron being trained to grow around it; the modern lamps had bases like bent coat hangers, and white paper globes for shades; there were piles of books and papers on the floor, a life-size bronze sculpture of a dog scratching. — Isn't he wonderful? Phyllis exclaimed. — He's my little favourite. He isn't really mine, worse luck. I'm just keeping it for Paul until he sells it. You must have met Paul just now, in Nicky's room; he's really famous, sells his things through one of the big galleries. Bit older than the others, dark and quite short, grumpy.

— I hated him, Colette said, though actually she'd been interested in Paul and his scratchy, rude remarks.

— He's so dedicated to his art, it's all that matters to him really. And he can be very funny. But he doesn't like women much, he thinks they're frivolous. Or at least, he only likes them in one way. I know that you're not frivolous, but I am.

Phyllis went behind a screen at one end of the room. — You

see, this is my little kitchen, she called. — Bathroom's next door if you need to pee, we share it with the guy upstairs, he sometimes passes out in there, I had to take the lock off. I'll put the kettle on for tea. Are you hungry, darling? I could make you toast. It's a bit of a change from home, isn't it? But you see, I'm so happy. You look wonderful, Col, you've lost so much weight! And without your glasses!

— I don't want you to talk about that.

She was managing to take out her contact lenses and put them in the little case, jabbing her finger clumsily in one eye, while her mother was in the kitchen.

— All right, I'm not talking about it, just saying how attractive you look.

— Shut up, Mum. I don't even want to be attractive.

Phyllis made mugs of tea. There were a few spindly chairs, and a mattress on the floor was heaped up with cushions; she sat down on it beside Colette. — You'll have to share the bed with me, darling. I'll lend you something for a nightdress.

— Is this the bed? Don't you have bedrooms? And what about *him*, won't he be sleeping in it?

Phyllis said that sometimes Nicky slept in his room.

— Aren't you two supposed to be madly in love or something?

— Something like that.

She helped Colette off with her clothes, then brought her a loose shirt to wear in bed. — I might come and live with you here, Colette said vaguely, when she had her head on the pillow and her eyes shut. — Because it's awful at home. It's really awful, Mum.

— But what about school?

— I've finished with school.

Her mother was stroking her hair, placating her. — All right, I see.

— You couldn't have missed us that much, if you're so happy.

— I'm not happy all the time, Phyllis confided in a low voice somewhere close to her ear. — I did miss you, you'll never know how much. And Nicky isn't a good man like your father. He's very young, he isn't mature, he can be selfish. He sleeps with other women, but I love him. Everything's different here. I see everything differently.

— Did he sleep with Maggie?

Startled, she stopped in the middle of stroking. — Maggie? Why? I don't think so.

— *Tits like sugarplums.*

Phyllis couldn't help herself laughing, scandalised. — Is that what Paul said?

Colette nodded.

— My God, what would your father think? No, Nicky can't stand Maggie, I don't think it's her. Though you never know. Her tits *are* like sugarplums. Which counts for a lot with a man. But go to sleep now.

Colette lay listening to her mother moving about in the room, taking her clothes off and folding them, turning down the paraffin heater, putting out the lights. They hadn't shared a bed since Colette had a fever when she was very small, in Cairo. And yet when Phyllis climbed beneath the sheets, her vital heat and the smell of her hot skin were intensely familiar among the alien surroundings: the concentrated close presence of her body, the fine vertebrae in her turned curved back under a skimpy nightdress. This body had a new meaning, however, now that she had a lover. Shyly, Colette held off from touching against her mother anywhere. It was striking how sedulously Phyllis had been paying court to her, as if Colette were owed this concentration on herself alone; none-theless she felt the strain, on the brink of oblivion, of her mother's not having asked yet after Hugh. They lay awake in the dark without speaking. *How's Hughie getting on?* Phyllis whispered eventually, when probably she thought that Colette was already asleep. She whispered back that he was all right, seemed to be enjoying school. After a pause: *Does he say anything about me?* Co-lette didn't know how to respond to that, so told the truth. — He says he hates you.

Colette realised as soon as she woke the next morning that her mother was pregnant. She had taken in something different in her appearance last night, without understanding in her daze what it was that she saw, when Phyllis took off her coat; the bulge in her figure was very slight.

Phyllis was up and dressed already, frying bacon in the kitchenette.

— You're having a baby, Colette said accusingly, standing in the gap where the screen separated the kitchenette from the rest of the room; one of the floor-length windows was pulled up six inches, letting in chilly morning air around their feet. The shirt Colette had slept in was too short, she was tugging it down from behind, feeling the indignity of its not reaching all the way across her bottom.

A smile – complacent, pleased – flickered in her mother's

expression while she prodded the rashers. — You're too clever for me. You find out everything. I didn't think it showed yet.

— Does what's-his-name know?

Phyllis served up the bacon onto plates kept warm under the grill, then cracked eggs into the pan. — Nicky isn't happy about it. She laughed, as if this were amusing. — Of course he doesn't want kids yet, though I reassured him I'd look after it, he wouldn't have to do anything. Actually we had quite a row. He said he'd always thought I was too old – I mean, to get pregnant. Which, frankly, is what I'd thought too. So that I hadn't taken any measures, to prevent its happening. Is it too dire, darling, me talking to you about these things? That's when he stormed off and stayed the night with Liz.

— I thought you said Liz liked women.

— Sometimes she goes with men as well. Probably she did it just to get at me. I'm sure Nicky believed at first that I was deluding myself, that this baby was some kind of women's hysteria – you know, to do with the change and everything. But I'm booked into the maternity hospital now, it's definite. Anyway, he'll get used to the idea. And I'm so glad. It's a new joy in my life. There'll be another little brother for you, Col.

— I don't want another brother.

Phyllis said that she'd been nauseous at first, but now she'd got such an appetite, and must be careful not to get fat; she had a craving for raw cabbage and could eat a whole one, if she didn't stop herself. — This baby's a toughie, I'm not afraid for him. I'm feeling so strong, Colette! It's amazing, since I moved here I don't get my sick headaches any more. Now I see I was only ill in the past because so much was false, in my old life.

— How d'you even know it's a boy?

She said that she'd asked the old woman downstairs, who told fortunes. — And anyhow, I just know.

They ate their breakfast sitting on the bed, mopping up the egg yolk with sliced bread. Phyllis tried to explain how she was so different now. For instance she'd gone along in March to the Vietnam demonstrations in Grosvenor Square. — I wondered if you might have seen me in the news on telly. Someone said they saw me. Of course I knew what Roger would have thought.

Colette said that the news was boring.

— It did get out of hand, Phyllis said. — Nicky wrote about it, a lot of people didn't like what he said, but it was true: that some on the left were provoking the violence for their own political purposes, not caring if anyone in the crowd was hurt. They were throwing ball bearings at the police and using their banners as lances, trying to unseat them from their horses. But it was part of a big game for the police, too: that opened my eyes. They drove us deliberately into the square and trapped us there, jeering at us. We stood under the trees, because on their horses they couldn't get in there to use their truncheons on us. A girl I know was kicked by a policeman, she was covered in blood.

— It sounds idiotic.

— Everything isn't what it seems in Otterley. The state isn't benevolent, Col, it's violent. It's not there to protect people. Politicians inflict violence all around the world, in support of big business and economic greed.

— So are you a communist then?

— Nicky says I'm more revolutionary now than he is. I haven't grasped all the complexity of the ideas. But I do see that the way we're living is all wrong, there has to be a better system.

— *The only problem with communism is human nature.*

Colette parroted this in a silly voice, imitating her history teacher, the one who made them copy out notes from Trevelyan. — Or perhaps, Phyllis suggested, — human nature was distorted by capitalism.

How could she be so transformed and yet the same person? Everything she said excited Colette and at the same time humiliated her. An old world was crumbling, and this new continent of experience, with its dizzily altered perspectives and intoxicating freedoms, should have been trackless – yet her mother's footprint was on the sand everywhere ahead of her. Before Colette even had time to explore, Phyllis had taken possession, making the new world over according to the same old feminine mystique, the same perpetual drama of her self and her body.

Hugh was alone in the house, sticking his new stamps in their places in his album, when his aunt Marnie rang the doorbell. He knew it was her because when the bell rang he padded quietly in his socks to peer from behind the curtains in his parents' bedroom, recognising with a shock of distaste his stout aunt on the porch steps, in capacious khaki mac and rain hat, one gloved hand gripping the painted handrail. In Hugh's memory, Marnie had never before arrived here uninvited. The Otterley family always went to Guildford, because Grandma Fischer was more or less a fixture in that house; only once or twice a year, after extensive negotiations, she might be transported to Otterley for Sunday lunch.

It wouldn't have occurred to Hugh to open the door to his aunt, except that as he stood spying on her, waiting for her to make her dejected way back down the path, she spun her head around suddenly at uncanny speed – like a zombie, he thought – and skewered him at the window with her look. He should have been prepared for this, because although his weird aunt passed as a grown-up, she preserved a core of childhood cunning – giving sly pinches and playing practical jokes, picking up on hints not meant for her. Now she waved at Hugh frantically, gesturing for him to open the front door. Doomed, he dragged his feet on the stair carpet, jumping down one reluctant step at a time, descending through the still air whose privacy and secrecy seemed more sensuously velvety, now they were invaded. This was his last day, before he went back to school. Roger was still at work, Colette had gone out somewhere, hinting to him mysteriously. His solitude in that house had seemed oceanic, rocked by the rain and wind outside, with seas of time between him and the dim grey line of tomorrow on the horizon. When he opened the front door a crack, keeping on the chain he'd fastened earlier, khaki mackintosh filled his vision; he preferred not to look up past the brooch in the shape of a Scottie dog, pinned on his aunt's collar.

— Now, aren't you going to invite me in? Marnie said archly.

— There's no point really, Hugh said. — There's no one here but me.

— In any case, Hughie, it's you I particularly wanted to see.

— But you saw me the other day, he protested reasonably. — When we came to lunch.

— I want to find out all about school: you hardly told us anything.

— There's nothing to tell. It's exactly how you'd imagine it would be.

He thought of pushing the door quickly shut, like a resourceful boy in a cartoon, and then crouching until she'd gone away, with his fingers in his ears, in his old hiding place in the cupboard under the stairs. But Marnie shoved at the door sharply from her side, protesting that she was left out in the rain, and had come all this way on the train especially. — Open up, Hugh, don't be ridiculous. What would your father think?

With adult resignation Hugh undid the chain, then stood back in the hall while his aunt underwent a mammoth disrobing, draping sodden garments on the hallstand, shaking off her hat, putting her umbrella in the porch to copiously drip, unzipping her boots and putting on shoes which she'd brought with her in a bag. She puffed with the effort and her jowls shook, the red spots in her cheeks were hot, she mopped at her wet neck with a handkerchief. — You shouldn't be running around in socks, she said.

Hugh looked down at the socks in surprise: he'd been unconscious of himself until she came. He had no idea what to do with his aunt, now they were confronted in the house – he supposed that he ought to offer her tea, but didn't know how to make it. Luckily Marnie took charge of the tea herself, banging around assuredly with the kettle and tea caddy in the kitchen, opening tins in search of cake because she said her blood sugar was low. Hugh didn't like tea, but submitted to it as a penance. They sat down to drink it at the kitchen table, Marnie groping in her stiffly upright black handbag for cigarettes, then snapping its clasp shut with a hollow echo. — You can see that this isn't a home, she said, lighting up and shaking out the match. Hugh fetched her the brown coronation ashtray, ringed with animals he knew off by heart — elephant, kiwi, beaver, kangaroo, eland.

She added that you couldn't blame the girl for it.

— Which girl?

— Whoever cleans and cooks here.

— Her name is Verey, Hugh supplied.

His aunt relaxed into her cigarette; her glance, from those eyes like polished black beads, was everywhere in the room. Monumental in her dark blue suit, seated incongruously here at the heart of the house, she blotted up the rainy light and blocked Hugh's view through the window, dropping ash on the slopes of the fearsome mountain of her bosom. The kitchen's sunshiny colours were meant to be hopeful and cheerful but through Marnie's eyes he saw they were tarnished and foolish.

— So, Hugh, where are they all?

Her voice was trumpeting, and sometimes she hummed dementedly between sentences: he and Colette had perfected an imitation of it. He kicked out his legs from the stool in a show of unconcern. — Oh, do you mean my family? Well, my father's at work, my sister's gone off into town. I'm here, obviously. I ought to get back to my stamp album really, I've got tons to do.

He wouldn't even think the words to himself, that this was *his last day*.

— And how about your mother? Where is she? Don't bother to tell me that she's in Leamington, because I know she isn't. I've telephoned there.

Hugh shrugged vaguely, as if it didn't much interest him. — Well obviously I haven't seen a lot of her, as I've been away at school.

— Oh, come off it.

She was as rude as a boy, unforgivable: scalding tea rose in Hugh's throat, he was so violently affronted. On the other hand, why should he waste time defending his mother? It was Phyllis's fault that Marnie was able to sit here at her kitchen table, persecuting him, devouring the few hours of freedom he had left. Why not betray his mother to her? He *wanted* to betray her, she deserved it. She and his aunt were as foul as each other, they belonged together. — I gather that she's living with someone else, he calmly said, as if it were an ordinary thing.

Marnie gleamed triumphantly at him through her puffed smoke. — I knew it! I knew that this had happened. I've always known she wasn't right for Roger. Poor Roger: she wasn't up to his standard, that was clear to us from the start. I haven't said anything yet to Grandma, but it will break her heart. And do we have any name for this *someone else*?

He didn't care. — I believe he's called Nicholas Knight.

That stopped her in her tracks. Her cheeks flushed suddenly, and she clashed down her cup so that it slopped tea in the saucer. — Don't tell a naughty fib, she cried. — And anyway, how do you even know that name?

They were nakedly enemies now. Hugh stood down from his stool to face her, although he thought she might twist his arm or hurt him in some way – he almost wanted her to hurt him. — You asked me, he said, boiling with indignation, — and so I told you. Nicholas Knight came here. I saw them together.

SEVEN

Roger found out from Colette that Phyllis was pregnant. Colette had asked her mother if she should tell him, and she had said, *Why not?* It was a horror to him, and his secret knowledge was a heavy burden. He felt it very bitterly, although he didn't show this to his daughter, but kept up in front of her his appearance of a resigned cold calm. It haunted him that Phyllis had had such difficulty in conceiving children with him, and now – in this situation as fatally twisted as a Greek drama, and at her age too, and with that boy, his own boy – fell pregnant with casual ease, like an ignorant teenager. He wrote to Jean to tell her, and to say this changed all their plans. *Now, of course, we can't act to separate them. In fact, we can't act at all. This paralyses us. I shan't ask Anne to visit her.* He didn't trust himself to talk to Jean on the phone, and thought that at least for the moment they should not meet in person. He imagined his letter arriving at Cressing, and Jean's foreboding intuition at once, before she even opened it, of the bad news it must contain. Perhaps her housekeeper would bring it in to where she sat, at a spindly eighteenth-century *escritoire* in weak spring sunlight in the morning room – if there was really a morning room, or for that matter an *escritoire*, or sunlight. He couldn't remember much of the detail of the house.

She would be paying bills when the letter arrived, he imagined, signing cheques worriedly with a heavy old fountain pen. Roger didn't care materially about Cressing – he'd have been perfectly happy if Jean had given it up, and they'd gone together to live in a bothy in Scotland. But his fantasy of Cressing was inseparable from his idea of her solitude. He was almost resentful of his own image of her privacy and detachment.

Colette began to go back and forth between her parents. When Roger remonstrated with her, she pointed out that since she'd first visited her mother her attendance at school had actually been better. At the very moment when she was considering giving up her education altogether, she returned to her classes and made serious new efforts – which seemed somehow more like play – at mastering her subjects. She made lists of the names of birds and trees and vegetables in French, practised idiomatic phrases for her oral. In the reference section in Otterley library she read through books on the French Revolution and Restoration, also on parliamentary reform, and the cycles of popular unrest and repression in nineteenth-century Britain. She had the sensation of straining her mind forward all the time, through multiplying detail, to attain a critical overview – commanding and controlling what she learned, not merely submitting, as the other girls did, to the torrents of information. She might as well pass her O levels this summer, whatever she chose to do with her life afterwards. And in any case, this new knowledge was a liberation in itself. She could use it for her own ends, to contrive a position in the world.

So sometimes when the school day was over she came back to the sober house in Otterley, and warmed up whatever supper Mandy had left for them. Hugh by this time was back at

Abingdon. She put out place mats on the dining-room table, and she and her father chewed their way through their food more or less in silence, or asked each other politely how their day had been. Each night, Colette tried to put smaller and smaller portions on her own plate. When she'd stacked the dishes in the kitchen, she went upstairs and did her homework dutifully and assiduously in the pink-and-white bedroom, smoking cigarettes to suppress her appetite. The evenings were lengthening and on warm nights she opened her window onto the garden to smoke, inhaling the odorous thick peace of the suburbs, growth pushing in the earth, restlessness of the river flowing out of sight. As light thinned in the sky, its tension, like a high struck note, roused her to a pitch of nostalgic longing.

Later, when she and her father watched the news on television, extraordinary things happening in Paris and America and even London seemed continuous with her reading about revolutions in 1848 or 1870. They rarely commented on what they saw, but she could tell that Roger was pained and offended by the young protesters. Their contempt trapped him in his middle age, trampling his experience underfoot like so much junk – but he wouldn't be caught out huffing and puffing at them like an old fool. Only once, when they saw snatched, censored footage of a girl streaking naked into a lecture, upsetting a distinguished elderly philosopher, Roger called her a *silly tart* under his breath. He said then that these people should be afraid of themselves, unleashing so much unkindness. They have no idea, he said. Colette dreaded catching sight of Phyllis among the crowds. When she was in Otterley she could see it all from her father's point of view. It was so easy to break things, he said. Putting them together was long and slow.

On other days she caught the train into town after school, and joined in with her mother's much more chaotic life. Phyllis's neighbour Mrs Feinstein had a telephone and Colette could leave messages with her, to let her mother know if she was coming. She wasn't ever sure how much Phyllis really wanted her there. She was affectionate and enquired with close interest after what Colette was doing, but never greeted her again, after the first time, with that ecstatic eagerness which had torn through, for a moment, the wary history of their relations. Colette even wondered sometimes if her mother had hoped, embracing her so passionately on the stairs at the Everglade, that she came as a messenger from Hugh. But this was probably not true, or only partially true. Phyllis would touch Colette's hair sometimes with a secretive smile, as if her presence were at least a relief, a reprieve from guilt. And her having absconded from Otterley put her on a new footing of equality with her daughter; sometimes they chatted almost like girlfriends. Colette was surprised by revelations of her mother's personality, seen from this perspective of their new intimacy. She hadn't known that Phyllis was so rash, quick, improvising: indifferent to other people's judgement. If she'd stayed in Otterley, Colette would have dismissed her as conventional.

Often she was working when Colette arrived, sitting at a rickety small table with her new reading glasses on, frowning over the figures in Sam Harris's account books. Also she'd begun dressmaking for some of the local women, taking up hems or putting in a new zip, making a skirt from a pattern; she'd gone back to Otterley again with Paul, to pick up her sewing machine. *I want to pay my own way,* she said. Her new life was far more sociable than the old one; she had belonged to all those clubs, but she used to make fun of them with Roger, she'd called them her *Mothers' Meetings*. Now there were always friends dropping in to the long room; she sewed big cushions for them to sit on, out of Indian cottons and silks she found in the street market. She cooked up pots of curry and rice or stew in the tiny kitchen, bought in cheap wine from the Spanish shop round the corner. Parties sprang up spontaneously, you didn't have to formally invite anyone. In the fine weather they flung the windows up and put music on the record player; sometimes Sam Harris or someone else played the guitar and sang. Phyllis found an old piano put out on the street, and paid a couple of removal men to bring it upstairs.

Colette put on a show of sulky reluctance, but she was intoxicated by this easy sociability. Some of her mother's new friends were from the same tribe as those bewitching individuals she'd admired in the crowds on the King's Road, when she couldn't think of any way of getting close to them: good-looking and unsmiling, men and women both, flaunting their outrageous clothes, rank with smells of sweat and marijuana. Now she was actually sitting among them and eating with them, cross-legged on the floor. She was mostly silent, and when she introduced herself didn't always say that she was Phyllis's daughter; she noticed that Phyllis didn't hurry to explain this either. Probably few of these friends realised that Phyllis was forty, and mother to a sixteen-year-old. They were often closer to Colette's age than to her mother's; no doubt they were Nicholas Knight's friends really. When there was talk of history or politics, Phyllis was out of her depth: some of them had read so much, some were university teachers. She would listen to them respectfully, careful not to make a fool of herself or say too much. There was something suppliant in her mother's attitude which irritated Colette, who would have liked to argue with these men – it was mostly the men who had strong opinions, although there were certain clever women too, who joined in, or got shouted down. But Colette couldn't join in yet. She didn't know enough, she wasn't ready.

And these men didn't care about her opinions anyway, nor about Phyllis's: they wanted their noisy arguments with other men, and the smokes and company and music in the long bare room. Phyllis served them with food and drink, or danced with her reflection in the window, to Dylan or Joan Baez, in the candlelight. She worried about her figure when her pregnancy began to show, but mostly the men seemed to feel sentimentally about it, liking her swollen shape. The prospect of a new baby fitted in with their charged idea of the future; the political ones were emotional now with the importance of this moment, when history was happening. This is the revolution, they said. Someone came fresh from the Hornsey College sit-in and said all the art textbooks should be burned, someone else said that only fascists burned books. They all ate hungrily, and Phyllis kept spare mattresses for anyone needing to crash.

Nicky had gone off to Paris apparently, with a couple of friends, because he wanted to write about it. Then Phyllis announced excitedly that he was back, he was exhausted, it had all been amazing, he was working on an account of the uprising for the *New Left Review*. Every time Colette arrived in Ladbroke Grove she thought she might encounter him, and seemed to see herself again in that hideous pink dress she'd worn when they first met, although she'd thrown it out long ago, burying it deep in the dustbin. She remembered their strong antagonism at the front door in Otterley – although she'd had no intimation then of how far he could disrupt their lives. Nicky's clumsiness had only seemed ordinary; he had been gangling and incapable and drunk, foolishly self-important, spilling wine on their tablecloth, blundering into their furniture, pushing up his glasses nervously on his nose with those big boyish hands with swollen red knuckles. All that had been tiresome but familiar, nothing new.

When finally she saw him at her mother's place, she hardly recognised him. He came in late one evening, when a few friends were sitting around talking quietly. Phyllis was filling the coffee percolator and for a moment, as Nicky stood inside the door, only Colette was aware of him: in a dark green blazer, dark hair down to his shoulders, his shadowed face conscious and aloof – with its crooked beaked nose, full-lipped mouth. She thought that he was good-looking now, tightened and concentrated like an old portrait of an unknown youth. If Nicky was aware of her awareness, he didn't return her look: probably he'd forgotten who she was, or that she was visiting, if Phyllis had ever told him. He was bored, she thought – crossing the room in his slow lope, in tatty gym shoes with the laces missing, joking casually, hands in his blazer pockets, cigarette stuck wetly to his lower lip – by finding them all here, when he only wanted Phyllis. Everyone stirred, because he had arrived; he changed the atmosphere, people wanted the beam of his attention turned upon them. This alteration in his significance couldn't only be because he was among friends here, or because he'd just come back from Paris. Something had changed and refined Nicky since Colette last saw him, made him more powerful. She supposed that part of what had happened must be her mother. It must be sex, she conceded sourly. Sex and his grown-up relationship with her mother.

Phyllis finished pouring out coffee and sat down beside Colette, touching her hair again; she was watching Nicky nervously, to see how he reacted to her daughter. He seemed hardly to notice her; or rather, Colette saw that his policy was to treat her like everyone else – not unfriendly, but not making any special effort either. The old ties of family relationships were obsolete, square, bypassed in a superior new world: you could make up your relationships for yourself, out of your free choice. It didn't matter to him that she was the daughter of the woman he slept with. And anyway, how could anything personal be important, besides what was going on in France?

Nicky explained how they'd travelled via Ostend because you couldn't get in any other way, then driven down from Brussels, where the students were occupying the university. They arrived in Paris in the middle of the night, but there were still people on the streets and fires burning, stink of tear gas, glass from the shop windows underfoot everywhere. He and his friends had enlisted in the *service d'ordre*, they were billeted in the Beaux-Arts, in rue Bonaparte. What you didn't want to be, he said, was a revolutionary tourist: there were plenty of those. He was chased one day by the police wielding batons, took refuge in a smart art gallery whose owner opened up for them; his friends went to support the Renault workers at Flins, who flew a black anarchist flag over the factory. In a pitched battle there with police, one worker-comrade was killed; his friends were lucky not to be arrested and hauled off to *les cages*. You had to be careful not to hitch-hike, Nicky said, because the rightists pretended to give students lifts, and then beat the shit out of them.

So will the government collapse? the others asked. And the bourgeoisie, will that collapse? *Billeted*, Colette thought: how ridiculous, what showing off, as if they were real troops in a real war. Nicky had only been in Paris for a fortnight. And whenever these revolutionaries talked about *the workers* they had a silly solemnity, like a girl with a crush. But couldn't any one of them have been car workers if they'd really wanted to, if being a worker was so wonderful? To be fair to Nicky, he was a brake on the extravagant enthusiasm of some of the others: sardonically he described the splits between the different factions, and the criminals taking advantage of the chaos. Colette wasn't on the side of the political types anyway. She was more drawn to the ones who talked about drugs and art and music, were often stoned and not at all in earnest. They weren't waiting for the students and factory workers to bring about a new era. As far as they were concerned it had arrived already, they were helping themselves to it wholeheartedly.

At the end of that first night, when the others had gone, Phyllis said she would put down a mattress in the kitchenette for Colette. Nicky told her not to bother, he'd go back to his room, it was easier. Colette saw how her mother longed for him to stay: brightly she encouraged him, touching her hand lightly on his neck under his hair, smiling up into his face. *Colette doesn't mind, really!* But Nicky pulled away from her, though not unkindly. He said he was still shattered, it was better if he was in his own bed. Colette could guess what effort it took for Phyllis not to show her hurt at his rejection: *Of course, darling, do whatever suits you.* She was so afraid of boring him, becoming a drag. But Colette was relieved, she was wary at first of sleeping so close to her mother and Nicholas in bed together. In those weeks after he came back from

Paris her antagonism to Nicholas was renewed. They couldn't be gracious to each other, their situation was too awkward. And there was an asymmetry built into it: he had carried off her mother and ruined Colette's life, hadn't he? She was only a peripheral inconvenience to him. Sometimes he seemed to pick up the same chaffing, dismissive tone that he'd taken with her at Otterley. When he did that she saw through, for a moment, the new gloss of his sophistication, to something more rivalrous and childish in him.

Barbara Jones said that Colette shouldn't be hanging around in Phyllis's flat. She was a child, she was still at school. Didn't Phyllis know she needed somewhere quiet, to concentrate on her revision? Phyllis made a face of mock despair. — But this is my home, what am I supposed to do? Colette takes no notice of me anyway. If I tried to stop her coming, it would only make her more determined.

— Some of those ones you call your friends, I wouldn't let them past my door, I don't trust them. Aren't you afraid she'll get mixed up with the wrong sort?

— But you know me, Barb. The trouble is that I like the wrong sort, they're so much more fun. And I'm hardly in a position to tell her to be sensible, am I? All I want is for her to be happy.

Barbara hissed through her teeth. — Happy!

— What's wrong with happy?

Phyllis had been sure that Colette and Barbara wouldn't get on. Barbara would surely disapprove of the eye make-up Colette wore, and her flattening remarks. In Grenada, before she moved to live with her uncle and aunt in town, she had walked barefoot every day to a one-room schoolhouse, four miles there and back in her green-and-brown uniform. How could she appreciate Colette's dismissing her education so carelessly? Barbara was unbending and judgemental, and Colette didn't make any effort to be liked. She was mostly broodingly silent in company, then from time to time – with that gesture of tossing her head back and wrinkling her nose, even though she'd left off her glasses – said something which was meant to be striking, but more usually fell flat or trailed away into a mumble. When Barbara said that if Colette needed peace and quiet she could come to study in her room at the Everglade, Phyllis didn't think she'd take her up on the offer.

But Colette walked round to the Everglade with her bag of books from school, one evening when she knew Barbara was at home. Barbara was revising for her exams too; just imagine, Colette thought, if somebody's life depended on your remembering a diagram of the oesophagus. The young woman's stern discipline, her head bent down over her books, weary from her day's work on the ward, seemed admirable and moving, simplifying. They didn't talk together much – and Colette left to go back to her mother's as soon as Barbara wanted to go to bed. But when Barbara put the kettle on mid-evening, they allowed themselves then a lull in concentration. Setting down a cup of sweet tea on the desk, she put her other hand on Colette's forehead, feeling for her temperature. — You OK, girl? Eat biscuits, you too skinny. Are you working too hard? I'm jealous of my sick patients sometimes. I think, you come on out of that bed, lazy so-and-so, and I'll just hop into it in your place, behave a lot better in it too. Imagine nothing to do all day but lying there with your eyes closed.

— But I suppose they're suffering, said Colette doubtfully.

— I suppose they are.

She was reading Colette's revision notes over her shoulder. — Repeal of the Corn Laws, sliding scale, Speenhamland system: I knew all those. I studied all that too.

— Really? But why? It's not very relevant to where you come from, is it?

Barbara clicked her tongue and said she was a British citizen just like Colette. It was all part of her history: Castlereagh, Peel, Disraeli, the lot of them. — I had a natural aptitude for that kind of thing. To begin with I taught myself out of my cousin's books, he wasn't interested in it. Then he died anyway.

— Gosh, that's so sad, I'm sorry. How did he die?

— Cut his foot, blood poisoning, age thirteen. But without it I'd have never got to high school: I wouldn't be standing here now. My uncle found the money for my education after my cousin died. He was the last boy in the family.

She warned Colette against getting too mixed up with her mother's new friends. — Be careful with that crowd, don't let them take advantage. You know most men are looking out for what they can get. They don't care what happen after.

Colette had no intention of taking Barbara's advice, or being careful. She believed there was no safe passage across the threshold into experience and the real life awaiting her. Yet she submitted gratefully to the calm of those evenings when they studied together, the atmosphere of dedication to achievement and the future. The examinations were only a game to her, but she understood they meant something quite different to Barbara: for her they were an iron law, or a barrier across her path, which it would take all her strength to force open. She couldn't afford, as Colette could, to throw herself away. And this wasn't because Barbara was more timid or hidebound than Colette in her personality. It was simply a material fact, rooted in their different histories, the unfair accident of their different circumstances.

When her exams came round in May and June, Colette wasn't worried. At the last minute she topped up on details – quotations from poetry, sample glaciation features, dates for the accession of states to the Zollverein, the German customs union, and so on. She knew how to spread this information around, to make herself look expert and confident. It wasn't the same in maths and science, but she hoped she could scrape through those. She told Phyllis that when they were over she was going to leave school, and get a job and a place to live – but not in Otterley. Phyllis asked if she'd talked about this with her father.

— It's not his business anyway. What does he care?

— You're his little muffin, Col, don't you remember?

— He's changed his mind, he doesn't think that now.

At the end of one party night in summer, a few of Phyllis's friends slept over on her floor. Colette was on a mattress in the kitchenette, and her mother went off in the morning to an appointment at the antenatal clinic. When Colette got up eventually, everyone else had gone except Nicky, who was sprawled diagonally across the bed, face down, dirty bare feet sticking out of one end of a mess of sheets and blankets, his long narrow back with jutting shoulder blades exposed at the other end. The room was stuffy with sleep and smoke. Colette rattled up one of the windows, letting in the morning air, and then stood contemplating him, holding her sponge bag and towel on her way to the bathroom; she was wearing as her nightdress that same shirt which didn't quite cover her bottom. Nicky snorted once and broke wind, oblivious, face buried in the pillow. But her gaze must have tugged at him eventually, in whichever deep recesses of dreaming he was burrowed, because he roused and turned over on his back, opened his eyes and looked at her, as blankly as a sleepwalker.

Experimentally before his empty gaze, Colette lifted her shirt up over her head, dropped it on the floor. She was still inexperienced, and hadn't actually yet shown her new, adult nakedness to anybody; there had been some kissing and fumbling outside the pub, that was all, with those High School boys. For a long moment, as Nicky looked at her and she looked at him looking, it was as though they contemplated each other without barriers, as if the air between them were stripped of all the social and personal complications which in everyday life prevented them from seeing each other. It was almost, but not quite, not sexual. Then in the next instant he was scrambling up into a sitting position, kicking backwards away from her, pulling the sheets up around his chest defensively, dismayed. — For fuck's sake, Colette! What do you think you're doing?

Colette laughed. She picked up the shirt from the floor but didn't put it back on, and made her way out to the bathroom, swinging the shirt around like a striptease, waggling her behind at him jauntily. It was all just for fun, it was all a game. But if he'd invited her to join him in his bed, she would have done it.

———

Phyllis was huge, she couldn't sleep. She contemplated her distorted shape in the mirror one night, in the grey light from the street. When she'd been pregnant with the other two, she'd never looked so boldly at herself — she'd smuggled away her changing body as you were supposed to, disguising it under pretty smocks. She was in awe now at this eruption of raw life, swelling her like an animal. Nicky was fairly repulsed by it, and didn't want to make love to her in this condition; when she tried to show him the baby bulging and quaking inside her, he said it made him queasy.

She didn't care what Nicky thought. Somehow, in getting pregnant, she'd arrived past the point where everything depended on him: she loved him but also saw him more clearly, in a cool impersonal light. She saw how young and irresponsible he was, powering ahead according to his own purposes — and how easily she could become a burden to him. Also, now that they lived in daily proximity, she was more aware of his immaturity. He dropped his dirty clothes on the floor where he took them off, and made a fuss if he got ill with the slightest cold. Sometimes he moped or sulked, or was plaintive if his confidence needed bolstering. She tried to avoid falling into a pattern of mothering him. When she guessed he was going after some other woman, she couldn't help her jealousy. Imagining them together, delighting in each other's youth, taking their pleasure tenderly, shutting her out, made her feel sick and frantic. But she wouldn't show this weakness to him and she didn't accuse him, not after the first time when they'd quarrelled over Liz. Nicky didn't even like Liz anyway. He said he couldn't read her poetry, and since they'd slept together he'd been avoiding her. Phyllis found ways to hold back from her own desperation: in a part of her mind she could see that his subterfuges and bungling untruths were comical. And they could still be happy together. Often they were, they liked each other.

And anyhow, she thought about other men. Her life wasn't over yet; she reflected ruefully on all those years when she'd been a faithful wife. There was Sam Harris, for instance, who was handsome and such a gentleman, tipping his hat to her or lifting heavy lids when he looked up to smile at her: she loved his pencil-thin moustache and the disabused, weary comedy of his talk. And then there was Paul. Paul was such a shit, you couldn't expect anything good from him, but it was true that he was the real artist out of all of them; he and Sam were the real artists. If Paul was attractive, it was because of the power that came with this. Paul and Sam were closer to her own age, too. Something could happen one day, with one of them.

In low moments Phyllis was afraid of what she was bringing the new baby into, without a husband to help her, exposing it to danger and dirt like a poor woman's child. She remembered the cosseted world of childbirth in the nursing homes, flowers in every room, the layette of folded white shawls and perfect soft vests and bootees and little dresses. But in fact those places had seemed glib and fake when she was in them; the staff had left her to suffer alone for hours. She didn't want that cosseting any longer.

Colette's schoolfriends in Otterley were bored now the exams were over. The summer days these girls and boys spent congregated in the park stretched out to such thinness that their limbs ached with tedium and they made a nuisance of themselves, running around on the grass and screaming as if they were still children. They needed the keeper to come out from his brick hut and shout at them, call a halt to it. Somebody had a transistor and they took turns gluing their ears to its tinny leakage of pop music; they were mad about the Beatles and the Byrds. When 'Mr. Tambourine Man' came on one of the girls wept, though in school she was stolid and unromantic, with a short thick body and hair in mousebrown bunches; now her face worked helplessly and was ugly with emotion. When they lay with faces turned up at the sky, virulently coloured begonias and pelargoniums from the flower beds were printed on their closed lids. They were pent up in an interminable anteroom; ostensibly they were waiting for their results, but soon they'd exhausted that suspense in imagination, as if it were already past. Hungrily they looked up at every new arrival through the park gates. When Colette described things that happened at her mother's, or told Nicky's stories from France, they didn't sound true, even to her. She told them she'd met someone who knew Paul McCartney. Susan Smithfield said she wanted to come to one of these parties.

— They're not exactly parties, Colette said warily. — You wouldn't like it.

Susan insisted that she would. She had lost some of her lustre in these last weeks in the park. In the old days she would have filled up her holidays with sports practice, wholly absorbed in her role as netball champion. Now this no longer fitted her exactly, there was some new shortfall between her self and her gift. As if a spell had broken, her abrupt movements, which had been commanding, were now jarring, her clear skin was roughened, she'd done something to her bright hair which made it lank. When she met Colette on the station platform, to catch the train into London, she was wearing an outfit so wildly inappropriate that she could almost get away with it as fancy dress: a low-necked green satin evening gown, knee-length, that she must have borrowed from her mother, under a white bolero jacket. In a gesture towards her old style, she had her brother's Boy Scout lanyard tied around her neck. Her expression was less pleasure-seeking, more grimly set upon the kind of adventure pirates or intrepid explorers might have. The burden of steering Susan through her mother's world weighed upon Colette: she warned her about the pregnancy, and Nicky. — It's all quite weird, she said. — It's freaky. Don't be freaked out.

Susan's look was trusting, she put herself in Colette's hands. They went first to Phyllis's flat, where a few friends had come round to eat her curry served with rice and sliced banana, sultanas, mango chutney. Dumbly, Susan sat on one of the little dance-studio chairs, eating out of sheer shock, Colette suspected, asking politely for more water, dropping curry on her green dress and rubbing at it resignedly with a handkerchief. No one was interested in her, although they glanced in passing at the dress. — You didn't tell me there were darkies here, Susan said in an undertone – not resentfully, but as if this were an astonishing discovery. Colette advised her not to call them that. — So what should I call them then?

— Well, they're just people, aren't they? Don't call them anything.

Some of her mother's friends huddled in the kitchenette after they'd eaten, and Colette guessed that they were taking drugs, dropping acid probably – though not Phyllis herself, because of the baby. When Susan asked what was going on, she said they were making coffee. Then they all went out together because there was a free concert, on the wasteland where so many houses had been demolished to make room for the new road, the Westway. Passing the entrance to the tube station, Colette said they could go home now if Susan wanted, but she shook her head wordlessly with a distracted air. It was a surprise when they broke out from the looming tall terraces crowding the sky into a great emptiness of open space. The evening light was grey-blue, intensity gathering in the purplish clouds, the brick side of one house soaking up orange from the west, its windows flaring. The green dress gleamed like a phantasm, and when Susan tripped and fell her bolero was dirtied, she cut one knee.

A bonfire burned in the distance, its colour weak to begin with, sapped by the drama in the sky; as they made their way towards it the sky lost its light and the fire gathered force, its brightness and intent roar and crackling drawing them on across the rough ground where stubby thorn bushes had taken root, and poor, tufty grass grew among chunks of brick wall, mounds of stones, broken concrete stuck with rusted iron, enamel sinks, dumped refrigerators and mattresses. Colette confided to Susan that dead donkeys had been found in this place, and a dead woman once, and tramps lived here; she nodded as if all this were only likely. Their faces in the lurid light appeared smaller and more definite, like faces in a play. They seemed to be in a ruined city, or at a frontier: Colette half expected to be stopped by a sans-culotte with a musket, asked for a password. A reedy long line of music from a saxophone floated over to them, and the beating of rival drums. Someone said that the bonfire was built of sleepers stolen from the railway yards; their great scaffolding was black against the flames consuming it, shifting down into the fire and then collapsing in it, crashing in explosions of sparks, making everyone jump back shrieking. There were more people than you saw at first, and as they penetrated into the edge of the crowd it thickened behind them, with more and more arriving. Bands were competing in the vast space, which diffused the sound thrown out by the piled-up speakers – free jazz with a poet chanting, a rock band tuning up, ska music. The girls moved in and out of the different spheres of sound, distinctive as different rooms inside the spaces of the night.

Phyllis and Nicky were hanging on to each other, Phyllis balancing her heaviness on his arm and directing his aimlessness at the same time, Nicky lifting his feet up exaggeratedly as he stepped forward, explaining that he could feel the tarmac of the new road pushing up underneath them through this thin skin of grass and rubble. Colette found him irritating when he was high, with his expression unfocused and vacuous. Grabbing Susan's hand so as not to lose her, she pulled her away into the crowd. *Be careful you two,* Phyllis said warningly. *Don't miss the last train, don't forget.* Colette was disappointed in the first minutes they were left alone, anonymous among the walls of turned backs and the closed circles of friends swaying and partying together: they were in the mass but not of it – and even though she felt invisible, she was afflicted with self-consciousness. The smell of pot was everywhere, everyone was smoking or high, apart from them. Boldly she stopped a guy wearing beads and waving a joint around; he handed it over. *Peace and love, girls,* he actually said.

They passed it back and forth between them and as the pot took hold something loosened in Susan that had been fixed and tightly wound. She gave one barking laugh, threw her head back and shook it as if she were clearing it, and then led the way – shoving and dodging between strangers, dragging Colette after her – out in front of the ska band, where people were dancing. Susan at least had never known what self-consciousness was. Her dancing style was peculiar, for someone who'd been so graceful in netball: absorbed, frowning, stooped as if she were watching her own feet, shaking her fists not quite in time to the beat, Boy Scout lanyard flying in all directions. It seemed a dedicated and private ritual, she didn't need anyone to dance with. Nonetheless a guy began dancing opposite her, following her moves: skinny and white, with his shirt unbuttoned, spirals and peace signs drawn in greasepaint on his bare chest. Susan acknowledged him with a glance and a brusque nod. — Love the dress, he shouted. — Can I call you Queenie?

Stately, she granted him permission. Colette jogged uneasily up and down beside them for a while: no one came to dance with her and she felt herself shut out from the ska beat, its invitation to pleasurable abandon. Perhaps she didn't have abandon in her body, only this stiff clumsy resistance; even Susan Smithfield knew better than she did how to submit to it. When she mentioned the last train Susan only shrugged, and Colette said she could crash tonight at the flat if she wanted to, Phyllis wouldn't mind. Without much interest Susan responded – that was an idea, she might well do that. — I'll come back to find you later, Colette said, but thought that her friend hardly heard her. When she was making her way alone through the crowd she felt more free, although also more frightened; instead of lifting her above the scene, the pot made her feel lost inside it. She thought that individuals pushing past her, not seeing her, had faces as marked and haggard as masks, or alight with sly purpose, audacious; some seemed to come from a different world than anyone she'd met at her mother's – these weren't middle-class rebels, they were more like gypsy wanderers or adepts in a secret street life, at home in this underworld. And yet her own mother also belonged here. Everyone else knew how to be carried along in this turbulent river, while Colette watched from the dry land of herself. She felt the river's pull and its powerful romance, along with its terror, but didn't know how to let herself into it. A dirty-white swollen moon rose above the waste ground and shed its pallid light on the scene; she stood listening to the broken music of the jazz band. To steady herself she rehearsed in her mind the order in which German states had joined the Zollverein.

— Is it you? someone said from beside her. It was Paul the sculptor, whom she'd met first in Nicky's room. — Aren't you the child who came looking for Phyl Fischer? Are you allowed to be out here on your own?

It was a great relief to be seen at last: she was flooded with gratitude. Paul seemed suddenly like someone she'd always known, with his flopping jet hair and compressed dense scowling features. He cultivated as a style his indifference to his appearance: collar of his workman's jacket turned up to his ears, hands in his pockets, line of his jaw bristling with beard growth, wolfish in the dark. — I'm not a child, Colette said. — And I wasn't on my own, I was with a friend. But she seems to have got off with somebody.

He said, wasn't that what always happened to one's friends.

— I don't know. I've never been to anything like this before.

— Do you know your way home? Where is home? Don't you live in Otterley?

Colette said she didn't want to go home. — If I go home now I'll feel defeated, as if nothing's happened to me.

He was amused and offered her a cigarette, said it might not be such a bad thing if nothing happened. They were submerged in the straining, screeching jazz, and had to lean in close to hear each other. What was her name? he asked her. He'd forgotten it. When she bent her head to where Paul cupped the flame of his lighter, his brown stubby hands, with cracked, broad, childish nails, were an illumined cave, and she tasted his salty sour skin on her cigarette afterwards. He also had whisky in a flask. — You see, you've forgotten, she reproached him, — what it feels like to be in my position. Which is no position. It's an un-position.

He blew out smoke sceptically, avuncular. — So what does it feel like?

— As if I'm wasting my life. The minutes are racing away somewhere without me. It makes me desperate.

— And how old are you? Fifteen?

— Sixteen: seventeen in October. But age doesn't change anything, does it? I could die tomorrow.

— You're probably statistically more likely to die if you stay out here tonight.

— Why, is it dangerous?

He looked as if he might have lectured her on self-respect, then changed his mind. — Actually it's fucking boring. I've been watching something called a Destruction of Art Symposium.

— That sounds funny.

— It wasn't funny. It was depressing. These people appal me: moustaches and kaftans, intellectual level more or less vegetable, thinking they're going to change the world by destroying art.

— I suppose you love art more than anything.

— Jesus Christ, Paul said, laughing. — You're bringing it all back to me. What it's like being sixteen, how fucking horrible. If you really are sixteen.

— I really am! she said indignantly. — Almost seventeen. And anyway, what's wrong with loving art?

He dragged his hand in mock despair down the flesh of his face, but she knew he didn't mind really, she was entertaining him. — People who think they love art disgust me, he said. — Art's just work to me. It's how I make my money.

— I know you don't mean that really.

— Then you don't know anything. Because I do.

— All right, I'm open to your opinion, I'll think about it. In fact I worry sometimes that I don't really have opinions of my own, I'm just waiting for someone else to tell me what to think.

— Take it from me about the art lovers.

— I had a crush on a teacher at school, Mrs Bernhardt, and had to wait to hear what she thought about anything before I could make up my own mind. I think it's wearing off now, at least with her. Probably I'll transfer my loyalty to somebody else. I could transfer it to you if you like.

Alarmed, he said that he'd rather she didn't.

— Wouldn't it be wonderful to have someone hanging on to your every word? But I suppose you get that anyway. You must have loads of disciples. I know my mum is one.

— What, Phyllis?

— She loves your work.

He said that her mother hadn't the first clue about his work, and Colette was gratified, swigging more of his whisky; her consciousness went swooping overhead like a hawk, looking down on herself talking intimately in this crowd, inside the music's noise and the flickering hellish firelight, with this real grown-up man, an artist. When she said that she dreaded growing up to be like her mother, he said he doubted that she would.

— You mean because I don't look like her?

— Not just that.

— I know what you're thinking now. You're thinking how women always want to turn the conversation around so that it's about themselves and their looks. *Do you like me? Am I pretty?*

He conceded that he might have been thinking something along those lines.

— But do you though? Just out of interest. Do you think I'm pretty?

That question wasn't interesting, he said. Asking, she disappointed him. But if she wanted his opinion, she wasn't exactly pretty, no.

— So I'm plain.

— I didn't say that.

— Would you ever draw me?

— You wouldn't like it if I did.

— I swear I would. Even if I ended up as just two squares and a triangle, I'd see what you meant. I want to *see* myself, through someone's eyes.

— You'll grow out of that.

— But it's too ghastly when people tell you you'll grow out of things.

The band took a break and Paul began shifting his feet as if he were cold, glancing over her shoulder while they talked. Colette had no idea whether she was cold or not; she was wearing her PVC mac, her legs were bare, perhaps they were shaking. This man was losing interest in her: she had been a sideshow, a quirky child whose odd remarks were briefly comical. — Anyway, I'm off home, he said. — I think I've got everything I can out of the Destruction of Art. Why don't you go and look for Phyl and Nicky? I saw them, I think they're still somewhere around.

— They don't want me.

— Better go home then, back to Otterley. Won't your daddy be worried?

She nodded and said she'd go, OK. But when Paul began to move away through the crowd, she wound after him. He turned round abruptly, frowning to put her off. — Are you following me?

Colette said that she wasn't, but kept on following.

— What is this? What do you want? Leave me alone.

— I want something to happen, she said. — I want to come home with you.

— You can't. I don't like little girls. I'm not interested in babysitting.

Colette said she wasn't a little girl, she was just herself. Juliet in Shakespeare was only thirteen. And she added that she was sure he'd have taken her home if he'd just met her randomly, hadn't known she was anyone's daughter. Swearing at her, he turned his back and resumed pushing through the crowd; she followed after, shoving past the knots of people, apologising. Once or twice, Paul looked round for her, exasperated, over his shoulder. Then when they were away from the crowd, and their footsteps were sounding on the roads beyond the wasteland, he paused to wait for her under a street lamp. He reached out as she came closer, gripping her arm so that it hurt; with his other hand under her jaw, he tilted her face towards him, examining it deliberately in the light, unsmiling. — I'm not one little bit romantic, he said in a harsh, hostile voice. — If you're trying to pin some romantic shit on me. I don't have love affairs.

She said she wasn't trying to pin anything on anyone.

— But you know what will happen if you come home with me.

She nodded and then he kissed her, as if he were testing something or meant to disabuse her of any illusion: these kisses were hard and perfunctory, derisory. Colette had been kissed by a couple of boys, never before by a grown man, whose mouth was so hot and tasted so fiercely. She melted and was shot through from head to foot by desire, so that she could hardly stand. If Paul had said anything caressing or seductive, or if he'd tried to flatter her, then the moment would have been spoiled.

— And what about your friend?

— She's fine, she's with some guy.

— Do you know who the guy is?

— He looked kind. He had peace signs drawn on his chest.

— Oh well, that's all right then, with the peace signs. He must be OK.

Colette laughed. — He really did look fine. He looked weedy.

— They're the worst.

————

And actually Susan Smithfield did go missing for thirty-six hours, her parents had the police out, but she turned up at home in the end more or less unharmed, saying she'd stayed overnight with friends she'd met. Mrs Smithfield telephoned Roger when Susan was safely home, to rant at him. Apparently Susan had told them she was going with the Fischers to a classical concert; now she was forbidden to leave the house for all of the rest of the summer. Mrs Smithfield said she understood that things were difficult for Roger, without his wife, but did he have any idea what his daughter was getting up to when she went into town? It was more or less an orgy, from what they could gather from Susan. Drugs, people of all sorts, no kind of supervision and in some no-man's-land, Susan couldn't even describe exactly where it was. Perhaps Roger really didn't care what his own daughter did, but if anything had happened to Susan – Mrs Smithfield raised her voice, wavering on the brink of tears – she would have held him personally responsible, in a court of law.

Roger was diplomatic and conciliatory, he put all his old skills to use. But he was irritated, put into this absurd position. Didn't Kay Smithfield remember being young? These women lived such sheltered lives, believing they were insured by their class and respectability against danger or loss – or even anything ruffling the surface of their suburban routine. No wonder their children revolted. Of course, he had to make a scene with Colette, interrogate her about the concert, ask how she managed to get separated from her friend, and whose house it was that Susan had gone back to. But why should she have responsibility for any other girl? The scene meanwhile was hateful to Colette, because she felt the indifference behind her father's performance of an outraged parent. *He doesn't care,* she thought. In fact, Roger rather admired his daughter for her self-possession in the face of his assault. Jean had encouraged him to see things from Colette's point of view, and sometimes in a flash of illumination he could perceive, inside this sour-faced teenager, the clever, stubborn little girl whose company he'd loved. Probably, however, they could no longer be friends. She had cast off into her own life, and he must guard himself against her adult apprehension of him. He had not liked her seeing him humiliated, when Phyllis left.

One evening Susan telephoned, when Colette happened to be in Otterley: she was picking up a few things, because she was moving in with Paul. Paul didn't know she was moving in, but he hadn't objected to her staying over so far; Roger didn't know about Paul, but he guessed there was someone. He called Colette to the telephone and she took the receiver with a stony face, then pressed his study door shut against him, closing him out while she began to speak. She climbed with the telephone, so as not to be audible, into the kneehole of his desk, where she used to hide when she was little. Now she could hardly fit inside it and had to stoop her head at an awkward angle, cradling the telephone in her skirt.

— Thank God my parents have gone out for once, said Susan in a constrained voice, as if she too were speaking from some place of concealment. — To play lousy bridge. And I'm going mad, penned up here with only my brother – he's sort of like their Nazi informant, literally paid to spy on me. That's why I'm having to call you from the downstairs cloakroom, so that Jeremy can't hear – the flex just about reaches, but I have to lie on the floor with my head against the door. I'm pretending I've got my period, that keeps him out of the way. I told your father I was Linda, otherwise I knew he wouldn't let me talk to you. How are you anyway?

— More important, how are you? They said that you came home unharmed. Are you unharmed? If so, that's disappointing.

— Why, aren't you?

— Harmed, definitely.

Susan gave a low wolf whistle, appreciative: this was more like her old sporty self. — Really? Harmed – who by?

— A guy I met who's a sculptor. He's much older.

— Mine's called Stewart, and we did do quite a lot, but we didn't go the whole way.

— Well we did.

— I wish that I had, now that I'm locked up here. I might as well. Still, you might be preggers.

— He took care of it. And I've been the whole way over and over, since then.

— You shouldn't trust them to take care. But God: so what's it like?

— It's amazing. I can't describe it.

— No, you have to.

— I can't. You have to find out for yourself.

— Anyway, I'm still in touch with Stewart. He writes to me at Linda's, these ten-page letters all about living on the land and things, and I write back to him, though not ten pages. We're going to get together somehow, as soon as I'm in the sixth form. I'll tell them I'm going in for lessons and then I'll go to his place.

Susan murmured that she had to go. Before Colette rang off she could hear Jeremy banging on the cloakroom door. — You're not *allowed* to use the phone. I'll tell on you!

Sometimes during that summer Colette visited her aunt Anne in Highbury, where Hugh was camouflaging himself to fit in with the gang of his older cousins. But she spent most of her time in Paul's room in the Everglade. Enthusiastically she adapted to Paul's routines: they stayed up all night with friends, then didn't get out of bed until the afternoon. When he went to his studio to work, or to the foundry, she fell back into magnificent bottomless sleep – she could sleep twelve or fourteen hours a day. She would have cooked for him, but he only had one gas ring. Then she joined the Notting Hill Gate public library, and climbed into bed with her books, reading with an exhilarating consciousness that she wasn't accountable to anyone any longer, for what she thought or knew. Paul wasn't a reader. It was Nicky Knight who recommended things and lent them to her: Herbert Marcuse and Lukács and Thomas Szasz; the *Marat/Sade*, Ginsberg's 'Howl', *The Making of the English Working Class*.

Certain elements in Paul's life were a surprise to her. She had had no idea at first that he had money: his room was austere, with only an iron-framed bed in it, an ancient broken-springed armchair, and a bronze crow hunched, untidily disconsolate, in the fireplace. But he took her out to expensive restaurants, and parties at the houses of his wealthy, fashionable patrons. He bought her clothes too, things she'd never have dreamed of choosing, from exclusive shops where she was struck dumb with shyness, turning round slowly when he instructed her, under the critical gaze of the assistants. Although Paul was indifferent to his own appearance, he liked Colette to be glamorous, in clothes that showed off her young body. When they went out with gallery people, or the ones who bought Paul's work, she pretended to be bored because she didn't know what to say. She watched him play up to the role they required of him: the untamed working-class genius, contemptuous and dangerous.

Phyllis was odd about the whole thing with Paul, curt and disapproving. — Seriously though, Mum, Colette remonstrated, — you can't get at me about this. I mean, you just can't, after what you did yourself.

— I'm sorry, but to me you're still a child, Phyllis said infuriatingly. — You're out of your depth. I know something about men, and Paul's not anyone to mess around with. I'm afraid for you, that's all. I'm your mother and I don't want you to get hurt.

— You're just jealous! Colette flung at her. — Because he likes me!

But Phyllis couldn't resist the dresses, the Ossie Clark and the Zandra Rhodes. She sighed when Colette put them on for her, touching the fabric and the seams yearningly. There was a comical contrast between her daughter's new stylishness and her own clumsy figure, huge with her pregnancy. — Oh, Col, you look wonderful, she said, with tears in her eyes as if she conceded something, giving way to youth. Colette's O-level results arrived, she telephoned home from the phone box, Roger read them out. She'd passed everything except chemistry and got four A's, which was better than she'd hoped, but she didn't really care. It was as if her old life carried on in the far distance, miniature people with their miniature fretting.

In her new full-sized real life, Paul did draw her eventually. He posed her naked, sitting on a hard chair in his filthy studio, which smelled of mouldy wet rags and cold clay; he switched on the electric fire for her. She was perfectly happy. *Open your legs. Wider, like that, wide apart. Feet flat to the floor. Now keep still. There.*

EIGHT

Marnie took a long time finding Phyllis, to tell her that Nicholas Knight was Roger's son. She wanted to deliver the blow to her sister-in-law, and see her reel from it – if Phyllis didn't know already. Even in all her righteousness, however, Marnie shied away from the blow's finality, appalled quite genuinely by these murky twists of fate. It wasn't *strictly* incestuous, she reassured herself: but it wasn't the kind of thing that happened to good people. Perhaps Hugh had made a childish mistake? Also, Marnie was afraid of her brother – if it were true about Nicholas, then Roger must know it, and he would resent her interfering. Simply, anyway, she didn't know where to find Phyllis, or Nicholas. So she put off her project of disclosure for months on end. Then one night in September when she was in London, at the theatre with a friend because the Guildford paper sometimes asked her to review for them, she bumped into Peter Knight, whom she hadn't seen for so many years. Jean wasn't with him, thank goodness; the woman on his arm was much younger, with coppery lacquered hair. Tactfully, Marnie didn't acknowledge her, so that they didn't have to be introduced. Peter had dried up in his years abroad, she thought, into a dull stick of a man. Because they had nothing to say to each other once they'd exchanged their opinions on the production of *Major Barbara*, she asked after his son, and Peter told her which papers Nicholas was writing for. Next morning she telephoned the office of one of these papers, predictably left-wing, and they gave her Nicholas's address in Ladbroke Grove. Now she had no excuse not to go there, and look for Phyllis.

She wasn't afraid of penetrating into these regions of darkest London – when she was a girl she'd worked for a while at a City Mission in a place like this, providing sports clubs and seaside outings for deprived children. Contemplating the dizzying staircase in the Everglade foyer, she decided to take the lift, clashing the folding double gates behind her: it groaned and wheezed on the way up, then stopped unaccountably between the third and fourth floors. Marnie stood quite motionless for a while in the deep silence, inside the little box of varnished wood, gripping the ivory duck's-head handle of her umbrella, refusing to give way to panic. Of course had the halt lasted more than three or four minutes, she'd have had to demean herself like anyone else: she'd have had to press the alarm, shout out for help, rattle the gates, kneel on the floor and beat it with her fists or scrabble at the wall. Fortunately, when, after a pause, she pushed the button again for the fifth floor, the lift restarted. *Yea, though I walk in death's dark vale, yet will I . . .* The words popped into her head, a memento from childhood, despite her agnosticism.

When she knocked at number 53, a woman came to the door who wasn't Phyllis: across her shoulder Marnie viewed a scene of just the sort of squalor she'd anticipated – bare walls, an unmade bed, bottles and glasses and dirty ashtrays strewn among clothes and books on the bare boards. It was hot up here under the roof.

Nicky was out, the woman said, he was delivering something. She was Liz. No, she didn't live here, but Nicky didn't mind her working in his room if he was out and it was too chaotic at her place. She was going through a sticky patch with a friend she lived with, a woman friend. And she had to have quiet in order to write, because she was a poet. Oh, that explains it, Marnie thought. She drank in the other woman with greedy curiosity. Liz was probably only thirty, but her thin face with its reddened eyelids and plucked eyebrows wasn't young, it was too knowing: Marnie saw herself reflected in it, the bulk of her and its absurdity and her plainness, which she carried about with her like a curse. Liz told her where Phyllis lived, only ten minutes' walk away. *On the first floor,* she said. *It's the door on the right. All these people come here looking for Phyllis, I can't imagine what they want her for.* The flicker of her quick false smile was teasing, and Marnie flushed. She used the staircase on the way down.

Phyllis's front door was open when she pushed it; in the weak light of a bare bulb, as Marnie climbed to the first floor, the stairwell's dun-brown paintwork seemed to express Phyllis's fall from grace. So it was a surprise, when Phyllis opened the door after she knocked, to see the room behind her full of sunshine. Phyllis with her back to it was for a moment only a shape, imprecise, nonplussed. — Marnie, it's you!

— Do you mind if I come in?

— But what are you doing here?

Marnie barged in past her: the time for niceties was over. Phyllis was softly shapeless, wrapped in a flowered cotton housecoat with her hair dishevelled; Marnie only took in these details as signs of her decayed condition as an unfaithful wife. The way the big light room was arranged wasn't squalid exactly, but it smelled stuffy, and was as bare as the stage set for *Major Barbara*, whose modernity had so disappointed her and her friend. In the longueurs of a play, what to resort to, if the scenery wasn't a feast of detail? Marnie's taste in home décor, although she was abrupt and unfeminine in her person, inclined to cosiness. Breathing heavily, not taking off her mac, she sat down on the nearest flimsy chair, hoping it would take her weight. — Are you living here with Nicholas Knight?

Phyllis laughed, and said it was none of Marnie's business, but yes, she more or less was.

— Because if you are, then there's something you ought to know.

Portentously, Marnie clicked open her handbag, fished for her cigarettes and lit up, her hands unsteady, her glance wandering in the room but not seeing it – she might have noticed, otherwise, nappies and tiny vests drying on a clothes horse. Phyllis fetched her an ashtray, then perched uneasily on the edge of another chair. She'd thought she had escaped from this family and its virtuous indignations, which couldn't follow her here. When Marnie said she had reason to believe that Nicholas was Roger's son, Phyllis at first could hardly take in what she meant, and was only sick with rage against her ex-sister-in-law, for having any power to perturb her.

— Whatever are you talking about?

— The Knights were good friends of Mummy and Daddy's. That's why Cressing seemed the right place to send Roger when he was on leave in the war, needing rest and recuperation. But when he came home from there, to say goodbye before he went back to wherever he was going – he couldn't tell us where that was, of course – I *knew* something had happened. He was different.

— He loved the Knights' place, Phyllis said, still making light of it. — It meant a lot to him in those years, he's told me that. You're letting your imagination run away with you.

— Then Jean had a son. More or less nine months later, after all those years of the Knights' marriage being without children. She wasn't young – although poor Roger was just a boy, in years at least. And we had to hear of this new son through a friend of a friend. I don't think they even put a notice in *The Times*. From that point onward, the Knights cut off all communication; we'd used to see them two or three times a year. It was Jean who cut it off, of course. Women take care of that side of life, don't they? Keeping in touch, asking after family illnesses. Daddy was still alive then, we were looking after him at home. She should have written to ask about him, at least. Mummy didn't notice anything, she was too preoccupied. Only I noticed, and put two and two together.

— To make five, Marnie!

— Not that anyone could hold it against him, in the middle of the war. Roger risked everything for his country. He deserved any pleasure he could get, if there were women who'd let him have it.

— Your nature's soured, Phyllis said. — Stuck at home all day with your mother.

Marnie said she'd felt it her duty to let Phyllis know the truth, if Roger hadn't told her. Phyllis sat very still, looking down at her hands folded in her lap. — How sure are you?

— After the war, when he came home from Jerusalem once, I found a letter she'd sent him, among his things in his bag, with a photograph of the boy.

— You went rummaging for it.

— If I hadn't already guessed, I wouldn't have looked for it. He should have burned it, if he didn't want me to find it.

— It was still dishonourable.

— Dishonourable: that's rich! Coming from you.

— But Nicholas came to our house, Roger invited him.

— He invited his son. I suppose he wanted to know him.

The baby was stirring by this time in his carrycot, which was on the floor out of sight, on the far side of the bed. When Phyllis picked him up, squirming and hot against her in his bundle of shawls, Marnie scrambled to her feet, her expression stamped blank with shock. She seemed to take in all at once, then, the signs of the baby's disruption in the room: drying nappies, milky smells, knitted matinee jacket hooked over a chair, changing basket with its talc and pins, Phyllis's own still swollen and softened shape. She had given birth only ten days ago; when she clasped the baby to her, she could still feel him healing what was torn inside her. — So I'm too late, Marnie declaimed melodramatically.

— The baby's all right, though: even if what you've told me is true. Look at him! He's perfect.

Marnie backed off, dismayed, waving her cigarette in front of her. Superstitiously, she didn't like the floppy limbs of babies. — Does Roger know?

— I suppose that he knows, Colette must have told him.

— So even Colette is involved in this?

— She adores her new little brother.

— And has Nicholas told his mother?

Phyllis shrugged, almost sulkily. She hadn't asked Nicky if he'd told Jean anything about them: she hadn't wanted to know.

Stubbing out the cigarette end in the ashtray, Marnie conveyed the heavy finality of her judgement against Phyllis's new life; she trembled with disapprobation, gathering up her things – rain hat, umbrella, glum capacious handbag. Phyllis didn't try to offer her sister-in-law tea, or anything stronger to drink: why should she? Anyway, it would soon be time to feed the baby. Everything must give way to that. — What will you do? Marnie asked austerely, without looking at her.

Phyllis had years of practice, fending off Marnie's interference. — I'll talk to Roger.

So she telephoned Roger and arranged to visit him in their old home. She could leave baby Michael with Mrs Feinstein, with a bottle to warm up for him if he cried. While she waited to hear the truth from her husband, her mind beat back and forth in panic over what Marnie had told her. She didn't speak about it to anyone; she sent a note to Nicky, making excuses not to see him, saying she needed to rest. Nicky was drifting away from her in any case, appalled by the encroachment of the baby's needs. At one moment Marnie's story seemed a mere accident of biology, a joke, and not to count for much, even if it were true; the next moment its intimate complications trapped and sickened her. When she walked up from the station in Otterley the pavement glinted with wet evening light and was printed with the dark shapes of leaves; a melancholy autumn tang rose from the black soil in the gardens. She didn't see anyone she knew. Without the baby's warmth against her, she felt weightless and emptied, unreal; her footsteps sounding against the house fronts were echoes from a past life. Roger's shape showed vaguely behind the opaque glass in the porch door, and then he was fiddling with the chain on the door and the lock, opening up to her; she was wiping her feet on the mat, he took her coat.

They sat in the front room, which was chilly and felt denuded, although none of its furniture was changed. Phyllis would have liked to switch off the bleak central light: Roger looked furrowed and elderly in its glare, and she knew she was blowsily fat, after the birth. But it couldn't be her choice, to turn on any lamps: the place wasn't hers any longer. How thoroughly she'd broken up this home, which couldn't continue in its old form without her. Roger brought out the decanter of whisky and poured for both of them, although Phyllis only sipped at hers, it made her nauseous. She told him that Marnie had visited, and what she'd said. In his chair drawn up opposite hers – they'd both avoided choosing the old places where they used to sit – he stared down at the rug, with his elbows on his knees, head drooped between hunched shoulders. — I'm so sorry you had to learn about it from her. I didn't know she knew.

— Marnie worships you. She was bound to find out, if something so momentous had happened to you. But why didn't you tell me?

He hesitated before he spoke. — There was something infantilising, I see it now, in how I kept this story hidden from you. Perhaps it made a pattern between us, prevented us from being close. I'm sorry for it, now that it's too late. When I first learned you were with Nicholas, I was looking for you, I was going to tell you the truth. But then Colette brought the news that there'd be a child, and after all it seemed better to say nothing. I thought that you wouldn't find out.

— This horror can't have hurt my baby in any way?

If she meant in its heredity, Roger reassured her, then no, there was no danger of any kind. — But what a mess we've made between us, you and I, Phyl.

Phyllis had been braced to defend herself against her husband. On her way to meet him, she'd summoned an idea of his authority, implacable and punitive, mixed up with his role in the world of Establishment power. Now she was taken aback by how he bent his head before her, opening himself so easily; his kindness drew one sob out of everything loosened and raw inside her. Roger put a hand out to hold hers and she gripped it. — Poor old thing, he said, and she was grateful. It seemed a long time since anyone had taken care of her.

— And should I tell Nicholas too?

— I don't know. Will you continue in your relations with him?

She laughed then through her tears because he sounded like a tribunal: he assured her, contrite, that this was the last thing he intended. In the actual presence of his wife, Roger felt his resentment against her drop almost to nothing, an irrelevance. She seemed a stranger strayed into this room, whom he neither strongly liked nor disliked; with her face and figure bloated from childbirth, she was touching in the stark light, nervously assertive. He'd felt this impersonal generalised sympathy for her before, after the birth of the other two children. It seemed such an abject fatality for women – to be split apart in agony, bringing forth the new generation. Males were sealed at least into their single stupid bodies, which ended, thank God, when they did. This was bound to make essential differences between the sexes. — I believe that I can't continue, Phyllis said, in a flat, small voice. — In my relations with him, I mean. Under the circumstances.

— I suspect that you're right. I'm sorry. It poisons everything, my old secret.

She also tended to think, she went on, that she wouldn't say anything to Nicky. Roger agreed that perhaps, now there was a child, they had best go on keeping the whole thing under wraps. He was musing, almost with a civil servant's absence of rancour, on the detail of the case, to get it clear in his mind. — When Nicholas came to dinner here, was that the first time you'd met?

— Apart from when he was a boy, and we visited them.

— And you began seeing him after that evening?

— I thought I was so desperately in love with him. No doubt it all seems very exaggerated to you. You're bound to think it was just a romantic delusion, which I suppose it was at first. Things are different now. Nicky didn't want this child, you know. And also he sleeps around. He's very young. I know what you must be thinking, it's all so predictable. From your perspective I made such a fool of myself: I mean, even without this last complication. But I don't regret anything. Everything's changed for me.

— I can imagine that.

— Do you think that Jean Knight knows about us? Did Nicky tell her?

— I told her.

Phyllis pulled her hand away from his, startled, peering into Roger's face while he poured more whisky into their glasses. — You did? Oh, Roger! You're in touch with her. You're still in love with her. My goodness, of course you are. After all this time!

— Phyllis, I'm almost fifty. I'm not in love with anyone. Jean is a very dear friend.

— And Nicky is so like you: how could I have not seen that before? The way you both frown, for instance, it's the same – luxuriating in it. That thick fold of skin under your eyes, too, and your expression – both of you, sceptical as if you expect someone else to do something stupid.

— Is that my expression? I wish it weren't.

— Although of course Nicky's taller than you, and much thinner.

— I'm bound not to emerge flatteringly from this comparison.

— How comical though! Don't you think? That I should choose your own son, of all people, in my flight from you. Though none of it's Nicky's fault, Roger. I went chasing after him, nothing was his idea. You mustn't hold anything against him.

He said he would try not to.

— He admires you very much actually. And he hates his father, you know – I mean, Peter Knight. As if he's intuited something, I'm thinking now: that he isn't at all like him. And he's terribly fond of his mother, I've been quite jealous of her. But it never occurred to me that I should have been jealous of her in the past, too, on your account. In my innocence, when I met her all those years ago, I only thought that she was frumpy and sweet. It couldn't have occurred to me to fear her.

Roger was thinking how, for all these months without Phyllis, his house had been sealed in its thick silence. Her chatter broke through it now, like piercing a skin: what would it be to have the place raised up again, to its old pitch of bright domesticity? It might require great efforts on his part, to bring himself back from wherever he was deep buried now, hidden. But he only asked

272 | TESSA HADLEY

whether Phyllis was hungry: he had bought chops, he said, in case she wanted to eat. He could cook these for her.

— Really, chops? Can you cook? That's news. But I have to be back for the baby. I promised I'd catch the half-nine train at the latest.

— There's plenty of time. Or we could go out, if you'd rather.

— Not out, I'm not dressed for that. I'm not ready.

— It won't be cordon bleu. But I've peeled some potatoes.

Phyllis followed him into the kitchen, where he unwrapped the lamb chops from their bloody paper, with the butcher's calculation in biro on its corner. Looking round at the dingy ruins of her old empire, Phyllis wondered how she had ever been happy here: she felt a revulsion from its routines, its too-familiar faded lino, Formica-topped table, weighing scale, cake tins, spoons – and the red clock with its inexorable loud tick. Roger peppered and grilled the chops and they ate sitting in the kitchen, talking cautiously about the children: how Hugh was getting on at school, Roger's worries over Colette. Phyllis refrained from telling him too much about Paul. — If you wanted to, Phyl, Roger said, putting down the chop bone on his plate, wiping greasy fingers on a napkin, — you could come back to live with us here. I would be happy if you came back. And of course the children would. Perhaps we could find our way to living together again.

— Just as if nothing had happened.

— It would always have happened. But perhaps that would even be good for us, shake us up. Think about it. You don't have to decide now.

— Visiting your mother and Marnie every Sunday for lunch.

He shrugged. — We could stop going there. Or you needn't

come with me. My first loyalty would be to you, not to them. And I'd be happy to bring up this baby as my own. I suppose in a roundabout way I am responsible for him. Does he have a name? It is a boy?

— He's Michael – though I haven't registered him yet. I was thinking that perhaps I ought to put *Father unknown* on the certificate.

Roger was dismayed by this idea. — You mustn't do that. Think how it would stick to him in his future. You don't want your son thinking any less of his mother.

He didn't say, *not this son too, as well as Hughie.* — You could put my name.

Phyllis felt his reproach as a pang in her womb, although she protested that she didn't want to bring Michael up in Roger's old world, where such things as shame or illegitimacy counted.

— I suppose we do both live in the same world, though, you and I, he said.

She shook her head vehemently. — You haven't understood: I've changed. I can't go on pretending that everything's all right when it's not. Everything's insane. I couldn't come back here. When I think about DDT, or homelessness, or the class system, or the Bomb: I just refuse it, all of it.

— But if it's how things are, you can't refuse it. You're part of it.

— No I'm not. I can refuse it.

— Of course you could work to try and change it.

— I refuse to be any part of it.

The kitchen's atmosphere was thick with the fumes from the grilled meat: Roger sat brooding across the table, amid the remains of their dinner, biting his thumbnail, looking at her. She picked up their plates to put them by the sink, wanting to beat her fists against this bulk of her husband, his rationalism and realism blocking her way, like an immovable boulder on a path. Perhaps he was thinking that her mind was disordered, because she'd given birth. — The more urgent problem, she went on, — is how I can go on living there, in my place among my new friends, with this thing I've found out about him and you? How can I explain to Nicky, without telling him everything, that I don't want to see him any more? Especially when I do want to. I can't bear not to see him. But I suppose that I will bear it.

— If I could remove him for you, would that help?

She was alarmed, imagining the reach of her husband's power. — What do you mean, remove?

— Find something to take him out of the country. I mean some sort of journalistic assignment, something that would appeal to him. I have some contacts. That would earn you a breathing space at least.

— I suppose you've discussed this already with his mother.

Roger didn't deny it. Phyllis set down the plates on the draining board, for Mandy to wash in the morning. — Maybe it's not such a bad idea.

— I could certainly try.

— Shall I put on the kettle for tea?

Roger said that he would like tea. In the aftermath of their arranging to part for ever, they shared this odd interlude of married calm, half an hour or so, sitting together over their pottery mugs at the table. — Nicky ought to travel again, Phyllis said thoughtfully. — He's restless at home. And he ought to write a book. I think he's very talented.

— I think so too.

— Oh, do you keep up with him?

— How can you imagine that I wouldn't?

— Yes, of course, I see that. And you wouldn't mind how fiery he is, either.

— I'm not that old, Roger said, — that I can't remember being fiery myself, once.

And then, when it was time, he backed the car out of the garage, to run his wife down to the station to catch her train.

Nicky was queasy and full of dread, telling Phyllis he was going abroad for a year, travelling in Iran and Afghanistan. He had an advance from a good publisher, to write a book about it. To his surprise she took it rather well. They were lying in bed together in the winter's afternoon.

— I think it will be good for you, she said, stroking his face, smiling into his eyes.

— But will you be all right?

— Do you mean, without you? I should think so. I seem to have managed so far.

The room was stuffy from the paraffin heater, the baby was asleep in his carrycot, Phyllis had pushed a chair under the door handle to stop anyone intruding. They'd begun making love again, but without any of their old ardent excess, very gently and slowly at first; he pulled out of her too, because they didn't want another baby. Nicky still resented Michael. He felt smothered, whenever he came to see Phyllis, by the sight of the second-hand pram with its fringed sunshade, parked on the chequered tiles downstairs in the hall. And he tried to avoid the sight of the child guzzling on her breasts. When Michael jerked his head around to look at him, pulling away from the nipple so that the milk went everywhere, mouth falling open in its toothless grin, bubbling blue-white, Nicky thought that the baby was gloating over the man he had supplanted. He also knew that his jealousy was absurd, and made him babyish himself: particularly as he wasn't even being faithful to Phyllis. He was sleeping with a girl who'd been his supplier until she was busted in the King's Road. She had a Victoriana stall in the Portobello Market, and her father was a High Court judge.

In fact he was looking forward to getting away from the whole scene: it was not only this contracted world of the baby's room, with its tedious cycles of feeding and burping and shitting. There were too many idiots seeing UFOs, or believing they could change the world through reciting *Sgt. Pepper* lyrics backwards. *If all the governments dropped acid at the same time everything would be OK.* Nicky wanted something better than this and more authentic. Thirstily he imagined the landscapes he would travel through: bare rocky hillsides, dirt roads, dry steppe, stone dwellings built into precipitous cliffs – and the unfathomable rugged pared-down lives of the peasants. He remembered villagers treading carpets in an icy river in Iran, spreading them across the rocks to dry; remembered the huge-eyed children of his father's driver. This time he must take photographs: he'd got hold of a second-hand Leica. Phyllis seemed – as he propped himself on his elbow to watch her where she lay close beside him on the pillow, with her warm autumn colouring, the fine creases at the corners of her eyes and mouth, her smell like clean straw – to belong already to his past. He could hardly recall now how she'd appeared to him, when first she came to his room: so improbable, with her groomed sophistication like a woman in a magazine. He had been mesmerised then by her expensive perfume and husky worldly laugh, her bourgeois good manners and values. Their love affair had been the entrance, for Nicky, into his adulthood; he was piqued now by how ordinary their parting felt. He'd expected her at least to be astonished and desperate. Guiltily, wanting more emotion, he tugged lightly at her hair. — You won't miss me then?

— I will miss you so much, she said in a charged voice.

But she managed to contemplate him steadily, bravely, without flinching.

Everybody seemed to be leaving. Paul got an exhibition in New York and a couple of major commissions: he asked Colette to go over there with him to live for a year or two and she agreed. Her father, dismayed, tried to persuade her not to go. — What about your studies?

— I am studying, she said. — Just not at school.

— You mustn't waste your intelligence.

— I'm not wasting it.

Phyllis went on resenting her daughter's relationship with Paul; she complained about it to Barbara. — She trots round after him, swallowing everything he tells her. She's like his little pet.

Unexpectedly, though, Barbara didn't disapprove of Paul: this was a surprise to Phyllis, and to Colette as well. — He's not a fool, she said. — He's a big success. Why shouldn't she have a bit of it?

— She's too young to be in a serious relationship, let alone with a man like him.

— Too late for that, Mummy, Barbara said. — You should have thought of it, letting her mingle with that bad crowd at your place. She could have done worse. At least the man is serious, knows what he's doing. You wait, no need to worry about Colette. She's biding her time. Let her see the world.

Later that year it looked as though Barbara might go back to Grenada if she passed her SRN exams: she was offered a good job at a hospital in St George's. Then she won a ten-guinea prize in the UK, coming second in an essay competition, 'Ways in Which the Nursing Curriculum Could Be Improved', and she decided to stay when she got money from a War Memorial Fund to go on with her studies, specialising in surgical theatre. Sam talked about going back, but he didn't go. Sometimes he called in at Phyllis's flat in the evening and she fed him. He appreciated her cooking, she learned to make saltfish fritters and pepper sauce, they joked together like old friends and talked about politics. Phyllis said that she hoped everything was changing, but Sam predicted that when the white boys cut their long hair and went back to their careers, the blacks would still be left on the outside. She listened carefully, she wanted to learn from him. One night when Michael was asleep in his cot and she'd had a few glasses of wine, she draped her arms around Sam's neck and kissed him on the cheek. It was a while since Nicky had left for Afghanistan. — I've always thought there was something good between us, Sam. Perhaps it could even get better.

Gently enough, but fairly coldly, he extricated himself from her embrace.

— You think so, lady? I don't think so. It good enough just how it is.

Phyllis was humiliated and burned with her own ignorance, the shallowness of her experience. Perhaps it was because she was white, perhaps because she was too old. Next time she saw Sam, it was as if nothing had happened, he was as friendly as ever, but now she saw the careful guard he set around himself, closing her out. There was so much she still misunderstood, in her naivety. It was a strange year for Phyllis, that first year of Michael's life. She took him to visit her sisters, but felt out of rhythm with them: their children were so much older and their concerns were different. Yet she never once looked back to Otterley. Nothing was finished for her yet, she thought. If she'd stayed in Otterley something would have been finished: instead, she had sidestepped her fate. More adventures awaited her, she was still alive. And in the meantime her little boy made her happy. He didn't look anything like Hugh. Michael was sturdy and stocky, dark and intently practical; she was relieved of that dread she'd always felt when Hughie was small, that because he was too beautiful she couldn't keep him safe. If Phyllis was in town she slipped into a poky, damp little church in Soho, which kept its doors open all day for sinners; she never told Barbara about this, or anyone. She put her pennies in a box and lit a candle, then knelt in a pew – among the tramps and derelicts keeping warm, and the girls on the game – closing her eyes to give thanks to God. She couldn't find her old God again, the one like a clarifying magnesium flare. But she was aware of something surrounding her in the mouldy musty air: some reassuring spirit, humdrum and animal and wordless, smelling of wet wool because the tramps dried their clothes on the hot pipes. She helped out at Christmas, when that church gave dinners to the homeless, and the old men took turns looking after Michael.

She got together with Hugh every so often, when he was home for the holidays: Roger encouraged this. She met him off the train from Otterley and took him to lunch, saving up her money and putting on her most conventional clothes, so as not to embarrass him. But Hugh was changed, she was afraid of him and scarcely knew him; he was taller and more awkward, with big clumsy hands; his face was pasty and sulky. He barely spoke to her on these occasions, only flinging out fragments of school jargon occasionally, like a code he knew she couldn't break. Phyllis kept up a running flow of talk as if nothing was wrong, giving him news of his Highbury cousins, repeating the stories Colette told in her letters, asking him about school. She tried not to mention the baby more than once or twice. Hugh focused on ordering large helpings of food, and having his glass refilled with lemonade or Coca-Cola. Once he'd finished eating and drinking, he couldn't wait to get away from her.

For a while Phyllis worked at a small manufacturers near the river in Fulham, making fruit pies: later she got a more suitable job, waiting in Helga's restaurant, in the evenings when Michael was asleep. Dawsons, where they made the pies, was a terrible old hole with no hygiene standards. They scooped the pastry mix from paper sacks left open, mixed it and put it through wooden rollers, then added the glutinous filling out of tins. You could see the weevils sometimes, wriggling in the rolled pastry. Phyllis burned her hands at first, until the girls began to accept her and showed her the right way to turn the cooked pies out from the moulds, ready for the next batch. When she looked back on this time afterwards, she thought that she was very happy there.

Most of the girls at Dawsons were younger than her, but after a while they included her in their camaraderie. They sang along for hours at their work, to whatever pop songs were on the radio: some were gruff but some had fluting sweet voices, harmonising skilfully. And they talked about their boyfriends – crudely, humorously, dreamily. In the spring and summer after work these boys would pick up the younger girls on their scooters and go blasting off into the evening, leaving trails of filthy fumes behind on the air, the exhaust's noise raw and flaunting, with a defiant braggadocio. The boys wore their shirts unbuttoned in the warm night, gold chains glinting in their chest hair; next morning the girls told stories of knife fights, and of sex down on the wastelands beside the river. They were chased by policemen or frightened by the ghosts that haunted the foreshore – of boatmen who'd drowned, or the victims from bombed air-raid shelters. One of the boys was killed in an accident and the grieving girls made a shrine to him at work, keeping plastic flowers and a pack of cigarettes in front of his photograph, a miniature bottle of Tia Maria; when somebody stole the Tia Maria there was a row with screaming accusations and hair-pulling. Mostly the women at Dawsons, even the married ones, lived at home with their mothers or their grandmothers, in houses full of children, often with no bathroom and an outside toilet. They weren't interested in politics: they didn't know anything about history, didn't even know the name of the prime minister. They had some terrible ideas, too, about the Greeks and the blacks and the Pakistanis, although a couple of them had black boyfriends.

Phyllis was discovering she wasn't much good at politics either. She got bored in meetings, and was too easily moved by any speaker talking about suffering and injustice. She was confused by conflicts between the different factions, the RCP or the IMG or Militant, and felt false and ashamed whenever she tried carrying a banner in a demonstration or chanting a slogan. Yet she still believed what she had said to Roger: that she could simply refuse to be part of any system that was so cruelly wrong. How could she refuse it, Roger had asked, when she lived inside it? But she felt that refusal in her body, in her daily life. It was like a transformation of all her cells.

And about this time she had a fling, too, with a man who used to hang around at Dawsons. He was one of their suppliers, delivering the foil trays and packaging: not at all a suitable match for her, wiry and lithe with a thin moustache, dark hair slicked back, weaselly narrow face. He wore stainless-steel bracelets on his rolled shirtsleeves, and a flashy ring, and she wouldn't have looked twice at him in her old life, she'd have found him sinister and cheap. In the small world of Dawsons, however, he had authority. The girls teased Phyllis about him, and she found herself anticipating his visits. He flirted with all of them, mocking and suggestive, always one step ahead of the girls' banter; but while he spoke, his glance roamed around restlessly, lingering on Phyllis, communicating a different message, apart from everything tawdry in the scene. She only went out with him a few times, when she could get a babysitter — she wouldn't have wanted to bring him home. They met at a pub after work, then walked together by the river and lay down on the wasteland there, and she never forgot the heedlessness and rapture of it afterwards: the lemon-yellow light under the bridges, the swallows' effervescent twittering, the stinking sluggish water and all the foul debris washed up along the Thames shore. His lovemaking was expert and delicate and showy, attentive to her pleasure as if this was a difficult trick he carried off, source of his self-esteem. He brought a blanket from the boot of his car, and she hardly wondered who'd been on the blanket before her, she didn't care. She didn't mind imagining herself the latest in a long succession of women who'd lain down there under the wide sky.

Roger drove up to Cressing one weekend. The road ran for a while alongside a high brick wall which marked the boundary of the estate; he pulled in beside a pair of black iron gates, then got out of the car to look through them at the drive, which was overgrown with burdock and thistle. Jean had warned him that these gates were kept padlocked. The stately great trees inside the park were mostly bare, and leaves lay thick on the ground in their hectic colour; pale grass had grown waist-high in places, or lay flattened and dirty where the wind had broken it. Water glinted like a reminder from between the trees: there was a small ornamental lake. This landscape designed for the human eye seemed withdrawn and secretive, as if it had attained to a life all its own, and didn't want any longer to be viewed. He thought that he shouldn't have come, it was too late.

Further along the road, he turned into the rough track Jean had described, which ran past the ruined greenhouses and kitchen garden, then emerged from behind the shrubbery: abruptly the house loomed overhead, filling up his view, its façade stuccoed greenish-white, the grey stone of the rear quarters stained with damp and the Gothicky narrow windows inhospitable, though a pallid electric light gleamed behind one or two of them. The track crossed the moat, which was empty, and ran up to a side entrance. As his engine died, Jean came out of the door in a plastic mac and wellington boots, scarf tied under her chin. It was as if she'd deliberately chosen to look — what was the word Phyllis had used? Frumpy. A muddy cocker spaniel bounced around her knees. — Go down, Flossie, down! Bad girl.

Roger knew that she let the dog distract her because it was too much for her to see him here, she didn't know how to greet him. — It's awful inside the house, she said, pulling at Flossie's ears, laughing like an awkward schoolgirl, glancing at him sideways. — I dread you seeing how the place has deteriorated. Let's go for a walk instead. Oh dear, are those your only shoes?

But he had brought walking boots, and a stout stick. Everything was better once they set out. Jean was less self-conscious and her pace was a good match for his, she swung her walking stick. The path led down at first and skirted the lake, where Flossie splashed into the water among the reeds, barking at ducks, the fur on her belly draggled with wet silt afterwards. Then they went up towards the woods patched with ragged, vivid colour, scribbled over with the wet ink-black of twigs and branches. Roger and Jean's talk as they climbed was desultory, only skimming the top of the afternoon. The sound of their steps, crackling cobnuts and beechnuts underfoot, expressed their closeness better than anything they said. — Do you remember this? Jean exclaimed at last, throwing out her hand at the view, when they got to the top.

The truth, however, was that he didn't remember it.

Roger might almost have believed he'd never visited here before. It was not that the reality of it was disappointing, but his store of treasured old images turned out to be shrunken and limited, beside the confounding actuality of the place – so messy and unfinished and complicated. Nothing was where he'd remembered it, and he had no recollection of this walk. At the top of the hill a wooden seat was put, almost too obviously, in the spot where they were bound to sit down to rest, looking back at the house – which was not desolate from this distance. Against its backdrop of more trees it looked like something out of a fairy tale, with its turret and its slate roofs shining like silver, its golden cockerel weathervane blowing this way and that over the stables. Roger remarked that he'd never been up in the observatory. — Golly, neither have I, Jean said. — Or not for hundreds of years anyway, since I was a girl. We should go up. I'll bet Mrs Chick knows where the keys are.

It wasn't a real observatory, she warned him, just a little round room in the tower at the top of the house, with a brass telescope and a truckle bed; a conical roof could be unbolted to open partially to the sky, trundling round on a rusted mechanism of wheels and cogs. The old gentleman who built Cressing had spent his nights alone up there.

— When I retire, Roger said, — I'll come here to live with you and watch the stars.

Surprised by joy, she turned to smile into his smile. — But, darling, I'll be long dead by the time you retire. And anyway, there's never enough money to keep this place up. Peter would cut me off, if you were here.

Roger put his arm around her shoulders, pulled her close against him on the seat. In their bulky coats, with scarves and gloves, they were only aware indistinctly of each other's shape under the padding.

— Then leave it. Come and live with me now, in Otterley.

He knew that he would need someone. He couldn't – he shouldn't – carry on for too long, deep buried in his home alone.

— Are you serious? Are you serious, really? Even with the whole thing with Nicholas?

He hesitated and then said that he was serious, but Jean had registered his hesitation. — I can't imagine myself in Otterley, she said.

— No, he admitted, resigned. — I can't imagine you there either. It's too small.

— Then where can we go?

He thought about it. — I could hand in my notice and you could sell this place, or just shut it up. We could buy somewhere very cheaply in Italy. Open it for paying guests. Or in Morocco or Tunisia, where at least I can speak the language. We'd have to be able to pay for Hugh's education, and give something to Nicholas, perhaps to Phyllis. Meanwhile we'd be out of the way, not drawing anyone's attention.

— No one would notice us.

— So, would you come in with me?

Jean allowed herself to imagine it, for a moment. Mrs Chick would agree to have Flossie. And all those plates and knives and forks could turn out to be useful after all, and the quantities of monogrammed linen bedsheets and pillowcases – perhaps even the chafing dishes and wine coolers. In a brief absence that was like a hallucination, she seemed to see – in place of the mossy, frowsty, damp, disintegrating English autumn scene around them – a stone well in an ancient paved courtyard, baked in glancing white light. A bucket hit the surface of water far below with a muffled smack, and she knew that the well water was pure and cold and good.

But then on the other hand she was sixty years old.

And Roger had his brilliant career at the Foreign Office.

It was too late.

A fitful wind drove the torn clouds, sent leaves scudding and skipping on the path. Squawking rooks, warning off a marauding peregrine, were flung against the sky, giving themselves to the wind like scraps of black paper. She squeezed his hand through the thick fabric of their gloves, promised him that she would think about it.

ACKNOWLEDGEMENTS

Heartfelt unending thanks to my brilliant publishers Jennifer Barth, Michal Shavit and Ana Fletcher, and agents Joy Harris and Caroline Dawnay. Thanks also to my lovely publicists Jane Beirn in the US and Lucie Cuthbertson Twiggs in the UK. When I told my friend John Williams I was writing a novel set in Ladbroke Grove in the sixties, he recommended that I read Jonathon Green's *Days in the Life: Voices from the English Underground, 1961–1971*. This fascinating compendium of voices turned out to be the richest possible source of atmosphere, anecdote, detail and attitude – and was published in 1989 by my dear Dan Franklin, who published all my fiction books before this one, which feels like a nice symmetry. While I was writing I immersed myself in novels by Samuel Selvon, Margaret Drabble and Nell Dunn, and in Charlie Phillips' photographs – from these first-hand witnesses and wonderful artists I've stolen a few explicit details, and I've tried to put into my own words what I learned from their work, about the spirit of those times.

ABOUT THE AUTHOR

TESSA HADLEY is the author of seven other highly acclaimed novels, including *The Past* and *Late in the Day*, as well as three short story collections, most recently *Bad Dreams and Other Stories*, which won the Edge Hill Short Story Prize. Her stories appear regularly in the *New Yorker*, and in 2016 she was awarded the Windham-Campbell Prize and the Hawthornden Prize. She lives in Cardiff, Wales.